I0612959

When the Bough Breaks

by

Allison Thorpe

A Family Tree Mystery

This is a work of fiction. Names, characters, places, and incidents are either the product of the author's imagination or are used fictitiously, and any resemblance to actual persons living or dead, business establishments, events, or locales, is entirely coincidental.

When the Bough Breaks

COPYRIGHT © 2022 by Allison Thorpe

All rights reserved. No part of this book may be used or reproduced in any manner whatsoever without written permission of the author or The Wild Rose Press, Inc. except in the case of brief quotations embodied in critical articles or reviews.
Contact Information: info@thewildrosepress.com

Cover Art by *Kim Mendoza*

The Wild Rose Press, Inc.
PO Box 708
Adams Basin, NY 14410-0708
Visit us at www.thewildrosepress.com

Publishing History
First Edition, 2023
Trade Paperback ISBN 978-1-5092-4839-1
Digital ISBN 978-1-5092-4840-7

A Family Tree Mystery
Published in the United States of America

Mason Street and I huddled together in the small cemetery as two workmen lowered my mother into the ground. We were the only mourners. The minister muttered a few brief comments, chanted a prayer, patted my hand, and rushed out of the raw March wind.

A lawyer, Mason had helped my mother with a minor legal matter and was kind enough to help me with arrangements. He was enticing in a dark, brooding way, but I knew who I was—an unexciting genealogist who loved her work and had no illusions about dark, brooding men.

He took my elbow and asked if I wanted a ride. When I shook my head, he turned to go, then walked back and reached into his inner coat pocket.

"I almost forgot to give you this," he said handing me a thin white envelope. I recognized my mother's scribbled lettering.

"What's this?"

"She said to give it to you after her death."

"What's in it?" I asked, gingerly reaching out.

"It was sealed when she gave it to me." He shrugged. "Call me if you need help, El."

I thought the walk back to my mother's house might clear my head, but the bitter air made me wish I had taken him up on his offer. I came upon a wooden bench with some semblance of a shield from the wind. I sat and contemplated the envelope.

Finally, I ripped it open. The loose scrawl jumped off the page with the simple sentence: *I'm not your mother.*

Dedication

For Taura and Julie and their grand ideas

Chapter 1

Mason Street and I huddled together in the small cemetery as two workmen lowered my mother into the ground. We were the only mourners. The minister muttered a few brief comments, chanted a prayer, patted my hand, and rushed out of the raw March wind.

A lawyer, Mason had helped my mother with a minor legal matter and was kind enough to help me with arrangements. He was enticing in a dark, brooding way, but I knew who I was—an unexciting genealogist who loved her work and had no illusions about dark, brooding men.

He took my elbow and asked if I wanted a ride. When I shook my head, he turned to go, then walked back and reached into his inner coat pocket.

"I almost forgot to give you this," he said, handing me a thin white envelope. I recognized my mother's scribbled lettering.

"What's this?"

"She said to give it to you after her death."

"What's in it?" I asked, gingerly reaching out.

"It was sealed when she gave it to me." He shrugged. "Call me if you need help, El."

I thought the walk back to my mother's house might clear my head, but the bitter air made me wish I had taken him up on his offer. I came upon a wooden bench with some semblance of a shield from the wind. I sat and contemplated the envelope.

Finally, I ripped it open. The loose scrawl jumped off the page with the simple sentence: *I'm not your mother.*

****

My mother and I had never gotten along. A deep-bottle blonde with scarlet lips and a cigarette constantly in her hand, she went through men like I went through genealogy sites. I hadn't even known about this last affair until her call begging me to come and take care of her. Misgivings aside, I made the journey to Parkville, hundreds of miles from the city world I knew and loved. It wasn't until I arrived that I realized her condition was far worse than she had let on. The man of the moment—a poor poet—had fled the second the dread diagnosis hit the air. We spent what little time she had left watching old movies on television, soap operas mostly, and I wondered if she saw her life in those dramatic, sordid scenes.

She refused to run any fans or open windows, so the house exuded a stale whiff of hovered death. The heat was stifling. During her naps, I raced to a local grocery or just walked outside to fill my lungs before stepping back into her bubble. She woke at all hours demanding water, a Bloody Mary, a cigarette. After a short few weeks, I felt like a zombie. My attempts at finding out what doctor had diagnosed her proved unhelpful. Much of my waking hours had been spent on the phone calling medical facilities and hospitals, but they wouldn't or couldn't tell me if she had been a patient. One place referred me to the hospice care center, which ended up getting all the information I could not. Even with their help, life for my mother remained a chaotic season of frantic pleas and scornful recriminations, eased only by strong painkillers.

One would imagine this the time of bonding, but whenever I brought up anything of importance, she reverted to a theatrical hand flung over her eyes that signaled silence and sleep. Even though I was her daughter, she treated me like an unwanted guest, often rebuking me.

In her dementia, my mother had aimlessly ranted: "Take care of Albie" or "You must see to Albie." I had no earthly idea what she had been talking about and assumed her long-gone poet love had been named Albie, her pleas so heartfelt and desperate.

"And don't go through my things while I'm sleeping," she'd demand.

Or "Wait until I'm dead before you touch my personal stuff."

As an only daughter, a good daughter, I had obeyed. She didn't seem to have much. I guessed I had inherited that gene. Her furniture came with the rented house, and the few papers I saw lying around weren't of much consequence. We had been separated for so long our name seemed the only thing connecting us. I had carved out a comfortable life for myself without her.

Much of my youth had been spent moving from coast to coast and a lot of places in between. I had never been in schools long enough to make friends. "A boring life in sales," my mother had always claimed with a grand sweep of arms whenever anyone had asked about her job and all our traveling. Her short laugh had usually quelled any further questions. I had known better than to ask myself.

It had been both exciting and lonely. As I grew

older, there had been summer camps and winter science camps and eventually random boarding schools. The link between my mother and I becoming increasingly more distant. Sometimes I saw her on holidays—stiff and awkward affairs—but more often I went home with one of the nice girls who felt sorry for me being alone. At that point, I was too shy to do more than stutter my name and marvel at the normalcy of a family who stayed in one place.

I never knew my father. He was a vague name on my birth certificate—*F. Turner*—and though, in my younger days, I had done half-hearted searches, it wasn't much to go on. I didn't even know if that was his name. My mother had lived for movies, dreaming herself a tight-sweater pin-up girl, and Lana had been one of her favorites. I shortened my name to El when I was thirteen and never looked back. It would be easy enough to research my birth certificate, but did I want to? I was settled into the person I had become. I put my slurry of questions on hold for the moment, finding it exceedingly odd that someone who investigated family trees for a living should be so uncertain about her own.

****

In the end, I decided to stay in Parkville. There was nothing here to hold me but nothing to draw me elsewhere. It was a pleasant place with a beautiful river, a ton of parks, and a mayor trying to get the community to live up to its name. The downtown was lined with local shops and filled with friendly people. There were band concerts in one of the parks on Sundays. It flirted a southern charm, and in some odd way, it felt like home.

I packed my mother's personal stuff into a few

boxes, wondering about their content, her final message heavy in my thoughts. Did I want to know what it meant? Did she have proof she wasn't my mother? Or was she just being hateful to the end? My childhood had certainly been unstable—moving often, a random selection of men, hushed voices in the night. She hadn't been a PTA sort of parent and liked me best when I was quiet. Also among her possessions was her car, a non-descript, beige vehicle that looked like a million others.

I called Mason Street and moved into an apartment building he recommended that held many young professionals, him included. My work was antisocial in that I spent it mostly with my computer. I make my living as a researcher, hunting connections, documents, historic houses, family trees. It was true a nice bit of my business always came from people desperate to prove Abe Lincoln or some Cherokee Princess existed as part of their past, or that they had ties to the DAR or the Mayflower crowd, often not finding the results they craved, but I loved the quest. I cheerfully spent my life finding old clues in stuffy library basements, dusty courthouse records, and online genealogy sites. I couldn't think of anything I would rather do. My jobs had fallen off during my mother's illness, but Mason threw a bit of new work my way.

The apartment also brought Rita Starr, a neighbor, who became the annoying little sister I never had. A short, frizzy redhead journalist, sharp quivering nose, she spent so much time in my apartment I wanted to charge her rent. After a quick meeting in the elevator, she had declared us besties. She usually ended her days by plopping down on my sofa or pacing the floor expounding on the ordeals of journalism, her growing list of sources, and getting the big story. My need for concentration meant little to her. She couldn't hold a thought in her head for more than five minutes, but she kept me current on local affairs and livened the hours of my otherwise staid life. It was an easy relationship in that she asked nothing of me—no past, no explanations, no feelings.

****

Late spring and several months after my mother's death, a pet store man knocked on my door.

"Here he is!"

"Here who is?"

"Your African gray parrot!" The man was obviously excited to have found me, like he was discovering plutonium or fire. He pointed to the large cage with *The Ravin' Pet Store* written across the dark cloth covering the bird.

"I'm sorry, but you must have the wrong apartment. I didn't order nor do I want any parrot."

"Are you Lana Turner?"

"Yes. That's my name, but I think there's some mistake."

Then he solved the confusion. "The bird belonged to a Mr. Sam Taylor, actually, but I understood your mother inherited him from Mr. Taylor. Mr. Taylor boarded him at the shop when he had to leave town suddenly. Your mother was listed as the contact person. I just learned of her death. I'm so sorry. It took me a while to track you down." He handed me the cage, beaming at his brilliance.

"What am I supposed to do with this bird? I really can't care for any pets."

"The bird belongs to you. If you choose to sell, we

would be glad to help. In the bag, you will find a book about African grays, food, treats, and a few toys." He put the large sack beside the door. "I will tell you grays don't do well being shuffled around a lot, so think carefully before getting rid of this lovely creature."

Then he was gone, and I was left holding the heavy cage. I placed it on a side table and lifted the cover. A pair of dark alert eyes stared back at me. They followed me around the room as I filled the water and food dishes. When I raised the door to put in the toys, a lethal beak nipped savagely at my hand.

"Hey! What the hell are you doing? I'm trying to help here." I shook my hand and then held it under cold running water. At least no blood surfaced, but the bite was evident.

The bird's eyes followed me as I took the booklet and scanned its contents. *One of the best talkers in the parrot family,* I read. I gave it a try.

"Polly want a cracker?"

The eyes stared and stared. It was starting to freak me out. I grabbed the cover and hastily draped it back over the cage. Even so, I could sense the eyes through the cloth. Feeling bad, I lifted the cover off.

"Sorry, Polly. It looks like you and I are stuck with each other for the moment until I can figure out what to do with you. Leave it to my mother to reach out from the grave and saddle me with this."

Since that day, we'd kept an uneasy alliance. I fed, watered, and did all the things the book said, but the bird refused to talk. If I got too close to the cage, she was ready to rip my hand off. She sat and watched me constantly while I did my work, but she was as still as a tomb.

She was a mystery that kept me from thinking of other matters.

Chapter 2

I've always been a sucker for early mornings, and today was one of the best. The light oozed over the horizon and quietly smothered the walls around me, colors letting loose across the sky like a party of wild teenagers flinging paint when their parents weren't at home. The crisp air dusted off night's dark bluster and hummed the dew to freshness. Birds chittered musically outside my window. I got my best work done at the computer during those hours before the phone started ringing and the world shook itself awake. That time was golden and safe and free from intrusions.

"El! El!" Rita Star yelled, slamming the door and stumbling into my apartment. "Timmy's dead! I can't believe it! Timmy's dead!"

"What in the hell?" I screamed, jumping up from the table and spilling my coffee over my notes. "Rita, you scared the living crap out of me!" I tried to dab at the unruly liquid. "How in the world did you get in here?"

"Don't you remember we traded keys a while ago?" She flopped down at the table, jarring everything on it.

"That key was for emergencies only!" I cried.

"But, El, this is an emergency! Timmy's dead." She put on her pouty face and drummed her fingers on the table until she got my attention.

"Timmy?" I reluctantly looked up from mopping the spilled coffee and shook my head. It was too early in the day to keep track of all her leads, work problems, and men. I wondered how soon I could take back my key.

"Yes, my friend Timmy! You remember," Rita wailed, leaping up, shaking the table again, and pacing the room.

"You mean that drunk you used as a source a few times?" I set my soggy notes to the side and took my cup to the kitchen. This was not the peaceful morning I had envisioned.

"Timmy did like his drink, but no, he wasn't a drunk. He used to be the caretaker at the Hill estates." She sniffed. "Police found his body in an alley."

"Oh, my goodness! What happened to him?" I poured another cup of coffee. "Wait. Hill? You mean the people who own that old mansion at the edge of town?"

"Yes. And those nasty people fired him. My poor Timmy!" She took out a tissue from her pocket and dabbed at her eyes. "He was forced into a homeless shelter and started drinking again. I mean, it drove him to drink."

"I didn't think anyone lived at the Hill mansion anymore. Who fired him?"

"Some distant relative, a nephew or something, lives there now, and he claimed my Timmy was snooping around, so he let him go."

"And now he's dead? How did he die? Was it an accident? Heart attack?" I asked, hoping she wouldn't stay long. My research had just taken an interesting turn.

"Someone stabbed him."

"You mean he was murdered?" I sat back down and tried to make sense of Rita's current crisis.

"Yes! That's what I've been trying to tell you." She paused and struck a pose. "And I was there!" Drama was Rita's middle name.

"You were where?"

"In that alley. Last night!"

"Whoa! Wait!" I waved my hands in the air. "Last night, you were in the alley where Timmy was murdered?" I walked around to face her. "Rita, isn't that what you journalists call burying the lead? What in the hell were you doing in some dark alley late at night? You could have been killed yourself."

She moved away and strolled around the room. "That's where we usually met when he had a tip for me. Timmy called me yesterday and said he had a hot story about the Hills, so I agreed to meet him." She gave a little shiver and put her hand to her mouth. "Oh, El! Do you think he was already dead when I got there?"

"Probably not," I said, trying to process her question. "Did you see anything suspicious? Hear any noise?"

"Nothing! It was so dark I couldn't see anything. I called his name a few times, and then I left and came home. I figured he had gotten drunk and, I mean, I thought he might have gotten involved in something else." She stopped and looked out the near window.

"How did you hear about it?"

"Reb texted me."

"Oh, yes, Reb." I shut my laptop and gave up any thoughts of getting back to work. "I don't suppose you happened to mention you were there?" I asked, shuffling the soaked papers.

She hedged, then tossed back her mane of red hair. "No need to. And what does it matter? I didn't kill Timmy."

"What else did Reb say? Do they have any suspects?"

"Too soon to tell. Reb said it was probably random. He also said they had a tough time identifying Timmy. No ID or wallet, but Reb's so good at his job, I'm sure he can find someone's identity in an instant."

Personally, I thought the only thing Officer Reb Wilson could find in an instant were Rita's enhanced body parts. Reb Wilson was Rita's sometime link to police stories/sometime boyfriend. I thought him a blowhard with bad breath who liked to shadow his bulk a bit too closely for my comfort. He wasn't my brand of tea, but obviously he ranked highly as Rita's current drink of choice.

"It all relates to the old Hill horror stories."

"What are you talking about?" I'd tuned her out.

"Oh." She paused for an instant and looked at me, arched her back, and brought a purple polished claw to her plump fire engine lips. Her attire was usually a short skirt, low-cut blouse, and heels to rival any skyscraper. I sometimes thought of suggesting she buy stock in a makeup company. My at-home work attire was a pair of blue jeans and a sweatshirt. I generally wore no makeup and pulled my plain brown hair into a ponytail. I was thirty years of comfort; she was twenty-five and a fashion freight train. "I forget you're not from Parkville," she continued. "Our infamous town founder has a mysterious past."

"Mysterious how? Did he magically disappear or

something?"

"Mysterious like he went crazy and murdered his whole family."

"The town founder went crazy and murdered his family?" The researcher in me lit up. "And where can I find all the facts about this gruesome town history?" Rita was drawn to spectacle like a drum majorette to a parade. This tale teetered on the edge of over the line.

"Everyone knows about it," she huffed. "Just ask around town. It's common knowledge.

"Are there specific accounts at the historical society or in the library?"

"Probably." She turned her waning focus to the contents of her large designer bag.

"What more do you know about Timmy?" I continued, hoping to get her back to the immediate issue and reality, but she seemed wrapped up in powdering her mirror image. Her hot and cold histrionics were annoying.

She leaned in and checked her makeup, smiled brightly, and patted the skin under her chin. Tears for Timmy had long dried. "I really have to go. My editor is going to let me write the story."

I sighed, hoping this might be her signal to leave.

"I'm sure Timmy would like someone he knew to write about him. Does this mean you're giving up the gossip column?"

"It's a social column," she drawled. "The society of Parkville counts on me!" She looked down and straightened her skirt. "Besides, everyone else is too busy so I'm doing double duty." She dug in her bag for perfume and saturated my room with a dense gagging scent of gardenias.

I took that to mean no one wanted to write about the death of homeless man in a back alley, even if he had been connected to the Hill family. A mayor's race was heating up to boiling over, the City Council was deadlocked in an ordinance fight, and vandals were spray painting old buildings down by the river. These were the more important issues for the good townsfolk of Parkville.

"What are you going to write?" I tried not to breathe the clouds of flowery mist that enveloped me.

"Well, he was a nice man. He was old, or at least he seemed old. He had gray hair and walked all bent over, but his face didn't look old. I don't know." She shrugged her shoulders. "It was hard to tell. He was always kind of messy looking, but at least he never smelled." She waved her hand in front of her nose.

The researcher in me had a habit of constantly popping up to the surface. I began to crave more facts. "Don't you need to know his last name? How old he was? How long he worked for the Hills? And why does a grown man go by the name of Timmy?"

"Oh, I guess his name is Tim or Timothy, but everyone calls him Timmy. I mean, called him Timmy. I don't know anything else yet, but I'm going to find out. I'm going to write a wonderful piece about him." She squared her shoulders and adopted an air of theatrical determination. I wondered if she practiced her poses in front of a mirror. "I'll get all the facts, El. Don't worry. I'll write this to make you and Timmy proud."

"It will be a different style of writing for you. Good luck." At this point, I was weary of her gaudy exhibitions. It was like living with a show poodle. "Let me know when you find out." The air was still ripe with perfume.

"El! I'm talking about writing a real story! Finally, an important story! I was *meant* to be a serious journalist." She tugged the front of her blouse down even more and pursed her lips.

"Well, again, good luck. Can't wait to read about it."

"Speaking of high society." Rita picked up a lost thread of the conversation and pointed to the old painting that came with the furnished apartment. "When are you going to take this hideous landscape picture down off your wall? Something like this could ruin a girl's social life."

"It could if I had a social life."

"Your choice." She shrugged, slinging her bag over her shoulder. Her crisis had evaporated like an ice cube in August. "Well, toodles!" Rita had lately taken up the Gidget chant with a vengeance. The girlish façade clashed heavily with her more mature attributes as she slammed the door.

The silence was delightful. I opened a window to share gardenias with the world.

Chapter 3

Afternoon splintered the room when I finally looked up from my computer. After Rita's exit, I had thrown myself back into my work. Phyllis Anthony's quest to prove Susan B. Anthony was her long-lost relative wasn't going the way Phyllis had hoped it would. There was no connection I could find.

I stretched and decided to take a stroll.

"If you were a dog, I would take you along for a walk," I said to the bird. "What does one do with a bird? What good are you?" I pondered giving the bird away or selling it back to the pet store. "Why couldn't you be a Polly and want crackers?" I enjoyed a simple life and didn't need complications.

Outside, I took a deep breath of fresh air. I knew I spent too much time at the computer or digging around in musty archives, but it was my safe, passive path toward mirroring some movie action hero without the whip or snakes. Maybe I needed a hat of some sort? Maybe I could meet a man in a hat? I laughed out loud in the crisp sunlight. What sort of man wore a hat these days? A baseball cap maybe.

Even with the beaming sun and the idea of men in hats, my thoughts, whether I wanted them to or not, kept drifting back to my mother. Why had she sent me that message? Was she being cruel? Was it a reality I had to face? And if she wasn't my mother, who was she? Why had she raised me? Did I want to know?

I pushed those thoughts aside, not quite ready to dig into my mother's boxes or our pasts. I concentrated on Timmy or Tim or Timothy no-last-name and a different line of inquiry. Why had he been murdered? What was his big story he never got to tell Rita? I had the feeling there were things Rita wasn't telling me. Had she seen something she shouldn't have? Did she know something important? All the questions swirled around my brain like dusty tumbleweeds. I put them to rest and let my eyes take in the scenery.

Parkville extended along the banks of the Roma River, a questionable run of water that rushed in beauty most of the time, especially after the rainy season, but dawdled to muddy ripples when the summer suffered from too much dryness. It was getting close to that now. The downtown area where I lived was a huddle of buildings where small shops like juice bars, electronic centers, and lamp boutiques hobnobbed with taller structures housing banks and other corporate importance. Reaches that had once been outliers were now absorbed into the city limits, and the growth seemed to be continuing in that long panorama.

I wandered leisurely over to my favorite park and chose an out-of-the-way bench where I could indulge in the light and watch whoever happened past. The lovely weather drew a wide variety of people outside, and I mindlessly observed their journeys, vicariously participating in the family laughter and facial joy.

Whatever mayor had initiated the creation of parks throughout the area did a fantastic job. It seemed the only requirements to be designated a park were a tree and a patch of grass. Somewhere along the line in their formation, the mayor decided to honor the signers of the Constitution. Thirty-nine men with pen in hand now each had his own park, complete with a metal plaque. Washington received the honor of having the biggest, most-central, and best-tended park.

Over the years, the town had unknowingly chosen certain parks and dictated their designations. Basset Park quickly became known as the dog park. Not wanting to be left behind, the cat people captured Morris Park for their socializing. When the local library needed a bigger building, they quickly situated it near Read Park. The veterans liked to hang out at Sherman Park and petitioned the city to place a small tank in its midst. Clymer Park slowly developed into a tangle of jungle gyms and other structures perfect for wearing out legions of energetic children. Mifflin Park eventually became overshadowed by Mifflin Muffins, a popular bakery that couldn't keep its products on the shelves for long. People ambled over to eat breakfast or lunch takeout across the street in the park, an overwhelming favorite of most of the birds around.

"Buenas tardes, Señorita Turner."

"Oh, buenas tardes, Señor Marquez."

G. G. Marquez stepped quietly into my vision. He owned the small market near me and was my supplier of newspapers from around the country. I think I was born a newspaper junkie, or maybe it had developed over the years living in a large city. Whatever the case, Mr. Marquez fed my addiction. Not long after moving into my apartment, he had begun the arduous task of trying to teach me Spanish. He was a gentleman of the old world in that he favored extreme politeness, a kind manner, and serious bowties. With his bushy gray eyebrows and dashing white mustache, he was hard to miss.

"*Te gusta el parque?*"

"Do I enjoy the park?"

"*Sí.*"

"*I mucho gusta the parque.*"

"*Me gusta mucho el parque,*" he corrected me.

"*Sí. Me gusta mucho el parque. Gracias.*"

"*Puedo unirme a ustedes?*" He pointed to the seat next to me.

"*Sí por favor.*"

"I have brought my grandson to the park today. There he is kicking that soccer ball with the others."

"A handsome boy! You must be very pleased."

"Yes. He makes me feel young inside. And you? You spend the day delighting in the sunshine and nature rather than working?"

"I decided to take a break and delight in the sunshine," I agreed.

"Yes, and the river also is very beautiful today though it is running low. I wanted to fish, but the boy loves soccer."

"Have you lived in Parkville a long time?" We passed the time but did not often indulge in personal lives.

"*Toda mi vida.*"

"Your whole life?"

"*Sí.* My grandfather come here to build the early settlement."

"Was he a carpenter?"

"Back then, men did whatever they needed to do to survive. He was very handy with tools. Men cut logs, lashed them together into rafts, and floated them down the river. It was sometimes very dangerous."

"Really? That's interesting. I'm sure you must have some fascinating stories of that time and his life."

"Sadly, he died when my father was very young, and he spared my grandmother the details of that life. It was a time of hard labor, with many men dying from the conditions. But my grandfather was strong and passed that gene down to us. Hard work is in our veins, and see what we have achieved!"

"Yes, you can be very proud of your success. Your shop is my favorite place to go every day. What did your father do?" It felt relaxing to speak of things not related to Timmy or my mother.

"He was a builder as well and worked on many houses and structures throughout Parkville. He thought I should follow in his footsteps, but it did not suit me. I find joy in what I do now like you find joy in what you do."

"Yes, I do love my work. Many people might find it dull, but I find it fascinating."

"And is your family here?"

He had no way of knowing, so I switched the subject as quickly and subtly as I could. "I didn't know you could trace your history to the town's beginning. Your family must go back as far as any in the Hill family."

He rose abruptly from the park bench and spit on the ground. "I must go. *Adios.*"

"*Señor Marquez!* I am so sorry if I have offended you. Please accept my apologizes. *Lo siento.*" I had no idea what nerve I hit.

He waved his hand through the air. "*No importa.* That time is long gone, but that name still rings in anger. It is I who must apologize to you for my rudeness. Now I will let the sunshine and gentle breeze restore my countenance. *Buen día.*"

"Yes, *Buenos dias, Señor Marquez. Lo siento mucho.*"

His outburst, as well as Rita's mention, stirred my curiosity. What in the world had Clark Hill done to kindle so much anger? The Hill mansion stood quite a distance outside of town. If that began as the center of a community, why had the downtown been built up somewhere else? And why did that mansion now sit sad and forlorn as a forgotten outsider? Questions surrounded me like empty wrappers at a candy convention.

Something was up, and I couldn't shake the feeling there was more to the Hill saga than was hitting the surface of this town. And what did Timmy have to do with anything? Somehow his killing did not seem like a random murder. Maybe Rita had gotten more answers. I headed home to find out.

A brisk rush of air rustled the still-green leaves. The sun was sinking, and the temperature was cooling accordingly. Summer was moving on. Time to get back to work.

****

Email to El Turner
Dear El,

I am getting married soon, and I want to employ your services. I thought it would be a great surprise to give all the wedding party their own horoscope. I have everyone's birth day and year, so it should be easy for you to chart their stars. I know this is last minute, but my future wife and I have run out of ideas, and then I happened upon your ad, and it seemed like fate.

How soon would you be able to do this? I will send the information as soon as I get an answer with amount owed.

You will be saving our wedding.
Hoping to hear from you,
Paul, the future groom

****

Email to Paul, the future groom
Dear Paul:

Thank you for your email, and congratulations on your upcoming wedding!

Unfortunately, I am basically a genealogist (research family trees), not an astrologer (horoscopes).

I think your idea of a horoscope for each member of the bridal party is a wonderful one. I wish I could refer you to someone, but I don't know any astrologers. You can probably search online to find one that will work with you.

Again, congratulations, and good luck.
Best,
El Turner

Chapter 4

Somewhere a woman was screaming. I blinked in the early light and realized I had fallen asleep at the computer in my clothes.

I went to the door, running a hand through my tangled hair and checking the peephole. Deep male voices rumbled in the hallway.

"Police brutality! Help! Police brutality!" I recognized Rita's voice.

Opening the door slightly, I saw her waving her arms at two policemen who seemed to be in shock at her attitude.

"Ma'am, just come with us, please."

"I won't go anywhere with you." She saw me looking out. "El! Help! These big brutes are trying to arrest me!"

I unlocked my door and stepped into the hall. "What's going on?"

"Ma'am, please go back into your apartment. This is official police business."

Rita hit out frantically at the air and yelled at the top of her voice register. I heard another door open, and Jenny Lane's purple head popped out.

"Ladies." One of the policemen moved toward us. "Please go back into your homes. We can handle this." Jenny listened to them. I stepped closer to Rita.

"Help! Help!" Rita kept up her frenzied

commotion. "They're trying to arrest me. Call the police."

"We are the police," the other man in blue said, shaking his head.

"Gestapo! Citizen's arrest! Call my lawyer! Police brutality." Her tirade was nonstop.

"Ma'am, we aren't arresting you. We just want to ask you a few questions." The older man tried to talk over her screams.

"Rita, calm down," I shouted. "What's the problem?"

"El, call my lawyer. They're arresting me for Timmy's murder! They're getting ready to slap handcuffs on me, El!"

"Ma'am," the closer policeman said to Rita, "we are not arresting you. We want to take you down to the station for questioning," he repeated. "That's all."

"Why would you question me? I don't know anything about Timmy's murder. I hardly knew the man."

"Rita." I tried to make some sense of the situation. "Just go along and tell them what you know. Just tell them the truth that you were in the alley but don't know what happened to Timmy."

The hallway suddenly got quiet, and the policemen froze. I saw Rita's face droop, and she scrunched up her mouth. Nothing came out.

"You know for a fact this lady was in the alley the night of the murder?"

"What?" I looked at Rita's face and tried to back my way out. "I don't know anything about an alley."

"Are we going to have to take you in for questioning as well?"

"Okay." Rita piped up. "So I was in the alley. Big deal. I didn't see Timmy. I didn't see his body. I don't know anything about his murder."

"Then you wouldn't mind coming with us, would you?"

"El, call my lawyer to meet me at the police station."

"Who is your lawyer?"

She paused, then brightened. "Call Mason. He lives in the building."

"What if he's not around?"

"Look online. Find someone. Anyone."

I noticed a policeman stayed behind outside Rita's apartment.

****

Mason Street wasn't answering his phone. I got his answering machine. Didn't the man have a secretary? I searched online for local attorneys, trying office after office. No luck. Was there a lawyer reunion I didn't know about? I glanced at the clock and realized it wasn't much past eight. I left messages all over town: *Call me. Call me.*

A long hour later, I had given up connecting with anyone when there was a knock on my door. Were the police back for me? I got up warily and inched forward.

"El, it's me." I heard Rita's voice, hoarse and raspy.

I checked the peephole and yanked the door open, shocked she had bothered to knock. "Rita! What are you doing? Did you escape?"

She shook her head and croaked, "They let me go. I'm a person of interest now. Suggestion not to leave town. Suggestion to be where they can reach me easily." She flopped down on my couch.

"Rita, I'm so sorry I blabbed about you being in the alley. I hope I didn't get you into any trouble."

She threw one arm over her face and waved me off with the other. She could have put Sarah Bernhardt out of business. "I would have told them anyway."

"What did they ask you? How come they sent the police to bring you in? What did Reb have to say? Do they know who killed Timmy?"

"Well, it seems when I walked into the alley, I accidentally stepped on the knife that killed him. I almost broke a heel on that thing! I thought it was a stone or something really gross."

"Rita!" I was shocked at her cavalier attitude. "Rita! Please tell me you didn't do this."

"You know me, El! I could never do something like this!"

"But how come they didn't arrest you? How did they know you were even there?"

"Seems there was a witness who saw someone go in and come out of the alley before I arrived. The witness happened to see my car, which the police are now checking for blood, and they took away the clothes I wore last night. I'm sure they will find evidence. My shoe stepped on the knife. The police department also sent an escort to follow me around." She crossed her heart. "I thank whoever was watching in the shadows, but I can't go anywhere without my tail."

"Are you going to call Mason? No one called me back."

"My editor got me a lawyer. I'll come by later." She sounded like a rusty foghorn. "My voice is gone."

"Well, you did do a lot of screaming." I noticed the

police had gotten to her before she had applied her makeup and styled her hair. No wonder she had screamed.

"This person of interest is going home." She struggled up.

"No work today?"

"My editor said to finish my article at home since I can't go anywhere. At least I don't have to wear one of those clunky ankle bracelets."

"How did he hear about you being at the station?"

She looked at me like a naïve child. "Police scanner."

"Of course."

"Let me go home and get in a bathtub filled with bubbles, finish Timmy's article, and then I'll come back." She mouthed "Toodles" and left.

I turned to the bird. "I don't know what's happened to my sane life, Polly. A woman I thought was my mother died, an uncommunicative bird has entered my life, and now I'm involved in a murder. What else can happen?"

I should have known better than to ask.

****

"So what do you think happened to Timmy? Did the police tell you anything?" I had been anxious all day to hear Rita's story.

"Not a thing, but I know those Hill people were involved in his murder. I have a reporter's nose about this!" Rita was back to being her normal pacing self.

"Do you think we should offer the policeman in the hall something to drink or a chair?"

"After the way they treated me?" Rita scowled.

I went to the door anyway. "Officer, would you

like some coffee or a chair? Rita will probably be in here a while."

His gruff exterior melted a bit at the word coffee. "Thanks, I could do with a cup. Black, please."

I searched for a clean cup, poured his drink, and took it out to him.

"I noticed a small seating area at the end of the hall. Please let Ms. Starr know that's where I will be and not to get any ideas about sneaking away. We don't look kindly on that sort of thing." His crusty façade returned.

"I'll see she doesn't go anywhere, officer. Just let me know if you need more coffee."

He touched the brim of his cap and moved down the hallway.

I shut the door, anxious to get back to Rita's tragedy. "I thought you said Timmy didn't work for the Hills anymore. Why would they care about him? And why murder him?"

"They fired him for a reason. He had a big story, and I was this close to getting it!" She gestured with her thumb and finger a hair's breadth apart.

"But was it enough to kill him?" I asked.

"I don't know, but I'm going to find out." She stomped into the kitchen. "Can't you work your magic on that computer and find out more about him? There must be a reason somewhere. El, you have to help me solve his murder. I think the police have given up, so it's up to us! I can't be the only suspect!"

"I can't just type in 'Timmy' and expect his whole life to unravel before us." I wasn't at all sure I wanted to be included in her ragtag school of solving crimes. "What was his last name?"

She snapped her fingers. "I'll have Reb find out. I'm seeing him tonight."

"I thought you couldn't go anywhere?" I asked.

"We're staying in, and he's taking over Officer Whatshisname's shift."

"In the meantime, tell me about the Hills." My researcher's mind couldn't contain itself.

"Okay, so a long time ago, like a million years, this guy who founded this town was rumored to have killed people. Whenever someone dies mysteriously, the Hill name comes up."

"Really? What kind of town did I move to?"

"Clark Hill was supposed to have killed all sorts of people—his wife for one. Everyone said it was because she had this child who grew up to be another nut, and they chained him up in their attic, but nothing was ever proved."

"Well, that's certainly gruesome!" I had a hard time sifting out the truth from Rita's drama-queen hyperbole.

"He had this outrageous temper. He found out his wife was cheating on him with one of the workers, and that child wasn't really his, so he killed them all. Or maybe the child belonged to one of the sisters, and she was the one he killed. I don't remember." Rita adjusted her vivid purple blouse, yanking it even lower, and picked up her large, orange designer bag. She resembled an ample peacock. I wondered why she carried a purse when she was going from her apartment to mine.

"Why haven't I heard about this? It sounds like a TV movie."

"That's what people always said."

"So Clark Hill might have had a son? And the son was fathered by either Clark or one of the laborers, or he may have belonged to one of the sisters?" Rita spewed gossip and scandal as readily as a rampant geyser.

"This town wouldn't be alive without its dirty little secrets."

"As a researcher, I found out most towns thrive on their dirty little secrets."

"I think this one has more than most." Rita threw herself onto the couch.

"What does a possible past killing or killings have to do with Timmy's death?" I couldn't see the connection.

"To keep Timmy from telling me his story," she argued as though the fact was perfectly obvious.

"But what is the story?"

"That's what I have to find out! For now, my editor wants some other angle to Timmy's murder." Her voice was still raspy, but all frogs had left the building. Heavy makeup and high-fluffed hair were back in full force.

"Tell me more about what happened at the police station."

"No time now. I need to think of something gruesome to write."

"How about devil worship?" I tried sarcasm.

Rita clapped her hands. "Perfect! I can work with that."

"With what? I was kidding. You can't just make things up," I countered. Facts were my livelihood.

"No time!" She raced toward the door. "El, you are super!"

Then she was gone. The room seemed suddenly

like a balloon with all the air sucked out. Rita's nervous energy gone again with a door slam. I was thankful she hadn't plastered my apartment with one of her cloying perfumes.

I heard the officer's heavy steps in the hallway and the clink of the cup against my door. Rita was lucky she wasn't in jail. Who was her mysterious witness? I tried to get back to Phyllis Anthony's story, but there were enough loose ends floating around my brain to knit an afghan. They clogged up my thinking.

Chapter 5

Just as I was finishing up my report to Phyllis Anthony, I heard a knock on the door. I wondered if Rita had returned, but then I remembered she didn't usually knock. When I looked through the peephole, I saw Mason Street. Opening the door, I was taken aback. Seeing him in person always took my breath away. He was taller than I remembered, sharply dressed in clothes I was sure were designer inspired, and had a lopsided grin that lit up the hallway.

"Mason! Hello. Come in." I ran my fingers through my hair. Had I brushed it today? Tried to smooth out the wrinkles in my sweatshirt.

"Hi, El. How are you doing?" He ducked a bit when I motioned for him to come into the apartment. He looked a lot fitter than the last time we met.

"I'm good, thanks." My brain seemed to be on vacation. "Oh, and thanks for helping me get this apartment. It's perfect."

He smiled and looked around. I saw the place through his eyes: computer on the kitchen table, papers everywhere, broken-down sofa. "I'm glad things worked out."

"Sit down, please," I said, shuffling some of my paperwork to the side.

"Maybe another time. I'm late for an appointment. I just really wanted to find out about Rita. I got your message. Does she still need a lawyer? I tried knocking on her door, but no one answered. There was a policeman walking the halls. Is he here for her?"

"I'm so sorry. I should have called you back and canceled. Her editor found someone. She probably didn't hear you knock because she's working on a piece for the newspaper and sometimes wears headphones. And, yes, that officer is here to make sure she doesn't bolt. She's a person of interest, whatever that means."

"So she wasn't arrested, just taken in for questioning? Something about a murder? Our sweet journalist isn't out killing people, is she?" He wore that concerned look I had come to know.

"No, she isn't, but she was at the wrong place at the wrong time." I didn't know how much to reveal.

"What did she say about what happened? Did this man Timmy say anything to her before he died?" He seemed to move in a bit closer. His interest seemed a bit intense.

"You know who got murdered?" I asked. "I didn't think the police had released any information."

He took a second longer than he should have to answer. "Well, it's a small town. Things get around." For a moment, he looked almost awkward.

"She didn't see him the night he died. I think she had talked to him earlier."

"Really?" he asked eagerly. "I mean, she said she talked to him that day?" He leaned against one of the kitchen chairs, trying to appear nonchalant. "Did she say what they talked about? What had he told her?"

I felt a chill run from the back of my neck down my spine that I couldn't understand. Like he had said, it was a small town, and I didn't want to get Rita into any more trouble. I also didn't understand his interest. It seemed to go beyond mere curiosity. "I think they just arranged a meeting time and place."

"Oh. I just wondered." I saw his shoulders relax slightly. "I better get going." He pointed at the table. "Looks like you have a ton of work as well."

"Just doing a family tree for a woman who wants to be connected to someone famous." I followed him as he headed for the door.

"Sounds fascinating." He turned, and the confident smile slid back into place. "I better let you get to it."

"Thanks. I'd be glad to do your family tree sometime. It's on me; I owe you that much."

"No!" His voice came out curt and loud. He laughed to ease the moment. "I mean, not necessary. I'm just glad you've settled in nicely." He turned the door handle. "Besides, I don't want to expose all the pirates and crazy uncles on my side of the family." He laughed again, and the strange moment passed. "Keep me in the loop with Rita. I'll be glad to lend an ear or advice. We have to take care of each other."

"Thanks, Mason. I appreciate you stopping by."

He waved and headed toward the elevator. I turned and found the bird staring at me. "What are you looking at? Maybe you think I should have offered him coffee or told him what Rita said?" I shook my head. He was the same Mason Street who had helped me with my mother and getting settled in Parkville, but there was a certain shifting that had occurred. Maybe I imagined it. After all, he was a lawyer and a nice guy. He was bound to be privy to certain information the public might not have. I was seeing boogie men where none existed.

Nevertheless, my sleep that night was not an easy one.

****

I was out of pumpkin seeds.

My go-to, stress-relief, can't-leave-the-computer snack. With Rita on the warpath, I needed all the stress relief I could get.

I grabbed my cart and set off for The Village Market. Even though the signs at the entrance to Parkville stated it was a city, it had a small-town feel. The downtown featured a mix of old-fashioned charm and new age allure. My rolling cart came in handy when I had to restock my other favorite foods—soup and coffee.

I wondered about Timmy and hoped that Rita had gotten more information. When my researcher brain saw a puzzle, it wanted to dive in and solve it. Timmy may have appeared homeless, but there were so many pieces of this jigsaw that didn't fit. Would we ever find out what big story he had for Rita? Could that have been the reason for his murder?

The Hill saga also summoned big questions for me as I filled my basket. For someone who had founded a city, why was there little evidence of his achievement? No streets named for him. No buildings bearing the Hill tag. No statutes. Not even a park. Why had Clark Hill been almost erased from the history books? I knew who to ask.

The first thing I did when I got back home was open a package of seeds and chew my way toward calm. Then I called Ida Parks.

"How's my favorite librarian?" I asked when she picked up the phone.

"Just dandy. And how's my favorite house whisperer?"

I grimaced. "You have to stop calling me that. That's not what I do anymore."

Before I moved to Parkville to care for my mother, I had worked for a company that produced a television show called *Haunted Histories.* I had been hired to investigate houses that people thought were haunted, excavating property deeds, tax documents, wills, and probates to see what secrets might have been buried by people who had lived there. I never spoke to the current residents; that job belonged to Barb Lipton, moderator of the series. I flew to whatever city was chosen and did the pre-work of getting information. Living in hotels and eating in restaurants for a week or more sounded glamorous in the beginning but soon developed into a boring necessity when one was all alone. Information I discovered was presented to the staff and discussed. The present-day owners were then brought to a studio where Barb revealed the house's history results to them—good or bad—on live television. It wasn't like the shows that looked for ghosts; we looked for reasons.

Sometimes I uncovered real evidence of past crimes or reported strange activities, but often the outcomes turned up nothing. But Barb had a good nose for finding just the right personalities, whatever the results. Often those homeowners who were told nothing was wrong with the house were the most adamant and stubborn, roaring their disbelief or screaming claims about all the curious happenings that had occurred while living there. Those live reactions of skepticism were often the most entertaining and brought the highest ratings. Though the show was a hit, I never really connected with the rest of the staff. They worked together to prep background and ready guests; I worked alone, gathering the data they would later sift through over beer and pizza. It was a jolt seeing my name in the credits, and the money was good, but it hadn't been that hard to let go when my mother called.

"Okay, how's my favorite researcher? Is that better?" I pictured her in the library, tall, black, statuesque. Her small red glasses firm on the end of her nose, the attached silver chain glittering around her neck, her hair a slicked-back bun of neatness.

"Much!"

"What can I help you with today?"

"I'm wondering about the town's history."

"Ah, someone's been filling your ears with mystery and mayhem." She laughed. "I'm not sure how much there is." Her tone turned serious.

"Come on! There are always tons of background documents."

"Usually, yes." She dropped her voice to low. "There was a fire long ago, and after that, someone or some ones did a great job of erasing what little there was. People don't think it's a good idea to poke around in the past or stir up trouble."

"Now, Ida, you know I just like to find out about where I live."

"Well, come in and dig around the old microfiche and microfilm. See what's there. I know the city government likes to think we popped up newly sprung as Parkville. Most all that's left are old rumors more suited to Halloween."

"I think it's time I unearthed that past." I could sense her hesitation over the phone.

"A word of caution. Some secrets aren't meant to be unearthed."

"Such as?"

"I have no idea. Clark Hill is not a popular person."

"I'll just do a bit to satisfy my curiosity." I tried to sound indifferent.

"And, you know what they say about curiosity."

"I've done enough digging into haunted pasts in my former job. No ghost has ever reached out and strangled me in my dreams." I shifted topics. "By the way, have you heard anything about the homeless man who was found in an alley? Timmy something? Do you or anyone there happen to know his last name or anything about him?"

"Not much has filtered through the gossip mill," she said. "Personally, I don't know much. He was always just Timmy. He lived in that old caretaker's cottage on Hill grounds for a few years. Sometimes you'd see him hitchhiking into town. Why?"

"Just curious. Does anyone know where he came from?"

"And there's that word again. Caution ahead!" She paused. "Not to change the subject, but you know we do have a historical society, don't you?"

"Really? I didn't see anything about that online."

"I doubt the person in charge would have anything online."

"Where is it, and who's in charge?"

I heard Ida laugh. "I'm not sure what's there."

"What aren't you telling me?"

"The building is at 1309 River Road. It's a house. The caretaker is Cassie Troy."

"Cool. Thanks. Should I call first, or is the society

always open?" I asked.

"I'm not sure she has a phone. You can try just popping in."

"Will do."

"I'll be interested to know what you think."

"About her or what I might find?"

The laugh again. "Either."

****

Letter to El Turner

Dear Ms. Turner:

I saw your ad in The Genealogist Gazette and thought I would write to you. I have a curious problem and don't know where to turn.

Let me explain. I come from a family where all the women have double, sometimes triple, chins. I am now in my thirties and worry this could happen to me. Is there some way to check the family tree to see if this is something inherited? I know my immediate family (the women) all have this problem (although they don't consider it a problem), but if I could see if it goes back further, I might then go to seek medical help.

Please let me know your thoughts on this matter. Thank you!

Sincerely,

Jennifer Chennly

PS: Do you think this has anything to do with our name? If it does, I would be glad to legally change it.

PPS: I hope you do not think this is a joke. I am truly serious. If you are in doubt, I can send a check or money order to convince you of my sincerity.

PPPS: And please don't laugh. I get enough of that in my family when I bring up the subject. That is why I hope an "outsider" can help.

****

Letter to Jennifer Chennly

Dear Jennifer,

Thank you so much for your letter. I can see how this might be a concern for you. My best suggestion would be to go through family albums that might show women in your family. If that is not feasible or does not give the results you want, you may wish to canvass the people in your family to see what they remember, despite what they may think. It sounds like they do not understand how important this is to you. Maybe if you describe how serious an issue this is, your mother or another close family member might be able to help.

I don't believe investing in family research would help you since photos and personal knowledge are the few items that might give you more information in this instance. Physical characteristics such as double chins would not usually show up on birth/death certificates, obituaries, or even medical records. You might express your concerns to your family physician. I'm sure there are medical procedures that may address this issue, and your doctor may be able to point you in the right direction.

Sorry I couldn't be of more help.

Good Luck,

El Turner

PS: I don't believe this is connected to your name in any way.

PPS: I can see how serious you are about this and would never laugh at your inquiry.

Chapter 6

Rita banged on my door early the next morning. I had told her I somehow misplaced my key and had to ask her for the other one back. She wasn't happy. I wasn't sure which was worse: having her barrel through the door unannounced or beating on it like a bongo several times a day.

"My story is in! I even quoted you for part of it." She waved an early edition in my drowsy face.

"Me? What for?" I turned on the leftover coffee and hoped it would heat swiftly. "I didn't know anything about Timmy."

"I wrote two articles: one about Timmy and one about the Hill family," she cried.

"But I didn't give you any information." I looked quizzically at her radiant face. Something told me I wasn't going to like what was coming.

"You had the idea."

I felt like I was swimming in mud. "What idea?"

"The idea about devil worship. It fit in well, and my editor loved it." She shook her head when I didn't respond like she wanted.

I was alarmed she mentioned me at all. "What exactly did you say?" I was wide awake now.

"I quoted you. You're my source." She grinned like a child. "Besides, it's nice to get your name in the paper. It might bring you some business." She looked into the hall mirror and puckered her lips.

"I have all the business I need." I poured out the reheated coffee, took a swig that only partially scorched my mouth, and reached for the paper she was reading.

"*Devil Worship Back in Parkville?* That's your headline?" I quickly scanned the article, my fears growing with each sentence. "Oh, Rita! You say Clark Hill was a possible suspect in several murders! You also imply he might be somehow connected to Timmy's murder. None of those things has been proven! You can't just go and speculate about this!" I downed another scorching slug of coffee, not even noticing the burn. I couldn't imagine a worse start to the day.

"Oh, phooey! That's just good journalism. It's a hook. It's how you get people to read the article. Besides, Clark Hill's dead. He can't reach from the grave and sue me." She grabbed the newspaper back, sulky at my criticism.

"I wish you hadn't used my name." She wasn't listening to me. "Rita!"

"What?" She reluctantly looked up from her article.

"Please, in the future, don't use my name without asking!"

"I thought you would be happy. You brought it up."

"I was being sarcastic. You can't just play loose with facts. And devil worship?" I hovered between anger and anguish. "I hate that people think I had anything to do with this. And besides that, you call me an International Researcher. That's not my title. I'm not international." I was sinking rapidly toward absolute embarrassment. My hands holding the hot coffee were shaking with fury. I wouldn't be able to show my face at the library for months. What would the people there think of all this?

"My editor loved it!" Rita was still a bit put out I wasn't heaping praise on her.

"Rita! Don't do it again!" She had dug a hole and put me at the bottom. "And what about Timmy? I thought he was the big story. You barely wrote a paragraph about him and didn't even mention his name."

"The story has become bigger than Timmy. I'm sure he would understand." She had certainly distanced herself from her supposed great friend and story source in favor of newspaper sales.

"Aren't you concerned about him?"

"The police are taking care of that. That's their job. Mine is to tell readers the human side."

"Just yesterday, the police weren't doing their job, and you wanted us to solve the murder. And, by the way, you are still a person of interest in the murder. Is it legal for you to write about what happened to Timmy?"

"I didn't mention his name in the Hill article. I left things very vague. We have a legal department that passed it."

"Rita, I thought you wanted to be a serious journalist. This kind of misdirection and innuendo is not what I would call serious."

"Spoilsport! You know what I mean. There are other levels to his story." She picked up the paper and waved it in front of my face. "I didn't say anything about the information he might have had. He did work for the Hill family, and he did have some kind of dirt on them. If only I had gotten to that alley sooner. Who knows what he saw or heard?"

"Did you get his last name or find out anything about him? I could research his background." I was trying to find a nugget of gold among the ashy disaster.

"Like I said, the police are handling that."

"What's going to happen to him?" I sank into my chair.

"What do you mean?"

"Did anyone claim him?"

"Claim him?" She appeared bewildered. "I think he's still in the morgue."

"Did anyone in his family claim him? For a burial, that is."

"He was homeless!" she exclaimed as if that answered the question. She went back to staring at her name in print.

"Homeless people do have families."

"Really?" She wasn't listening.

"Would you ask Reb Wilson what's going to happen to him? Maybe he was a veteran? Find out his name. Now that you got me involved, I would like to know more. Try to get my reputation back."

"Oh, Reb is so proud of me! He said he would buy a dozen copies of the newspaper with my stories." She strutted around the room, a fuchsia-skirted peacock today, her lime blouse thin as well as revealing. "I've never told anyone, but sometimes I see him following me around. You know, like tailing me when he thinks I don't see him. That man can't do without me. I just wish he didn't have such a jealous streak."

"Would you ask the man who can't do without you to get Timmy's name? Please."

"Oh, all right. I don't know why you care. He was

just another homeless man."

"Somebody gave birth to him. Taught him how to read and write. Took his hand crossing the street. Laws usually require police or the city to make an effort to locate next of kin." I shook my head and went to get another cup of coffee. "Besides," I shouted from the kitchen, "I thought he was your good friend."

"Yes, he was. And I never thought about it that way." She stared off into space, suddenly somber. "I guess the city will be responsible for burying him if they don't find anyone." She brightened a bit. "Maybe if he was a veteran, the veteran people will put him in a special cemetery. Maybe even give him a medal."

"In old days, indigents and people with no families were put in what were called potters' fields or unmarked paupers' graves."

"Oooo, paupers' graves. That sounds spooky." She grabbed her bag. "Maybe I can use that in my next story."

"Just leave me out of it! Don't quote me on that or anything else. Promise!" I shook my finger at her.

She grabbed the paper off my desk. "Gotta run. My editor wants more. Maybe tomorrow morning I might just see if I can get through the gates of that Hill place and interview the person living there now. See if they have a statement in response to this story. There's also a lady who lives across from the Hill house who seems to know all about them." She took out her lipstick and smeared hot red all over her plump lips. I wondered if she had had any kind of lip enlargement. With the bright paint, they looked almost bee-stung.

"What happened to your police tail?"

"The police had other matters to deal with, and Reb

vouched for me. Told them I wouldn't run off."

"Well, just don't go running off; Reb gave his word. And don't mention me in your article, Rita." I hoped she would find out more about Timmy. "Do you want to borrow my tape recorder for the interview?"

"Silly, I have my phone."

"Right. Your phone." I still carried an aged flip phone and had a landline, too old-fashioned for my own good. I just wasn't a smartphone and social media kind of girl.

"Wish me luck! Double toodles!"

"Promise me, Rita! Nothing about me in any article," I shouted as she ran out.

Once more, the quiet settled like a welcome friend. I threw on some clothes and walked down to the local newsstand, dreading the task but knowing I had to read her article.

Mr. Marquez greeted me with a grand wave, our talk in the park forgotten. "*Buenos días mi amigo.*" His dark eyes twinkled as he curled his hefty mustache with his fingers. Usually, we spent the time in bi-lingual chatting, but today was not the time for it.

"*Buenos días Sr. Marquez.*"

"*Qué puedo hacer por ti hoy?*"

"Today, I would like a newspaper."

"El, you only learn Spanish if you speak Spanish."

"*Me gustaría un periódico por favor.*"

"*Un periódico para El Turner.*"

I put my money on the counter and picked up the newspaper. I hoped he had not read the article.

"*Mañana.*"

"*Mañana. Gracias, Sr. Marquez.*"

Even though I hurried back home, I puttered

around aimlessly, paying more attention to Polly than usual, ignoring the article but wondering just how bad it was. The newspaper taunted me from the table where I had thrown it. When I couldn't stand it any longer, I sat down and read it from start to finish, the short paragraph about Timmy first. The other was a typical scare-the-townspeople bit of overdramatic fluff. Devil worship is coming to your neighborhood so beware. Maybe I could change my name before too many people read it. I was doomed!

The parrot had an I-told-you-so sort of look.

Chapter 7

Cassie Troy was not what I expected.

A wig of blond ringlets cascaded down onto her shoulders. Bright red bows rested like two devil horns on the top of her head. She certainly rivaled Rita in the makeup department: spots of rouge highlighted her cheeks, and her false eyelashes could have reached out and touched me. Her bustled brown dress captured the 1800s, and she carried a faded pink parasol with dangling fringe. I had no idea how old she was under all the trappings. A short, stout little woman, she looked quite like a child dressed up for a party.

"Hello! Hello! Welcome to the Parkville Historical Society and Preservation Center. Please come in." She flung the door open. A swift rush of mothballs and stale air freshener slapped me in the face.

"Thank you. My name is El Turner."

"And I am Cassie Troy, curator of the Parkville Historical Society and Preservation Center."

"I didn't know Parkville had a historical society. How long have you been open?" My jaunt to the historical society seemed a safe journey for today. No one knew me there. No one would be talking about the article or looking sideways at me. I wouldn't have to explain anything, and I could find out more about Parkville. Maybe even see if there was a connection to Timmy and the Hill family. Researching someone else's family was a far saner option than thinking about my own.

"The Parkville Historical Society and Preservation Center began on April 1, 1998."

"Oh, April Fools' Day."

Her thin, arched eyebrows came together in what I took as reproach.

"You've been open that long? Wonderful." I hoped to regain her enthusiasm.

"Yes. Well, it got a slow start. It took me ages to collect everything you see here, but we are very proud!"

The room dozed like an unused parlor. Heavy red curtains shrouded the windows. She lit several oil lamps that swathed the room in an archaic atmosphere but caused the air to reek from the smudgy smoke. My eyes encountered clutter on every surface. She had peppered the walls with old photos and maps. I felt my heart leap at the possibilities before me. It seemed like a researcher's dream. I couldn't wait to start digging. Questions sprang to mind like spring tulips.

"I can give you a tour if you like."

"That would be wonderful, Mrs. Troy."

"Miss Troy." She twirled her parasol and bashfully looked down at the floor.

"Miss Troy, yes. Thank you."

"Should we start with the maps?"

"Of course."

"Now, these maps show the progress of Parkville. You can see they are dated according to year. Here, for instance, is the beginning construction for the Parkville Mall. The next year shows how far the workers got. And so on." She closed her parasol and used it as a pointer. The floppy fringe proved a rapid distraction. I refocused on the worn maps. They appeared more like battered copies than originals.

"These maps are all of the same area."

"Yes. They show the progress of the area where the Parkville Mall was constructed. If you look closely, you can see each year is represented."

Even in the limited lighting, I could tell the maps were all identical. The dated years were handwritten on each with a shaky pen. The copies were so faint it was hard to tell land from street. I had no interest in the Parkville Mall whatsoever.

"What are these maps over there?" I hoped to move on to something more in line with my quest.

Those eyebrows rose again as if I had breached some unwritten etiquette.

"Next on our tour are the overhead views of the same area for the same years represented. I think it shows the depth and dimension of that project."

I was getting dizzy trying to find differences among the blurred photos. I couldn't tell if they were horrible shots or too dust covered to be clear. "Yes. They certainly show a depth and um."

"Dimension?" Miss Troy offered.

"Exactly! Just the word I was looking for." I made a show of being engrossed.

"And then the tour takes us to the train and bus schedules over the years. Folks just love to look at those."

Tacked to the wall were worn brochures that were so difficult to read they could have been supermarket flyers for all I knew. My enthusiasm was sinking faster than a torpedoed boat.

She continued, moving us along the room. "Now,

these you might find exciting. They are genuine original paintings I did as a child. This one highlights our home, this very house in which you are now standing. It has been in my family for decades. And here we have my family—dearly departed mother and father with me in the middle. My parents always said I should have been an artist."

Leaning in to get a better look at the jagged lines and abstract figures, I accidentally knocked over a tiny knickknack from a nearby table. Fortunately, I didn't hear anything break, but Cassie Troy leaped into the air as though snake bitten.

"Oh! My childhood tree ornament! Oh goodness!" She picked it up off the floor and patted its roundness, cooing and coddling the object. "Lucky for you it did not break. That ornament is priceless!"

I considered myself lucky indeed as she placed the scratched and dented silver decoration back on the table. A thick layer of dust surrounded the exact circle where it had rested. She gave it another loving pat before turning back to me, parasol shaking at me like a scolding finger.

"Please use the utmost care around these historical objects. You destroy anything and it is like destroying history. You don't want to destroy history now, do you?"

"No, ma'am." I felt like a wayward six year old. I wondered how soon I could politely depart.

She lowered her parasol and gave a short smile, once more the kindly docent figure.

"You can see the tables are full of treasures from the early Parkville period."

"Where did you find so many treasures?"

"Many were in the attic. Some hidden away in the basement. Naughty little jewels!" She worked her way around the room, humming, caressing objects, stroking, and speaking to them randomly.

Careful not to move suddenly, I inched around seeing dolls with eyes and hair missing, jacks with no ball, a lead pencil with bite marks, a school primer, a pair of old scuffed tap shoes, a baby dress edged in yellowed lace, and truck loads of other odds and ends. Now I knew why Ida had laughed.

"Can I get you some tea, dear? You must be exhausted after my lengthy tour. I do tend to go on."

"No, thank you, Miss Troy." I tried to calmly work my way toward the door while keeping up a prattled conversation. "You said this home had been in your family for decades. Were you born in Parkville, Miss Troy?"

"Why, yes. My grandfather was one of the founding fathers of Parkville."

"Really?" A glimmer stirred as my hopes again rose. "He was a Hill?"

"No, but he knew the Honorable Clark Hill."

"Honorable? Oh, I didn't know Mr. Hill was a judge."

"He was the most honorable man in these parts of the United States!" She shouted, swinging her parasol over her head like a sword. "A giant! A legend!"

I moved out of the way, wondering if I should make a run for the door, but she lowered the weapon and smiled. I still hoped there was information to be mined.

"How did your grandfather know him?"

"The Honorable Clark Hill gave him a job. Him

just an immigrant with little command of the language and no money in his pocket received the blessing of a job." Her eyes swam in dreamy remembrance.

"Was he one of the workers who helped build the Hill house?"

"The house already stood in its magnificence when my grandfather arrived. The other buildings were nearing finish, and he became the storekeeper. A job with prestige and responsibility."

"Fascinating! Too bad there are no pictures of that time."

"Oh, but I do have one old photo of him."

"Where?" I was eager now. "I thought a fire devastated most everything of that time." Maybe there were nuggets of history yet to be unearthed in this misleading wasteland.

"This was taken before his journey here. It was snapped not long after he arrived in America. He carried it with him always."

She pointed to an old sepia picture of a man, hesitant and guarded, looking warily at the camera. He wore a high-necked white shirt and a dark suit too small for him. Bony wrists and rough hands jutted out of the shirt sleeves. "Wasn't he handsome?"

"Yes. Very handsome."

"I wish I had known him." She sighed.

"How long did he manage the store?"

"Until the fire took the town. He only survived because he had traveled to get supplies that day."

"When exactly was that?" Dates would be nice to have.

"Not long after the century turned to another age. All that history up in smoke." Tears trickled down her cheeks, causing the rouge to forge red tracks to her chin. "A town just beginning then destroyed." She appeared to be looking back into history like some sort of crystal ball, her chest heaving with sobs.

"Were people killed in the fire?" I turned away to give her time to collect herself.

"Some of the workers lost their lives. And all those buildings! That hard work! Mr. Hill was heartbroken."

"Is that what your grandfather said? That he was heartbroken?"

She spun around almost angrily. "Of course he was heartbroken! To lose everything he worked to achieve."

I wanted to say he didn't lose his house or his life but decided to hold back on my comments, fearing another round of hysteria from Cassie Troy.

She lumbered off to stand in front of another old picture. A small broad bull of a man with a fantastic beard, long dark hair, and thin sneering lips stood between two women who sat stiffly forward in their chairs. One of his hands rested on each of their shoulders. Even with the antiquated photography and worn exterior of the picture, one could see the beauty of the women shine through. Hair parted in the middle and pulled taut behind their heads, graceful uplifted faces, bodies trim and tidy in elegant lacy dresses, their essence was breathtaking.

"Delilah and Felicity, Clark's sisters. Like all the Hills, they had the beautiful black hair and green eyes. And that child is little Boris."

"Ah, so they were his sisters. I thought one might have been a wife. Lovely! I bet they had to fight off the men."

"What do you mean by that?"

"I just meant being so beautiful and all, they probably had many suitors."

"People talk, say they dallied among the working men, but I never believed that!" She stared at the picture then shook her head. "That man who was killed was in here not long ago asking me about the family.

"Timmy?"

"I don't know his name. He wanted to know the whole history of the Hill family and what they looked like. I think he was getting ready to steal my picture, but I asked him to leave before he could."

"When was he here?" Like Rita, I wished we had known what information Timmy had on the family, especially the nephew who was living there.

"Last week or the week before. He wanted me to tell him everything I knew." She looked around to make sure no one else was listening. "I think he had been drinking."

"What exactly did he want to know? What part of their history?"

"Strange questions, like how tall they were, what color hair they had, did they have extra-long ear lobes, what were their fingers like. All ridiculous things he was asking. I don't remember. A thousand questions. He was most insistent. Very ungentlemanly." She started waving her arms around in the air. "I had to ask him to leave, but he just hung around looking at the photo. He grabbed it and made for the door, but I hit him repeatedly with my parasol until he dropped it. He made me so angry that I could have killed him." She stopped then, her head wobbling back and forth. "I chased him for several blocks before he got away from me. For an old man, he ran fast."

"I wonder why he was interested."

She just stared at me, a scowl growing on her lips.

"Did he mention the Hill nephew who is staying there now? Do you know anything about him? Did he say what he knew about them?"

"I won't discuss the matter any longer." She wedged her parasol between us.

I brought her quickly back to the picture, hoping for a peaceful distraction. "Did the sisters marry?" I longed to grab the picture off the wall and examine it more closely myself. "That looks like a child on her lap."

"That lady is Delilah, and the child on her lap is Boris." Cassie returned to her calm hostess self.

"Her brother or her son?"

"Yes, he was the youngest Hill."

I squinted to get a better look. The child was on the smallish side, but on closer inspection, his face had the look of an old man.

"Was he the son or a brother?" I asked again. "I remember hearing there was some trouble in the family."

"Oh, people in this town do nothing but talk! He couldn't help it! He couldn't help it." She repeated. "They have no idea what a great and magnificent family the Hills were!"

"So the gossip about Clark possibly killing anyone is not true?"

"I won't hear such nonsense!" She put her hands over her ears.

"I'm sorry. I didn't mean to disturb you. I was just trying to get the correct information. I'm a researcher," I finished lamely.

She lowered her hands. "I'm afraid we must close early today. I will show you to the door."

"Of course. Thank you." She was shepherding me toward the front of the house with a shooing motion. "Miss Troy, I know this is a lot to ask, but could I possibly take that picture and make a photocopy?"

"Certainly not! One does not make copies of history!" She almost pushed me forward.

"You are quite right." I tried to appease her. "The original aspect of history is extremely important." I kept my mouth shut about the map copies. "Would it be possible for you to take the picture down off the wall so I could get a better look?"

"If you know history at all, you know that touching such items could tarnish them forever! I simply cannot take that chance!"

"Could I use my flip phone to take a closer shot then?"

She made a strangling noise and clutched a nearby table. I thought she might pass out.

"No problem, Miss Troy. Please forget I asked." I decided to change tactics and get some last-minute information before she propelled me outside. "What does this town have against Clark Hill?"

Based on her other reactions, I shouldn't have been startled, but I was still unprepared for her outburst. "They were out to get him! He was a great man! He didn't do the things they say he did. I know he didn't! My grandfather would not have helped a man who could do those things."

"Who was out to get him?"

"Unfounded lies!" Again the parasol swung through the air. With the red tear streaks across her face and the righteous look in her eyes, she gave off the impression of being totally demented. "I have gone to every City Council with the truth, but they refuse to listen! He never killed anyone! Unfounded lies!" She echoed.

She had backed me into a corner near the picture of the family. "I'm sorry to upset you, Miss Troy. Perhaps I should leave." I began to wonder if I should call the police. Was this anger what Timmy had dealt with? Could she really hurt someone?

"A kind man," she continued looking back at the picture. "A most wonderful man." She glanced my way as if seeing me for the first time, then rushed toward a door near the back, sobbing uncontrollably and charging through the room with her parasol before her like a lance.

I leaned in and took one more parting glimpse at the photo, then hurried for the entrance, afraid Cassie Troy might return. An over-decorated shoe box stood on a chair near the door with a sign that read *All Donations Welcome.* All I had was a twenty-dollar bill, but I pushed it through the slot and left.

Outside, I took a deep breath. Ida had a lot to answer for!

Chapter 8

The day was still young, and I decided to drive over to the alley where Timmy had been killed. What I hoped to discover, I wasn't certain, but it seemed like a good place to start digging and a way to get my visit to Cassie Troy's historical center out of my brain. Maybe I could find clues that would help clear Rita. After all, I was a researcher, and this was field work.

Yellow caution tape still hung across the alley entrance where the police had placed it. Would I gain any information by peering into the inky depths of the narrow passageway between the two buildings? I sat in my mother's car and wondered if I could even slip under the tape. Was there a policeman standing guard somewhere? Would I be arrested for going into the alley?

As I pondered my next move, I happened to see people sitting on the porch of a house down the street. I drove closer and stopped the car. An older man and woman were swinging the afternoon away on a porch glider. It couldn't hurt to ask them a few questions. See if they knew anything about the murder.

They started waving at me before I had even taken a few steps in their direction, so I headed over.

"Hi. How are you folks today?"

"Oh, we're just fine, honey. Take a seat." She pointed at a few dilapidated cane chairs. I eased my body onto the least rickety one.

"Lord, I hope she ain't selling anything," the older man mumbled. He had a bundle of thick, white hair and sported a mustache and dimpled cheeks. A pair of long thin legs kept the glider moving.

"She's not a salesperson, Hubie. Can't you tell?"

"So what do you want, Girlie?" He was a bit more forceful this time.

"Hubie! Where's your manners?" Rosy-cheeked and grandmother-sweet, she pushed her wire glasses back up her button nose and smiled. Her feet were nowhere near touching the deck. "I'm Susie Q, and this old grouch is Hubie Hawkins. You want some sweet tea, honey?"

"That's very kind of you, ma'am. Thank you."

"Now, Hubie, you let me off this wild ride so I can get our guest her refreshments."

Hubie stopped the glider with his foot. They shared a secret smile before she went inside.

"This is a nice street." I tried to make conversation with the old man.

"Used to be." He spit out words like watermelon seeds.

"Well, your front yard flowers are beautiful."

"Not my doing."

"Here you go, honey." Susie Q's sing-song voice saved the awkward moments as she handed me the tea.

"Thank you." I took a large gulp hoping to bolster my confidence. Instead I tried not to choke on the overly-sweet liquid.

"Something wrong, honey? Do you want me to add more sugar?"

"No, I'm fine." The man glared at me, so I went

on. "My name is El Turner. I love the name Susie Q. It's unusual." I wondered if I could accidently spill my drink in the flowerbed.

"Well, my daddy was from Louisiana and enjoyed that rockabilly music. When Hubie Hawkins came calling, my daddy saw us as the perfect match!"

I must have looked puzzled because Hubie shouted, "She's too young to get that reference, Mama."

"Well, it's pretty all the same." I tried to switch gears. "I was just curious about the incident in the alley."

"See, I told you, Mama." The man slapped his leg. "Another lookie-loo."

"Well, it's just human nature to be curious, isn't that right, honey?"

"I don't suppose you folks were outside here when it happened?"

"Well, you suppose wrong!" Hubie's gruffness reverberated in the stillness of the empty street.

"We love our porch, honey. We enjoy the night sky, trying to see the moon and any stars." She looked longingly down the street. "Used to be more homes around here, but they got moved aside by business. All our friends and neighbors gone. We loved to walk along the street and visit with other folks sitting out savoring the evening. One by one they got bought out, but Hubie wouldn't hear of moving."

"No one's chasing me out of my home!" The old man waved his fist in the air.

"Now all those outside business lights kind of detract from the heavens." Susie Q sighed.

"You call them shops, businesses?" Hubie

rumbled. "One sells candles, and the other sells drinks called kommie-something. Can't call them regular businesses."

"It's kombucha, Hubie." Susie Q's laugh sounded like a gentle wind chime.

"Did you see anything?" I asked, trying to get them back on track. "I know it was dark when it happened. Were you still outside?" I tried another swallow of the tea, hoping it had improved. It hadn't. If anything, it tasted sweeter.

"We sit outside in all kinds of weather, day or night." Susie Q beamed as if she had won a blue ribbon.

They must have seen the doubt on my face because she followed up with, "Oh, we're not scared of sitting on our porch at night. Hubie keeps a rifle just inside the screen door."

"And I ain't afraid to use it!" he shouted. I was sure whatever was left of the neighborhood knew it.

Susie Q patted his knee. "Well, we talked to Timmy earlier that day, poor man."

"You knew Timmy?" I was startled. They didn't seem the kind of people to mingle with Timmy. "Sorry for interrupting, but I didn't think he had many friends around."

"Wasn't our friend. Just came and sat on our porch." Hubie's voice rumbled like thunder.

"He just came along that afternoon and said his name was Timmy, and he had to wait for someone and wondered if he could sit a spell on our porch steps." Susie Q explained. "I gave him a big glass of sweet tea, and when we came out later, he had dozed off."

"Sleeping like the dead, he was." Hubie chuckled at his own joke.

62

"Hubie! Be kind now. Kindness is about all we have left in this world to give to one another." She patted his knee again. It seemed to be a familiar gesture and appeared to soothe him momentarily. "Isn't that right, Ms. Turner? About kindness, I mean."

"Yes, ma'am. I'll have to agree with you there." I tried to imagine how wonderful it would be to have grandparents like this. To come and visit, maybe have Sunday dinner. Something homecooked. Then to sit out on the porch and look for the stars. My thoughts about spilling my drink vanished. I knew at that moment I could only show my kindness to these two people by finishing my tea.

"We went into supper, and I was going to fix him a plate, but he had disappeared," Susie Q said. "We didn't know where he had gone until some nice policeman in a dark Homburg hat walked over and told us the next day." She suddenly looked dreamy. "I do love a man in a Homburg hat." I conjured up a picture of a grizzled detective with a gruff voice under a stodgy old hat.

"Now, Susie Q, I ain't wearing no hat. We been through that." Hubie shook his head, but he wore a hint of a smile.

"Anyway, we did see a tall thin man go into the alley," Susie Q continued.

"Looked like a weasel the way he slunk around!"

"Do you want to tell the story, Hubie, or should I?"

"You go ahead, Mama." He looked like a chastised boy.

"A while later, we saw this bright yellow car pull up, and a little red-haired lady got out. We could see her a bit before her headlights turned off. Hair big as cotton candy. She went in, and then this bulky man started moving around in the shadow of the building."

"Looked like a brick! And don't shush me, Mama! I got a right to my say."

"Yes, he was a very large man, but that's all we saw. Then the lady came running out, got in her car, and sped away. We didn't see the large man again, but the tall thin man snuck out later. If he had a car around, we didn't see it. With all those shadows there, it's hard to see. Hubie had his spy glass, but it was pretty dark."

"Spy glass?" I asked. I held my breath and gulped what was left of my drink.

"Binoculars. Couldn't really identify anybody. That's what I told Mr. Homburg hat."

"Poor Timmy," Susie Q said, looking down. She folded her hands as if she were praying.

"Stay out of dark alleys is my advice, especially at night," Hubie muttered. "That red-haired little woman was taking a chance going in there alone."

"Hubie was getting ready to get his gun and make sure she was safe when she came running out."

"Like a bat out of you-know-where!" Hubie was clearly enjoying the tale. I wondered how often he had been through it.

"Well, I have taken enough of your time. Thank you so much for talking to me." I got up to leave

"Did you know Timmy well?" Susie Q asked.

"Well, I have a friend who knew him." I didn't want to get Rita involved more than she already was. "Again, thank you for the tea, and stay safe."

They both waved as I walked to my car. I marveled again at what it must be like to have a partner in life, to sit out on a porch swing and pass the time, to spread kindness and love. Would I ever find that, I wondered?

Then the questions flooded into my researcher's brain. Who were the men they had seen in the shadows? One was big as a brick and the other tall and thin. Maybe the big man was Reb Wilson. Rita had said he sometimes followed her around. Were Susie Q and Hubie the witnesses who had taken the pressure off Rita and provided her with an alibi?

****

Email to El Turner

Dear Ms. Turner,

I am writing to see if you could get my family more information on a newly-discovered aunt on my father's side. We are having a large family gathering shortly, and I would like to unveil the recovered information then. It will be a surprise for all of us.

I have attached a file with all the facts I have as to her name, location, etc. Please let me know your rates and if you need anything more.

Thank you. I hope to hear from you soon.

Sincerely,

Wanda Darren

****

Email to Wanda Darren

Dear Ms. Darren:

Thank you for your email. I would be happy to look over what you sent and give you some pricing information. With all the facts sent, it should be fairly easy to follow her trail.

However, I strongly recommend looking over the results before announcing it blindly at a family reunion. Sometimes the information can be sensitive or even upsetting. I will get back to you shortly.

Sincerely,
El Turner

Chapter 9

The newspaper article was clipped and shoved under my door the next morning. I found it on my way to make coffee. Decided it was better to read it after the coffee was made.

Researcher Convinced Recent Murder Connected to Past

I would absolutely choke her! I couldn't believe she had written another article quoting me. And this time, I was the center of it all! No wonder she hadn't come knocking. It was humiliating. The story was full of fantastical claims and fiendish rituals. There was no way I would ever be able to show my face anywhere in Parkville again. What would the ladies in court records think? The article was slipshod in style and made no pretense of even remotely sticking to fact. I had cautioned Rita not to jump to any conclusions regarding the death of Timmy

Tears came to my eyes. I was so angry. Article in hand, I raced down the hallway to Rita's apartment, battering on her door as she had done mine. I was close to breaking it down, yelling and screaming for her to open up and face me. Some of my frustration evaporated as I continued to hammer the door and realized how much I was hurting my hands. I began to kick the door, but my slippers made the task almost impossible.

"El, what's the matter?" Jenny Lane leaned her purple-haired head out of her apartment door.

"Oh! I'm so sorry, Jenny." I added lamely, rubbing my aching hands on the sides of my pants. "I was just looking for Rita."

"I think she went out early when I was doing my Tai Chi."

Jenny Lane was a seventy-something new-ager. Tall and agile, she celebrated yoga and meditation, downed the vitamin supplement of the moment, and dyed her long braid every shade of purple possible. She wore ballet shoes and floated volumes of chiffon-like gauze with her every movement.

"I just got a new relaxation CD. Would you like to come in for a listen and have some kombucha? They can help calm a churning spirit." Her dangling earrings flashed and chimed in the silence.

"Thank you, but I can't today. Again, I'm sorry to have bothered you." As I hurried back to my apartment, I realized I still had my pajamas on, hadn't combed my hair, and wore a face decorated with tears.

I went inside, locked the door, and buried my head under the pillow. When the light got too bright, I felt bad for the bird and lifted the cover. I tried a mean stare-down contest, but I lost. The parrot wasn't very colorful, just a bit of red on her tail. Her coat seemed dull and matted. I wondered if I needed to brush the feathers or anything. To avoid thinking about my present life, I spent time reading the booklet until I knew more than I wanted about African gray parrots. Then I read it again.

I looked up into her eyes. "If you're so smart, why don't you talk? It says here you are the *Einstein of birds.*"

I wondered if she had talked at the pet store. I called Josh, but he wasn't in the store.

"E equals MC squared?" I tried again, babbling out nonsense. "Who's a pretty bird? Who's pretty as a picture?"

Being the lesser evil of items I didn't want to dwell on, I started to think about my mother and pictures, or rather the lack of them. I didn't remember ever seeing any in all the time I grew up: no kid on a pony, no birthday party, no grandparents in the backyard. My mother had once mentioned that we lost a lot of things in our moves, and I had never questioned the explanation. Or was that just an excuse? Had I been adopted? Did I have a real family somewhere else?

What else had I missed growing up?

My mother's job, for another thing. Aside from her sales travel babble, I couldn't recall her mentioning any jobs she had or remember her ever working, yet we always had money. We had a nice car, nice places to live, and moving cash. Had her men supported us? A father paying childcare? And why had we changed locations so much? We had never left in the middle of the night, so it didn't appear we were short on the rent. Just one day she would set me to packing, and within a week or so we were off. I had images of her laughing as we placed our belongings in a vehicle as if we were starting on an exciting new adventure.

And where was my mother from? My birth certificate listed Los Angeles, CA, as my birth city. Was that her home state? She had not done a lot of talking, at least not to me. Was it even real, or had she somehow gotten a fake birth certificate for me? If the answers lay within her boxes stacked in my empty room, I still was not quite prepared to look just yet.

Stretching my shoulder muscles, I stood and thought about food. A slight movement off to the side of my vision startled me. Then I remembered the bird.

"I wish you could talk," I said. "I need to bounce this information off of someone, even a bird."

Her eyes told me *fat chance.*

It wasn't until later, when I picked up Rita's article again, that I noticed her note in the margin: *Off to interview whichever Hill opens the door. You're the best!*

The best would have cheerfully wrung her neck if she had been there.

****

It took a day or two of wallowing around the apartment before I noticed Rita wasn't around. She was probably still afraid to face me. I had purposefully been avoiding meeting anyone I knew and burying myself in my work. I had the feeling everyone was talking about Rita's satanic hogwash.

I let my phone calls go to voicemail, but I did answer one from Ida Parks.

"Honey, I just called to see how you're doing. No one here believes you had anything to do with those ridiculous articles. We know the kind of meticulous work you produce. You're a first-rate researcher. Where did they come up with this stuff?"

"Thanks, Ida. I've been too humiliated to stick my head out the door."

"Now don't you go thinking like that! Anyone who has ever worked with you knows you wouldn't say those things, claiming that some people from the past had anything to do with that homeless man's death." Her soothing words were a comfort to my sorry state.

"Rita definitely took this too far."

"Is she the lady who wrote the article?"

"Yes, she's my neighbor, and I thought my friend."

"Keep your chin up, El. This will blow over soon. You have friends in the library." I could feel the hug she would have given me if we had stood face to face. "Every few years someone on the newspaper revives those old rumors, but this demonic dribble is a new spin."

"Your call means a lot to me, Ida. Thank you!"

"I noticed the police have stayed mum on this man's death. Folks have been saying he got knifed in that alley. That he had stab wounds all over his body. Other people say he was poisoned. I swear, if a penny falls to the ground, it turns into a million-dollar bill by noontime. Between the library, the post office, and the grocery store, there seems to be no need for any actual facts."

"That's what gives Parkville its small-town mystique. In a big city, no one cares. They read the news or listen to it on TV, then go about their day. Here one can listen to ten theories while taking a quick trip out for stamps."

"Glad you still have your sense of humor about you." Ida's laughter was contagious.

"Speaking of a sense of humor, I never got a chance to thank you for the tip about the historical society."

The phone went quiet, and then I heard her hushed admission. "I'm so sorry, El. I do apologize. I shouldn't have sent you over there without prepping you first. At least not with all this other stuff going on. Cassie has some good days and some bad days, and you have to admit she has some knowledge about this town's history. Her family's been around a long time."

"Are her parents still alive?"

"No. They died when she was fairly young; they were in a freak boating accident on the river. Her grandmother brought her up. Once her grandmother died, Cassie's lived alone in that big old house ever since."

"She has a picture of the Hill family."

"I've seen it."

"Cassie seems to be one of the few people on Clark's side. A kind man, not a killer."

"Yup. She has always been very vocal about it. I'm not sure what her source is, but who knows the information lying in wait in that house?"

"Either a researcher's fantasy or nightmare."

"I'm glad to hear you laughing. I was so worried you might never come out of your door again!"

"Has anyone ever been inside the Hill mansion and lived to tell about it?" I asked.

"No one's done a search. Any members of local government over the years have ignored it or been rebuffed." Ida sighed.

"Amazing what documents might be in that house as well. How does one go about finding out who lives there now?"

"People come and go in that place. They don't cause the police any trouble, and the city doesn't care who they are as long as the taxes are paid. Some years it just sits empty. I think whoever pays the taxes also pays for mowing and upkeep."

"I wonder if the tax records would show anything."

"Specifically what are you hoping to find?"

"I'm not sure, but Rita, the lady who wrote the articles, seems to think the people who live there now had something to do with the homeless man's death."

"If that's true, I'd stay away and let the police handle it."

"You're right, but it couldn't hurt to just look at the records. They are public."

I could see her shake her head on the other end of the phone. "Honey, whatever you do, you be careful!"

"Noted. Talk to you soon, Ida, and thanks for calling."

Our mothers had brought Ida and me together. More specifically, the names our mothers gave us. Mine had hoped for a movie star; Ida's mother dreamed she was fostering another dedicated activist. Both mothers had been disappointed.

A bigger question remained and pushed aside my curiosity about the town: Where was Rita? It really wasn't like her not to be around and bragging about her journalistic success. Crowing about what Reb Wilson thought of it. Although the silence was pure heaven, I decided to walk down the hall and calmly knock on her door. Before I could get that far, I heard a soft rap on mine. It was too polite to be Rita's.

Through the peephole, I saw a badge, a tall rail of a man, and then a black Homburg hat. Still, I opened the door warily, the chain in place. "Yes?"

"Miss Turner?"

"Yes." This must be the man Susie Q had mentioned. He was younger than I had imagined, and grizzled didn't fit anything about him.

"Inspector Poe. Parkville Police. Can I ask you a few questions?"

"Have I done something wrong?"

"Not that I know of. I'd like to ask you about Rita Starr. She appears to be missing."

"Missing? But I was just talking to her."

"When was the last time you saw her?"

"Ah…" I thought back. Often I lost track of time. "Maybe a few days ago. She had just written a story for the newspaper, and she showed it to me."

"Do you know her well?"

"She's in my apartment all the time, but I don't know her favorite color or book if that's what you mean."

A slight smile played across the man's lips, but it was gone before I could tell if it was real. He had a kind face. There were laugh lines around his mouth, but his eyes held mine and seemed to keenly measure every movement I made. I didn't want to be on his bad side. Yet, I felt an urge to ask him in for coffee.

"If you hear from her, please let us know." He handed me a card through the small space of my still-chained door. A spark shocked each of us as his hand briefly brushed against mine.

We both laughed a bit awkwardly.

"Shocking to meet you, Miss Turner." His mouth moved upward.

I looked down, feeling like I had to give some explanation. "The carpet in these hallways can produce that effect." It sounded like idiotic drivel. I switched it up quickly. "Can I ask what happened to Rita?" I stared at the card he had handed me, afraid to look back into those steel blue eyes.

"That's what we're trying to find out. She's a person of interest in a murder investigation. We need to get a hold of her. Which apartment is hers?"

I took the chain off the door and pointed down the hallway.

He stopped and looked into my apartment. "Is that an African gray in the cage?"

"Yes. I inherited the bird, but it hasn't said a word, though."

"Beautiful birds. Give it time. Then you might just wish the dang thing couldn't talk." He tipped his hat and moved down the hall to Rita's apartment. I wanted to follow him, but he glanced back at me, and I went inside. I noticed Jenny Lane's lilac halo peeking out into the hall.

Rita missing? What had happened? Had she ever made it out to the Hill house? Had she asked one question too many?

I relocked the door and went nervously back to my research, the bird's stare not the only thing giving me the creeps.

Chapter 10

I spent the rest of the day delving into Wanda Darren's mysterious aunt. The start of any research was like a quest, a clean slate waiting to be filled. The information she had given me made the journey fairly easy. By the end of the day, I had most of the answers. I wasn't sure Wanda Darren would be happy with them.

There is a reason some people fall off the family tree, disappearing either by design or through shame and embarrassment. We are glued to people we may or may not like by the substance called blood. We may not like them; we may spend our entire lives feuding with them. In the end, we want to know all about them. We want to fit them onto one of the branches, even if they do not want to be there.

Kelly Emmett, Wanda's aunt, had been lost among the leaves of the family tree for a good reason. She had run off with a circus clown and traveled with the show for years. That is until she almost beat another clown silly because he had stolen her husband's clown car. The story made a few issues of the *Williamstown Herald*. It appeared she hit the man with one of the bowling pins used by the Zalenko Brothers, a juggling act, and they had been implicated in the trouble. After they were cleared of the charge, Curtis Zalenko's wife Mysteria—the circus fortune teller—tried to run Kelly over with the stolen clown car. She succeeded in badly bruising Kelly's shin. The two got into a hair-pulling scuffle that ended up in the wrestling mud pit. Rita would have loved it.

All involved were asked to leave the circus and find employment elsewhere.

I wondered if such a fate awaited me when I got around to digging into my mother's past. With all the uncertainties swirling around my head, two incidents floated up out of the forgotten mire.

The first was when I was maybe eight or nine years old. I remember the man of the moment was sitting in the living room of whatever place we were renting at the time and smoking one of his horrid cigarettes. My mother complained about them constantly, airing out the drapery and bombarding the living room with every spray freshener known to man. It seemed odd since she smoked cigarettes. But he hung around for quite a while, so she couldn't have minded too much. One day after school, he asked me what I wanted to be when I grew up.

After a few minutes of thought, I answered, "A jewel thief."

"That's my girl!" My mother had laughed, clapping her hands and looking all shades of proud.

Why it stuck with me or emerged when it did, I don't know. Was my mother a jewel thief? Was she dating a jewel thief? I recalled that she sparkled a lot of the time: diamond earrings and a diamond ring. Had it been a wedding ring?

The other memory was when I was younger. We had just stopped at a pawnshop. I knew I had misunderstood her when she said pawnshop. "Are we getting a puppy?" I had asked, thinking she had said paw and shop, as if that were the name of the store. Back then I imagined a puppy to be the best gift in the world. When we went inside, however, I didn't see any pets. "Are they behind the counter?" I continued my daydream. Instead, my mother received a wad of cash she fanned in front of me.

"This is better than a puppy any old day!"

She had treated me to ice cream, and I suppose I repressed the memory. I tried to dredge up any other visits to pawnshops but could not. What had she sold? Hot merchandise? The possibilities seemed endless and caused me to want to avoid the sealed boxes in my spare room at all costs. I wasn't ready for such excitement. I hoped Wanda Darren was.

I typed up my final report and invoice and sent it off to Wanda, asking her to read the material first and cautioning her again about revealing the results cold. I enclosed the hard-to-believe newspaper articles. I didn't think I wanted to be at that family reunion.

****

Once more, my morning was interrupted by a knocking on the door. I wondered if I could get a mat printed with *Unwelcome.* Or maybe steal a door marker from a local hotel that read *Do Not Disturb.* Or maybe if I ever got the bird to talk, I could teach it to growl or bark. At least this visitor had waited until a decent morning hour to come calling.

I got up from my coffee and computer and went to the door. Through the peephole, I saw Reb Wilson, crisp and polished in his uniform. This must have to do with Rita! Maybe he had some information. Unlocking the door, I pulled it wide.

"Oh, hi, El, ah, Miss Turner. I'm sorry to bother

you, but I wondered if I could have a few moments of your time." He stumbled over the words as if he had rehearsed then forgotten them at the last moment.

"Hello, Officer Wilson, please come in." I stepped aside to let his muscled bulk pass. He removed his cap and ducked slightly, entering the door. I never noticed his squared jaw line and squinty dark eyes. His head looked like a block with brown fuzz on top.

"You can call me Reb, ma'am."

"Okay, Reb. Then you can call me El."

"I feel like I know you already since Rita talks, ah, talked so much about you."

"Yes, she talked about you as well. Won't you sit down?" I had an instant fear of him sitting on one of my used kitchen chairs, having it splinter beneath his mass, and seeing him end up on his uniformed butt, but he chose the sturdier couch and settled himself.

He folded his hands in front of him, then clapped them slowly together, unsure where to begin. "You know Rita disappeared. I mean, we both know Rita. What I mean to ask is if Rita mentioned anything to you before she disappeared. What were her last words to you?" He shifted uncomfortably. "Well, I don't mean last words in the sense of final words, just the last thing she said to you."

I had only met him a few times in the hallway as he was leaving her apartment, but Rita talked about him so much I probably knew more than he would have liked. He drove an old restored Chevy that he and his father had worked on together, loved country music, even played bass guitar in a country western band on weekends, had never shot anyone in the line of duty, and preferred briefs to boxers.

I realized he was staring at me, waiting for an answer. Remembering her last words about visiting the Hill house, I thought they probably belonged to Inspector Poe. Telling Reb Wilson first didn't seem advisable. I had no idea what he would do with the information. Would he storm out to the Hill place? From what Rita told me, he could be a bit of a hothead.

"You can tell me. I'll pass the information on to my superior. This is just a follow-up. I know Inspector Poe has been here to question you." He had a clipped way of speaking as if that's what he thought people expected of police officers.

"She didn't actually say anything to me," I replied. Truthfully, she hadn't *said* where she was going; her last words had been written on the article slipped under my door.

"You see," he appeared to drop the policeman guise and suddenly looked like an overstuffed, lost, forlorn puppy, "we had this big fight the night before." He ended lamely. "I don't even remember what we fought about. Something stupid about those articles." He looked straight into my eyes. "I hoped she hadn't run away because of me and our argument."

"I'm sure that's not the case." He didn't look like he could handle anything other than that answer. Fragile was not a word I would have applied to him, but that's the very thought that rang in my mind.

"Really?" He brightened somewhat. "She didn't tell you about our little tiff?"

The big fight had dwindled to a little tiff. He was already dismissing it in his mind.

"She didn't mention anything about your disagreement. Honest." I had lowered the spat even further. "I'm sure she'll be back before we know it."

He kept nodding his head like a puppet. Still, he made no move to leave.

"Can I get you anything to drink, Officer Wilson?" He didn't seem to hear me. "Officer Wilson?"

"Yes, ma'am?" He looked around as if he wasn't sure where he was.

"Can I get you something to drink?"

"No, thank you, ma'am." We had shifted away from Reb and El.

He stared at the door as if Rita might walk through at any second.

"Where did she sit when she visited you?" he asked.

"What?" I wasn't sure I had heard him correctly.

"When she came here. I know she spoke about coming here often." He studied the room. "Where did she sit?"

"Well, usually, she just paced around the room."

He laughed suddenly, a loud, braying explosion that scared the hell out of me. "Yes, that's Rita. Too much energy."

"When she was off work, she'd often flop on the couch where you're sitting and paint her toenails."

"I could feel her vibration here." He sighed. "That's what led me to this couch." He ran his hand over the sofa surface.

I hesitated to tell him that I didn't have much furniture, and the couch seemed probably the best thing to hold his weighted bones. He wasn't fat, just big and bulky.

"I can see you really care about her."

"I love that woman!" He moved his mass to the

edge of the sofa. "I've never told her, but sometimes I just follow her around. When she doesn't know it, that is. I just want to see where she's going. It makes me feel closer to her somehow."

It sounded way too disturbing for me. "What do you think happened to her?" I asked.

"Ma'am, I have no idea. I've run down every lead I could think of, on duty and in my off times. I've gone to all the places she liked to hang out, our favorite restaurants, even the riverbank, though Rita didn't care much for the outside. *Too many bugs*, she said. But I checked the riverbanks, just to be sure. You never know."

I couldn't picture Rita walking the area along the river, her high heels sinking into the damp ground. It almost made me laugh out loud. Reb was right, though. Rita was not an outdoor kind of girl, but something about his tone had shifted, appeared darker.

He kept rubbing the arm of the couch and stared forward, seemingly in a trance again. His eyes narrowed, and his breathing grew heavy.

"Officer Wilson?" I wondered how long he planned to visit. I had work to do.

"Did you know we had a fight the last time I saw her?" His voice lowered and held a whispery quality. "She really got me angry. I flew off the handle. Those stupid articles. Why did she have to keep writing about that old stuff? Should have left it dead and buried."

Things had progressed from creepy to spooky.

"That night was almost like I was watching myself. Like I was standing off to the side and seeing me clench my fists and getting mad." He stopped, staring straight ahead. I noticed he was again clenching and unclenching his fists. Had he done something to Rita? She said he had lost his temper a time or two. Had he gotten so angry he hit her? Could he have done worse? He always seemed like an awkward, lumbering, nice guy, but this bizarre man before me set off some alarm bells.

"Officer Wilson? Are you all right? Can I get you some water?"

"I followed her that night. That night she went to the alley to meet her source. I wanted to make sure she was safe. Are you sure she didn't tell you about that?" he droned, not looking at me.

My mind reeled. Rita thought he had followed her, and now he had admitted to being in the alley the night Timmy was murdered! Had he done something to Timmy? I tried to sound convincing, making my voice light and innocent. "She didn't tell me a thing. Honest." If Reb Wilson was dangerous, I had no hope of getting out safely.

He threw his head from side to side, like a dog shaking off water. In an instant, he was back to being himself. He looked around the room. "Ma'am, I'm sorry to have taken up so much of your time. It's just I'm concerned about Rita." His voice now sounded a bit forced and unnatural. "That little lady is special in my books. I'd do anything to protect her. I can't believe anyone suspects her of murdering that homeless man."

I rose to my feet, hoping it would be a hint for him to leave. "Yes, she is a special lady."

"Would you let me know if you hear anything?" he asked hopefully. "Anything at all. Any time of day or night. Here's my cell phone, my office number, my email, my twitter, my address." He handed me a card stuffed with numbers and addresses.

I had grown extremely wary, but at that moment, I felt a twinge of sadness for the guy. From what I gathered, he was more into Rita than she was into him. But there was that whiff of uncertainty. He was a big man with admitted anger issues. I hoped he hadn't harmed Rita in any way. Or Timmy. He had been in the alley the night of the murder. He was the brick Hubie and Susie Q had seen. Was he overly jealous or overly protective? Surely, my imagination was working overtime.

"I will keep this handy, Officer Wilson."

"Thank you." He stood ill at ease near the door, shifting from foot to foot, and finally stuck out his hand for me to shake.

After closing and locking the door, I turned to Polly. "Outwardly, he seemed like one love-sick policeman. I hope I'm not wrong about him. That got weird back there."

The bird bobbed its head twice as if it agreed, but one question remained. Where the hell was Rita?

Chapter 11

I knocked on Rita's door off and on the next day and tried her cell phone, but it just zipped to voice mail. All her social sites remained open but inactive. She popped into my mind when I was doing research, looking out the window, or watching the news. Oddly, there was nothing on the TV about her. I wondered if I should tell the Inspector about her plans to go out to the Hill mansion and interview whoever lived there. Surely nothing could have come of that, could it? I called Poe's number, but he was out, so I left him a message.

Toward evening, I went for a walk, still thinking about her. Could her disappearance have something to do with the articles? Did her headline about devil worship stir up some old hushed secret? Was someone new in the Hill clan now a murderer? Did they come from a long line of murderers? I hated to think that Rita had met a dire end at the hands of a killer, but such things did happen in the world. I chastised myself for being silly and tried to think of lighter solutions: She had taken a vacation. Gone shopping in New York. Run away with Reb Wilson. I crossed off the last item; Inspector Poe would know if Reb Wilson was also missing. Plus, he had just come to see me. Maybe it was all an act on his part. As much as I eye-rolled Rita's constant interruptions, I now missed them. Where the hell was she?

Crossing the street to get a newspaper, I felt a hand grab my shoulder and wrench me out of the road and back onto the concrete just as a car whizzed past, taking my sandal with it. My leg jerked with the force of the wind. I tried to move.

"Stay down a minute," a low voice cautioned in my ear, hand now holding my upper arm.

"What? Let me go!" I struggled away from whoever was holding me down.

"Are you okay?" The hand holding my arm helped me stand up.

I turned. "I'm fine if you will just let go of my arm!" I demanded. The hand dropped. The hand belonged to a tanned beach body with curling blond hair, startling dark eyes, and flashing white teeth. A wolf grin to match. He wore baggy shorts and a T-shirt, and I almost expected to see a surf board nearby.

"Yes, ma'am! Glad to see you are still in one piece." His face came close to mine, and I smelled rugged surf and sand. "You need to watch where you're walking."

I rotated my shoulder and stretched out my back. Felt scrapes and bruises popping up on my arms and legs. "What happened?"

"You stepped into the street, and a car almost ran you down. If I hadn't pulled you back, you'd be riding the grill of that vehicle as we speak."

A small group of people had gathered to see what the commotion was and to ask about my condition. I realized I had no shoe on. My sweatshirt had been torn at the elbow, and my jeans were ripped in several places. Little pieces of dirt and gravel clung to my clothes.

"My sandal."

A woman bystander went to the street and retrieved it, the strap broken, the thin bottom crushed.

"Sorry," she said, dangling it before me.

I reached for it anyway. "I'm fine. Really." I began to walk away from the stares, only to have my leg buckle beneath me and almost fall. The hand was there to catch me.

"Here. Lean on my arm. I'll help you get home."

I took stock of the situation: bedraggled woman, hair in disarray, with one bare foot and one mangled sandal needing immediate assistance. If I wanted to get home, there was no other way since my legs suddenly acted like boiled noodles. I nodded and felt the strong arm surround my waist. "Do you want me to carry you?"

"*No!*" I cried a bit too loudly. "No," I tried again. "If we go slowly, I can make it." I was suddenly glad my apartment building had an elevator. I limped gingerly along, feeling every stick and pebble on my bare foot. "Thank you for helping."

"No problem. Glad I was there. I'm not even sure that car saw you. This is your building, isn't it?

I nodded, relieved it was close. "Yes, that's it. And there's an elevator."

"Great. My name's Jack, by the way."

"I'm El."

"L like the letter?" He stopped and stared at me.

"L for long story."

A deep chuckle. "Yeah. Names are like that. We could all use an upgrade in that department."

"You look very familiar. Have we met?" I asked.

That wolf grin again. "I think I'd remember."

I punched in my security code, and Jack pulled the door open. Albert, the daytime concierge, ran forward to help, wrestling the man for my other arm.

"Miss Turner! Oh my goodness! What happened?"

"I'm okay, Albert. Just an almost hit and run."

"Do we call the police?"

"No. Please. I'm fine. I'm not even sure what the car looked like. Are you?"

The man called Jack shook his head. "A dark car. Tinted windows, I think. I wasn't really paying attention."

Luckily, the elevator was waiting for us. Albert seemed reluctant to let go.

"This kind man can help me up to my apartment. Thank you."

"Call down to the desk if you need anything. Anything."

"El Turner," Jack said as we got into the elevator. He pressed the button for my floor. "Didn't I read your name in the paper recently? Something having to do with the death of that homeless man? That you were involved in some way? That's very exciting!"

"Guilty." I leaned a bit closer. He smelled like the ocean on a sunny day.

"The paper said you were some kind of important researcher."

"I don't know about important, but I do research." The elevator opened, and we stepped out. Jack turned to the left in the direction of my apartment.

I had little time to wonder how he had known which building was mine, what floor I lived on, where my apartment was, or how he had recognized me before we were at the door. I took out my key. "Thanks. I can take it from here."

There was movement down the hall, and I saw a woman in a knit hat slip out of Rita's apartment. Before I could say anything, she was gone. I knew it hadn't been Rita.

Where was Jenny Lane when I needed her inquisitive purple head?

"Let me help you in, at least, get you settled. We can look at your injuries and see if you need a doctor." Jack pressed his hand against my back.

Remembering Rita, I realized it might be too late to be wary. "I'm much better. Thanks again. Really. You've been so kind." I let myself in and closed the door. Quickly locked it. I listened to hear the elevator door open and close.

The guy was cute in a bright shaggy sort of way, but I didn't know who he was. Just for safety, I dragged a kitchen chair over, wedged it under the door knob, turned on every light, and hobbled to the sofa. My body screamed from every surface. Maybe I should have called the police or at least gone to the hospital. I thought about taking a shower and changing my clothes, but I didn't have the energy. Every horror movie I remembered that featured a disastrous shower scene suddenly ignited terrors in my brain and refused to go away. I pulled the colorful afghan around me in weak sympathy and tried to drown out the pain. I didn't even get back up to cover the bird.

I wondered about getting a dog instead. A big fierce dog. A big fierce dog with gigantic teeth and a slobbering snarl who would protect me above all else. What good was a damn bird that couldn't even talk? I sensed a strange wind hovering.

****

My eyes creaked slowly open, the light attacking like a horde of killer wasps. Someone was once again knocking at the door. Maybe I should get a doorbell. This early morning door alarm was getting to be the most annoying, frustrating, disturbing habit. Groaning and gently stretching, I felt the thousand aches and throbs. A cheese grater against my skin would have been kinder. I was an idiot not to have taken a hot bath the night before. My fears had gotten the best of me. Well, I would spend the daylight hours soaking in water up to my eyeballs. Maybe drag a bottle of wine or two in with me. I tried to remember if I had anything stronger.

"Coming!" I called out, my voice rusty, my throat dry and sore. I wondered if I had chipped any teeth in my fall or bit my tongue. It felt too big for my mouth. My head pounded like a heavy metal drummer at a rock concert. I limped slowly over to the door and looked through the peephole. Inspector Poe stood on the other side.

Smiling in spite of the stabbing pain, I mumbled, "Just a minute!" I did a hasty shuffle to the bathroom and ran a brush through my hair, ignoring the shambled mess that was my face. Tried to straighten the clothes I had slept in. Splashed some mouthwash between my teeth. The stinging sensations shot through my mouth, almost making me scream in agony.

I undid the chain and let him in. He took off his hat, and I saw the short wavy brown hair beneath. It went well with his deep blue eyes.

"Miss Turner. I got your message."

I moved aside to let him in just as he took a second

look.

"What the hell happened to you?" He took a step backward and rethought his exclamation. "Sorry. That sounded bad. What happened?"

"I had a run-in with a vehicle while crossing the street."

"When was this? Did you call the police?"

"It happened yesterday evening. I went out for a late paper."

"Was the car trying to hit you?" Inspector Poe interrupted.

"Why would a car try to run me over?"

"Just asking." He looked me over from head to foot. I was still wearing just one sandal.

"Why would you even ask a question like that?" My brain felt scrambled.

"It's my job."

"Now you're scaring me. What's going on? Have you heard something about Rita? Am I in danger?"

He quickly changed the subject. "Can I take you to the doctor? You look like you could use some stitching up."

I suddenly noticed the jagged scrape marks and dried blood on my elbow and knee. I sat back down on the couch. "Please tell me what's wrong. Please."

He lowered himself into one of the chairs. "Miss Turner. I don't know what or if anything is going on. Rita Starr is still missing." He hesitated a moment. Judging by my disheveled appearance and pleading look, he let sympathy win out. "No one knows where she went. Even her boyfriend, Officer Wilson, has no idea of her whereabouts. Her editor at the paper reported her missing, but he says she sometimes takes days away from the office. I'm stumped. I don't know if we have a kidnapping or just a woman off on a random pleasure spree. I can tell you that those articles have stirred up a lot of dust."

I remembered my anger about the articles. "That's an understatement."

His eyes again scanned my face. "Rita Starr is a person of interest in a murder investigation. She was told to stay where we could reach her. Officer Wilson could get in a lot of trouble; he gave us his word she wouldn't leave. If you know her whereabouts, please tell me now."

"Honestly, I'm as confused as you are."

He took out his notebook. "Can you tell me anything more about her visit to the Hill residence? You left me a message about that."

"Only that she was going to interview whoever was staying there."

"About that story she was writing?"

"Well, I guess so." I tried to find a comfortable spot, but there didn't seem to be one. My body was on fire. "That and to ask whoever lived there about Timmy. She was working on the theory that someone in that house killed him. Timmy told her he had a big story about them but never got a chance to tell her. I think she was also going to canvas the neighborhood to see what people knew."

"Was she trying for a scoop or trying to do our leg work?" He seemed irritated. "Do you remember what time she went there?"

"She was here first thing in the morning to slip her article under my door, so I assumed she went there after she left my apartment. Maybe her car is somewhere around there. Have you looked?" I asked, a tinge of exasperation in my voice.

"Miss Turner, we have searched several areas for her vehicle."

"Miss Turner sounds strange. Please call me El." I tried to make amends even though the pain interfered with any hospitality on my part.

"Okay. El it is."

"Did you talk to the people at the Hill house?"

"And are you working to take my job away from me too, El?"

I tried to stand but lost my balance. He caught me in an instant. "Sorry, Inspector Poe. I'm still a bit fuzzy from almost being run over. I didn't mean to tell you how to do your job."

"No harm. People do it all the time." He held onto my arm as I flexed my weary bones and plopped back onto the sofa. Men holding onto my arm was getting to be a habit. His eyes had grown dark, and I couldn't read anything further in them.

"If you don't mind, I think I better see about getting out of these clothes. Maybe slip into something more comfortable." His eyes didn't stop watching me, and I felt my face redden. "Wrong choice of words. I meant to take care of my wounds. Survey the damage."

"Yes, good idea." He cleared his throat. "I think I might go have another talk with our friend Joseph."

"Who?" I was beginning to feel sorry I had stood up. I gripped the back of the chair. My head was reeling. He was standing so close to me. His nearness sent sudden waves of warm energy through my body, almost erasing some of the pain. He smelled really good, not like the surf, but like the sky: crisp and clean.

"Joseph Kerr Hill. At least, that's what he told me. It's hard to keep track of who stays there. People just tend to ignore the old place."

"Did this Joseph person say Rita had been there? Did he talk to her? What did he say? Did he seem suspicious?"

"Whoa. Hold on!" He realized he was still clutching my arm and let go. "He said he never saw or talked to her, but I think I'll pay him another visit. Now I would strongly suggest you get into a hot bath, take some aspirin, and go to bed. Are you sure I can't take you to a doctor?"

"Absolutely positive. Thank you, though."

"Looks like your bird needs food and water. Can I do that for you?"

"Yes, thank you. The food is in the kitchen."

"The bird could use a few more toys. These parrots like to keep challenged." He put his hand in the cage with one of the treats.

"Careful! She'll rip your hand apart!"

To my surprise, the bird tilted its head and allowed Poe to briefly rub the side of her face.

"I don't believe it! Are you some kind of bird whisperer or something? She almost pecked my hand to pieces. I can't even get close to the cage."

"They're smart birds. I think he probably knows how you feel about him."

"I've been calling her Polly, but you said he. How does one know male from female?"

"Well, that might take some research." He looked me over. "That's what you do, isn't it?"

"I've never done a family tree for a bird, but I guess there's always a first time!"

He turned at the door as if he were about to say something more, hesitated, put his hat on his head, and was gone.

I locked the door and did the chair wedging under the knob. Maybe I should see about getting a stronger lock on the door. The apartment had always felt comfortable, but now I began to wonder about safety issues. I stuck my tongue out at the bird.

"So you know how I feel about you, huh? Well, I'm not even sure I know how I feel about you! For the time being, I'm the main source for your food and water, so you better be nice!" I limped over to the cage. "And what did that man have that I don't? You were pretty nice to him!" Polly tilted her head. I wished she could talk.

I checked that all the windows were closed and latched, ran the water as hot as I could in the tub, decided to forgo the bottle of wine and took aspirin instead, secured the bathroom door, pushed the hamper in front of it, and eased myself into the water. I ignored the initial sharp sting screaming from all the cuts and scrapes, letting the warmth work out the aches, stupid birds, Hills, and serious blue eyes.

****

Email to El Turner

Dear Ms. Turner:

Do you find husbands for people? I'm kind of desperate.

Please don't dismiss my question. This is an honest inquiry.

Yours,

Winifred Schnickelback

PS Do you think names define a person?

****

Email to Winifred Schnickelback

Dear Ms. Schnickelback:

Thank you for your email, but unfortunately, finding husbands is not one of my services. I mainly research family trees or find legal documents. May I suggest one of the internet dating sites? I know many people have used them with wonderful results. Good luck in your quest! Let me know how it turns out.

Best Wishes,

El Turner

PS: I definitely do not believe that names define a person. I believe we define our names. Many people are saddled with names they would not choose for themselves but rise above the issue. For example, my mother named me after an old time Hollywood star. I decided to shorten my first name to El and have never looked back. Have you thought of using a shortened version? Winnie S. has a distinctive flair about it.

Chapter 12

I lounged around, trying to give my wounds a day off, but the boredom soon got the better of me. The bath and aspirin had helped. I shifted my focus to Timmy no last name. I remembered Rita saying he had been staying at a homeless shelter. But which one? I picked up my phone and systematically went down the list only to hear, "Sorry, we can't give out that information" over and over. At the very last one, an exasperated woman said, "We've already answered all the questions for the police." Bingo!

After calling Ida to find out where it was located, I set off on my mission: Find out all I could about Timmy. Mid-afternoon, I dressed in the biggest baggiest set of sweats I owned, hoping they would be kind to my injuries. I drove my mother's car carefully looking for the address in question. At least it was an automatic vehicle with enough room in the front seat to accommodate my sore spots. However, upon arrival at the shelter, I was abruptly blocked by a power-mad little woman at the door. I focused my attention on several old men sitting outside.

I smiled innocently. "Did anyone here know Timmy, the man who died recently?"

I got a line of blank faces.

"You a reporter?" one asked, then spit a wad of chewing tobacco that just missed my foot.

"No." I didn't know how to describe myself. "I'm just trying to find out if he had any family."

"Sound like a reporter," the tobacco-chewing man said.

"Yeah. But she don't dress like one. At least not like that other one." Several of the men laughed.

"Did she have red hair?" I asked, certain they were talking about Rita.

"Didn't notice her hair." The man spit again. "Noticed her low-cut blouse."

"That's enough." A tall man with a tuff of white hair stood up. "Ma'am, come walk with me a bit. My knees get locked if I sit too long. Let's mosey across to the park." He wore a shabby sweater and pants that seemed too loose for him.

"Sure enough, Sarge." The man sat back quietly.

"Will Pepper." The tall man held out his hand.

"Hello. I'm El Turner." I shook his hand. "That man called you Sarge. Are you a military man?"

"Used to be. Before life had its way with me." He led the way to the park. I was extremely glad he was a slow walker. If he noticed my winces and hobble, he was too polite to comment. "What's your concern with Timmy?"

"I think the reporter who was here is my neighbor. She wrote a few articles for the paper, and now she's missing."

"That nonsense about devil worship?"

"That's the one."

"His name was Timmy Russert. Tim, I think. You know he used to work for the Hill family, right?" He saw me nod and went on. "He was caretaker there for quite a while. Watched over the place when it was empty. Helped out when some relative or another was in residence."

"The main family doesn't live there?" I asked.

"I don't believe anyone knows who that is anymore." He stopped and looked at the sky. "Town takes a dim view of them. Always has. Earned or not."

"Do you know why Timmy was fired?"

"Not really, but I had the feeling he was hiding out from something or someone." He continued forward. "I know he hated those who were living in the big house now. Didn't rightly think they were genuine."

"What made him think that I wonder?"

"That man had a head full of strange ideas, so I just dismissed it." He turned onto a path that seemed to circle the area.

"That rings a bell. I went to the town historical society, and the lady there said he was asking all sorts of questions if the Hills had any similar characteristics like hair or eye color. Now you say he thought this guy living there might be a fake." It all seemed too much of a coincidence to me, but I wasn't sure where it led.

"Seems he was onto something," Will Pepper said.

"But why? What did he care? Was he afraid they might steal something from the house?"

"He did seem to take an unnatural interest. I thought it was because he had been the caretaker."

"Did he do or say anything else odd while he was here?"

"You mean something besides hiding that bundle of money under his mattress?"

I stopped in my tracks. "Bundle of money?"

"Thought that might grab hold of your attention." He eased himself onto a bench in the sun. "He showed it to me one day. Big chunk of bills with a bank band around it."

"Did he steal it?"

"Can you steal something that's already stolen?"

"I don't follow."

"He hinted it was stolen money. I think he was getting ready to tell the story to your friend, the reporter."

"Did he say where it came from?"

"Not a word, but it might have been what got him fired."

"What happened to the money?"

"Gone." He shrugged. "All places got someone who will poke into a body's personal stuff. We had Danny Boy Cooper. I think he overheard and took the money. Anyways, it's gone, and so is he."

"So it's been stolen a third time?"

"I guess you got that right!" He gave a snort I took to be a laugh.

"Could this Danny Boy have been the one to kill Timmy? Like maybe he was looking for where Timmy got that money?"

"Well, I'd say no. He's a sneak, not a killer."

"Do you have any idea who would murder Timmy?"

He thought for a good while, then stood up suddenly. "Don't rightly know and couldn't guess. I will just say the man had secrets." He moved off back toward the shelter and stopped. Giving me a stare, he continued, "I don't think he was the drunk everyone says he was either. I think he played it."

"Played it?"

"Pretended. People tend to let their guard down

around a drunk. I think he used it as a decoy, a diversion."

"How old would you say he was?"

"Hard to say. He had gray hair and walked bent over, but, again, I wonder."

"Did he ever say where he was from?"

"No, ma'am. He said something once about his mother living here, but I don't know if he was putting me on or not."

"Did you tell all this to the police?

"No one asked us. Some big hulk of a cop spoke to Mrs. Rachett in the office and then left."

"I see." He had given me a lot to digest. "Well. I thank you for your time. At least now I know Timmy's last name."

"Sorry, I can't help more. He wasn't here that long." He cut the sentence short.

"Nice to meet you, Mr. Pepper." I shook his hand again.

"Just call me Sarge." He shuffled back across the street. "Everyone else does."

****

My excursion to the homeless shelter took more out of me than I had thought, my scrapes and bruises protesting once again, but I was anxious to get to my computer and see what I could find on Timmy. Will Pepper had given me some good leads.

Several hours later, I was no closer to any truth about the man. There were tons of Timmy/Tim/Timothy Russerts scattered all over the country. Searches for Parkville and the state yielded nothing. Other than the gray hair and bent body, I had no idea what he looked like, so online images did little.

If, as Will Pepper seemed to indicate, Timmy disguised his looks, his age could cover a wide range.

Research often resembled a squirrel running up a tree and checking out every branch or limb along the way. One by one, I eliminated possible candidates, finding them to be current bankers, students, or community stalwarts. I knew from trying to track down my father that if someone didn't want to be found, it might take years and a lick of luck to find them. People with no ties could disappear easily.

Sometime into the evening, I remembered Will Pepper's comment about Timmy's mother possibly being from the area. Very few Russerts appeared, and no one even remotely similar to Timmy or Timmy's mother. Maybe Russert was her maiden name when she lived in Parkville. Maybe Timmy had been born here and moved away. Randomly searching through birth certificates didn't seem appealing. However, a hot bath and bed certainly did.

Up to my chin in warmth and water, I chastised myself for being a bad researcher. From the newspapers I had read, the police had gotten no further in their inquiries either, asking the public to come forth with any information. But I had skills; this was my life!

I knew I was missing something.

With a head jerk that sent the back of my skull colliding with the tub, I realized I had fallen asleep, the rapidly cooling water around me sending chills through my body. As I hastened to get out and wrap myself up in a big warm towel, the thought almost got away from me before I called it back: Maybe Timmy's mother had worked for the Hills or been connected to them in some way.

I speed-dried myself and jumped into cozy pajamas. Then I settled back at the computer and tried to find any listing of Hill employees over the years. It proved a dead end. Surely someone in town might know: Cassie Troy? Ida? Mr. Marquez? I'd follow that thread and see where it led, but for now, the day and my sore body had caught up with me. I'd see what kind of mountain that idea looked like in the morning.

****

Letter to El Turner

Dear Ms. Turner,

I can't say I am pleased with the results of your research into my father's aunt. Your discovery that she ran away with a circus clown and got into all sorts of trouble was a complete disaster at our family reunion. I had hoped it would be a joyous occasion and one that we could celebrate in years to come. Instead it was a hopeless catastrophe! Poor Grandmother Tootie fainted when she heard the news and fell face first into Melba's scrumptious peach pie. As a further insult, the weather turned and we were completely rained out. Aunt Gertrude's world famous potato salad was a soggy mess. In a way, I am not surprised since it was my father's side of the family. They do have a wild gene running through them.

I firmly believe in situations like this you should warn people of what your report contains so they can decide what to do with it. If I had known, I never would have revealed the contents. I have half a mind to demand my money back.

You will not be getting a good recommendation from me.

Disappointed,

Wanda Darren

****

Letter to Wanda Darren

Dear Ms. Darren:

Please accept my apologies for what you describe as a disaster.

If you look back at our correspondence, you will see that I clearly suggested several times you view the material first before springing it upon your family. I would always advise that to clients.

I am refunding the money you sent and, again, I am so sorry your reunion did not go as you had hoped.

Best,

El Turner

Encl.

Chapter 13

When I woke the following morning, Rita was the first face I saw. Now that I knew a bit more about Timmy, I realized I had to do something to help find Rita. After a delicious cup of coffee, I stretched and rejoiced with fewer aches and no new pains. The old ones showed good manners and stayed quiet. I even made small talk to the bird.

"Sorry I've been ignoring you, Polly, but I needed to rest my bruised and battered bones." I hobbled around the cage, changing water and adding food. I quickly opened the door and threw a treat on the floor before the beak could descend, but the bird didn't move from the perch.

My eyes fell on the notes of research I had done. Timmy and his mysterious/mythical mother hovered around the room like intriguing butterflies that would have to wait for another day and a sharper mind.

Then it came to me: I would stake out the Hill house for traces of Rita and also find out if there was some connection to Timmy's murder. Maybe there were clues. How I would achieve that was something I hadn't yet figured out.

Rita, however, was another matter. The Hill house had been her last known stop. Maybe someone had locked her in a tower. Or maybe even a cellar.

"Now I'm thinking like Rita," I said aloud. "And

that's not a good habit to adopt!"

What I expected to find by watching the mansion, I didn't know, but I was sure something would raise flags. Maybe I could find someone there to talk to and see if they were up on the Hill history. Possibly they had records or photos that would help. I wondered if anyone had ever asked them for information over the years. The house must be a treasure trove of evidence. If I mentioned I was a researcher, they might let me look around. I would love to get inside and snoop, but I didn't see how that could be accomplished. A dangerous move if Rita agonized somewhere inside the mansion. It seemed like there was a boatload of maybes. Whatever I discovered on my stakeout, I would get to Inspector Poe.

Over my third cup, I started wondering if my mission was to learn clues to Rita's disappearance, find out Hill/town history, or see Poe again. Alan Poe. Those eyes of his were damn fine. The first time he appeared at my door, I felt an attraction. Maybe if I found some clues, he would see me as a hero! I dug through my closet and pulled out a dark sweatshirt, pants, and watchman's cap. It was what all the TV detectives wore to blend in. I threw an apple and my laptop into a bag and set off; the caffeine worked to help me ignore the soreness and throbbing that still persisted.

My mother's vehicle looked really dusty in the parking garage. Living in the city, I hadn't needed a car. I walked, biked, or taxied where I had to go. I remembered the day I had loaded my mother's few boxes of odds and ends. The boxes were still sealed, sitting in the darkest regions of my spare room. My stomach clenched at the thought of what might be hidden there. Today was not the day to find out!

I hauled my weary body into the vehicle. My driving, however, was all over the place, impeded by flashing recurrent pain and rigid discomfort, worse than yesterday. What had started out as an easing of soreness a few hours ago, now reared an ugly reminder of speeding cars and dangerous street corners. What made me think I was some super woman? I ignored the throbbing and tried to concentrate on finding signs of Rita.

I drove out in the direction of the Hill place, not sure I remembered how to get there. My mother hadn't believed in GPS, so I had several false stops and starts before I pulled up on the street across from their fading ornate gates. I wasn't used to the car, and today the steering seemed to be pulling to one side. Maybe I should have it looked at. Who knew when my mother had gotten an oil change or tune-up?

The town was expanding. There were a few new-looking houses, lots of big machinery, and freshly-poured sidewalks. The scene provided a wide bridge from the present progress to the stately old mansion. At least there were cars around, so I could park without being out of place. I could see trees a street over that I imagined was Few Park.

I wondered if Rita had gotten beyond the closed metal gates and talked to whoever was living in the house. Grass and weeds overran many areas, and the trellised porch of a gardener's cottage groaned with straggling ivy. Was that where Timmy had stayed? Big and grand as the place was, there was a decided air of neglect. I couldn't see any kind of intercom box outside the gates to announce arrivals. There were outbuildings besides the cottage: a gatehouse, several dilapidated sheds, and in the distance what looked like a weathered red barn. The house sat at the end of a long drive. I could just see the front door.

Now that I was here, I had no idea what to do. Was I just going to sit here all day? What if no one lived there? Why hadn't I brought binoculars? Or a book to read?

Just as I had about decided to leave, a dark car maneuvered into the drive and stopped at the gates. I tried to see the license plate, but it was too far to make out. Rolling down my window, I leaned out to get a better look. A raucous buzz startled me, and then the gate slowly opened, punctuated by squeaks and grumbles. The car drove through. In front of the house, the driver got out. Another figure appeared from the side of the house. The man in the car gestured with rapid motions, seeming vaguely familiar. Where had I seen him before? With a baseball cap and baggy hoodie, the figure was hard to make out. The gates slowly closed on the image.

Through the bars, the new arrival seemed to be yelling and menacing the other man, who then knocked off his cap. The unknown man stooped to pick up his cap and then he turned toward me. I saw the curly blonde hair. It was the guy who had rescued me after the speeding car almost ran me over! What was he doing at the Hill place? He was driving a car that looked similar to the one that had missed me. I didn't know enough about vehicles to tell one from another. Was I imagining things? Did he have something to do with the incident? What had he said his name was?

Suddenly frightened, I started my car and slowly pulled out from my spot. I didn't want to attract any attention from the two men. I drove around the corner and put my foot on the gas. What was I doing? Over coffee in my locked apartment, the idea of approaching a member of the Hill family had seemed snap easy. Now confronted with the idea of actually talking to one had me trembling. Someone had been killed recently.

I got about two blocks away when I felt the tire go. Racing down the road did not help matters as I clung to the wheel, trying to gain control. The car finally screeched to a stop. With shaking hands, I got out and surveyed the damage. The front tire was completely blown. What now? Like an idiot, I had left my phone at home.

Just then, another car came down the road. I waved my hands frantically in an effort to get it to stop, which it did. To my horror, it cruised to a standstill, and the same man who had pulled me back from traffic, the very one who had just visited the Hill house, stepped out of the vehicle.

"Well, well, look who it is! Miss El Turner." He aimed that radiant white smile my way and swaggered over to my car.

"This is a strange coincidence." I had no idea what to say to the man.

"Are you in need of rescue again?" He walked over to the tire and crouched down to look at it.

"It would seem so. The tire just went flat on me."

"Good thing I came along. What brings you way out on this side of town?"

"I just went for a drive." It sounded extremely lame, even to my ears.

"Your tire is shot. Looks like a puncture of some sort. Just enough to give it a slow leak. This doesn't seem to be your week."

The road suddenly stretched long and deserted, the houses few and far between. What did I hope to accomplish if I ended up dead? I should have told someone where I was going. But other than Rita, there were few people I talked to on a daily basis. The guy clucked and smiled in a thoroughly comfortable way, but a distinctive shiver ran down my back. A wrong chord chimed in my brain.

"No, it certainly doesn't seem to be my week." I edged toward the driver's door. What if this man was dangerous? I was still sore enough that running as an escape mode was out of the question, and I had no weapon to speak of. "Please tell me your name again. I was a bit frazzled the last time we met."

"It's Jack. Jack Beane." He held out his hand to shake. I took it. His hand felt warm and relaxed, not at all scary. He gave my hand a small squeeze.

"Jack Bean? Like Jack and the Beanstalk?"

"Okay. Pile it on. I've heard all the jokes there are. But it's Beane with an e at the end, so you can tell me from the green variety." He laughed and let go of my hand.

"Sorry. I didn't mean to make fun. It's just an unusual name."

"I've thought about changing it, but too lazy to do it, I guess."

I looked away from the tanned face and sparkling teeth and back to my tire. "I'm not sure I have a spare. It's my mother's car." I shrugged my shoulders in helplessness.

"Let's look in the back and see what you've got. We wouldn't want your mother to be upset." He strolled around the side of the car.

"She's dead." I sputtered, sorry the minute the words tumbled from my mouth.

"Who's dead?" He stopped and put his hands on his hips.

"My mother. I mean, it's her car, but now it's mine." I didn't know where to go from there and just shrugged again.

"Well, whoever it belongs to, let's see if there's a spare." He continued on around the back and returned with a spare tire and jack, proceeding to change the tire.

He wore tight jeans and a faded blue denim shirt. I noticed how broad his shoulders were as his muscles worked at the tire. For a moment, I forgot my suspicions and appreciated the fineness of the man. Wasn't a rescuer a good thing? And wasn't coming to my aid twice in one week an omen from the heavens? Weren't we all searching for that shiny knight? He must have felt me staring because he turned suddenly, looked me in the eyes, and gave me a lopsided grin designed to melt hearts.

"All done." He rose and dusted off his hands. "I'd get that tire fixed soon. You don't want to be driving on that spare for long. It doesn't seem in too good a shape."

"Thank you so much, Jack! I really appreciate it. I don't know what I would have done if you hadn't come along."

He put the tools and flat tire in the back when I remembered where he had been. A bit of courage returned and settled on my tongue.

"Were you out driving as well? It's a nice day for it." I hoped I didn't sound too curious.

"No." He stopped what he was doing and stared at me. I couldn't read his expression. "I got the roads mixed up, so I stopped at this big place for directions. I think it's called the Hill Mansion. Do you know it?"

My face reddened, and I wondered if he had recognized my vehicle parked down the street. "I've driven past it. It's huge." I blindly forged on and blurted out, "Who lives there now?"

He slammed my trunk and looked at his watch. "Oops. I'm late. Better be going. Glad I could help El Turner. I hope you don't need any further rescuing." He turned back and gave me one final flash of that white-toothed charm. "Or maybe I do!" Then he was gone.

Was I afraid of him or attracted to him? My life seemed to have too many pitfalls at present to worry about handsome men. Let it be, some part of me cautioned. I got back into my vehicle, drove home, and, in what was now habit, bolted all the doors.

The bird, unfazed by my return, stared at the picture on the wall.

****

Letter to El Turner

Dear El Turner,

I am responding to your ad in Living Today. My story is a bit involved, but I think you may be the person to help me.

When I was six or seven, I witnessed a hit and run accident. I think the man who was hit died. It caused me to go into a bit of trauma. When I was feeling better, I asked my parents about what happened, but they said I was imagining things, that the hit and run never happened. They said I made it up. I have thought about it off and on for almost seventy years. My children think I am losing my mind, but as I get toward the end of my life, I am determined to get a full account of what happened and discover if the man responsible was ever caught.

I am trying to include information that may help you. We moved around a lot during those years because of my father's job, but I remember living in Milwaukee, WI; Madison, WI; Fond du Lac, WI; Atlanta, GA; and Tallahassee, FL. I can't say for sure in which city it happened since I was traumatized for quite a while.

I know a lot of time has passed, but you have first-rate credentials, so I am positive you can find out what happened. Police departments must have records that can be accessed. My parents are both dead, and no one in my family of relatives has ever been able to give me a straight answer.

Please, I have to find out what happened before I die. Let me know the cost, and I will be glad to pay you. Thank you for your time and attention.

Best,
Essie Williams

****

Letter to Essie Williams
Dear Ms. Williams:

Thank you for your letter. What a horrible thing to have happened to you as a young child. I can see why the uncertainty of it has weighed on your mind over the years.

I would be glad to do a cursory search to see if I can get any leads. However, it would be helpful if you could narrow things down a bit. Can you pinpoint your exact age? Can you also put the cities in order of moving and give me approximate (the closer the better) months/years of living there. Also, if you can remember any of the addresses it would be a tremendous help. Maybe you have pictures or letters that would give some indication of time. Anything you can remember will help.

I will wait for receipt of your information. Please see the attached price schedule. If it is suitable, just let me know.

Best,
El Turner

Chapter 14

The next morning I took the car to the first place that said they could take me. I had called several before Mike's Auto gave the nod. After asking if they could change the oil and do a tune-up besides fixing the tire, I left the car in their care, slung on my backpack, and hiked the mile to the county records office. Better to walk out the remaining kinks.

Yes, they had old Hill documents.

No, they weren't organized into any one file. Was I looking for a census? Land transfers? Marriage certificates?

I spent time browsing, but generally, I found the same information I had gotten online. Very little. I recovered some of the later tax and census records, but I wanted something juicier. A vague company called Old World Inc. paid the property taxes and had for some time. There was no listing of servants or employees who had worked there, and I found nothing concerning Timmy or anyone named Russert. Maybe I was asking the wrong questions. I'd see what I could find for Old World Inc. when I got home.

I went from there to the library. Maybe they would have the lowdown on Hill history or a record of employees. When Ida saw me, she rushed over and gave me a big long hug. I almost cried.

"I am so glad you are back among the living! How

are you doing, hon?" She peered at me over her glasses and rubbed my arm. I tried not to wince when she hit the injured spots.

"Better. It's good to see you, Ida. Somehow the library always makes me feel like I'm home."

"As it should! That means we're doing our jobs right!"

"Yes." I put my stuff on one of the tables. "Let me look through everything you have. Do we know where the Hill family came from originally?"

Ida lowered her voice and sat down at my table. "It was rumored the family was Romani. Gypsies. People think gypsies came from Romania or Hungary, but I believe they can be traced back to northern India. No one is sure if Hill is even their name. Clark Hill certainly sounds more American than Romani."

"I did a general search and found no immigration record of anyone with that name arriving in America during that time period. They could have come to America as children for all I know. No one by the name of Hill, that is."

"Personally, I think he changed his name. Cassie feels the same."

"You hung out with Cassie? Tell me all!"

"I went to school with Cassie. She wasn't always this fanatical. As she got older, she just started spending more and more time alone in that house. Who knows what she found." She smiled smugly and looked at me. "You would love to dig around in that attic, wouldn't you?"

"I saw the picture Cassie Troy has on the wall. Clark looks powerful; I'm not sure I'd call him handsome. The women were stunning. Those were his sisters?"

"Yes, beautiful women!"

"No rumors of them killing anyone?" I tried to infuse some humor.

"Only for being mixed up in the dark arts?"

"Dark arts?"

"Fortune telling, sorcery, you name it, this town has brought it up. I'm sure somewhere in Cassie's large house there are other pictures. The problem would be sifting through all the other collectibles before finding treasure."

"She declared all her goodies on display as treasures." I shook my head, remembering. "Hasn't anyone gotten into the house to look around?"

"Neighbors, social workers, busybodies all tried to delve into her life at one time, befriend her, make sure she was safe, but it's never helped much. I think the big fear is the place will go up in smoke one day. Too much clutter. The town council even attempted closing down the historical society part and condemning the house. She would agree to clean up the fire hazards, but I think she hid most of the junk to pass inspection and then brought it all out again. In the end, they just left her alone, hoping she will die off one day or maybe just go mad."

"That's so sad. She's living in her own world."

"And happy to be there. She doesn't hurt anyone, hardly ever goes out. People bring her groceries and leave them on her doorstep. She wears either that brown dress or a green one. It's hard to tell what can set her off. Just as quickly, she returns to normal."

She shrugged her shoulders and continued, "Clark had power. The family had money. Where they got it, no one knows. They kept to themselves. Many of the workers thought they had magical powers. There was a fire; they weren't touched. That's how rumors start."

"Ida, do you know anything about the people who worked for the Hills in modern times?"

"No idea, honey. I think there is some service that has cleaned and restocked groceries over the past few years. I can ask around."

"Not an easy family to trace."

"And they liked it that way. You could try checking with Robert in our local history section."

"Thanks. Have you heard anything more about Timmy?" I asked.

"No facts, just conjecture and a lot of nonsense." Ida got up from the table. "Who's running the investigation?"

"A man named Inspector Poe. Do you know him?"

"Alan? Sure. When you've been at the library as long as I have, you get to know most folks in town." She peered down at me. "Why do you ask?"

"No reason. Just curious." I could feel a hot flush heading up my neck toward my face.

"Oh. So it's like that." She laughed and put her hand on my shoulder. "A girl couldn't do better than Alan Poe."

"I don't know what you're talking about. I just asked a simple question." I kept my head down, afraid to meet her eyes.

"Well, to give a few simple answers: He works hard and is good at his job, he cares about people, and he's worn a Homberg for as long as I've known him.

"I appreciate that you have a creative mind, but I am way too busy to be involved with anyone if that is where you are heading."

"Don't wait too long. A girl can't live on facts alone!" I heard her laughter echo as she drifted off to help a customer.

****

Hours later and no wiser, I journeyed back to Mike's Auto. The fresh air and clear day made walking easy, my aches and pains almost disappeared, but my mind swirled around all the facts. What had Rita stumbled upon? I wondered if it was too soon to call Inspector Poe to see if he had learned anything new. Maybe he had been back to talk to Joseph Hill.

When I stopped at a light, I felt the hair on the back of my neck stiffen. Looking around, I noticed a dark car with tinted windows pulled to the curb across the street. The engine was running. When the light changed to walk, I proceeded across the sidewalk, the car in my outer vision. I saw it pull away from the curb and turn in my direction. This time I was ready. I raced to the other side just as the vehicle swept past. If I had been any slower, it would have hit me. This was too much of a coincidence. Was I in danger? Could someone just kidnap me when I wasn't looking?

There seemed to be only one solution: Stop digging into the Hill family history.

A taxi drifted by, and I quickly waved my arms to hail it down. Luckily, he stopped. I told him where to go, peering out the back and side windows to see if the dark car was behind us.

"Someone following you, Lady?" The driver asked, glancing at me in the rearview mirror.

"I just thought I saw a girl I knew," I bluffed, facing forward, and scrunching down in the seat.

I shifted my body rapidly out of the taxi and into the auto garage like demons were on my trail—and maybe they were— hoping no one saw me. Was I being paranoid? Could I afford not to be?

After a short wait, a mechanic brought my car around. I stared out the front shop window, concentrating on the cars going past. Not one had tinted windows.

"Here's your bill. Looks like the tire was cut with something sharp. Have you got any enemies?" He laughed.

"Why do you say that?" I looked suspiciously at him.

"Just making a joke, ma'am." He ran my credit card through the machine. "Here's a list of what we did. You should seriously think about getting a new set of tires, though. The others are badly worn."

"Great. Thanks." I put my card away and picked up the keys. When it looked like fewer cars were in the street, I made a dash to the car and ducked down behind the wheel. Satisfied that there were no dark-colored vehicles with tinted windows around, I started the car and took back streets home, checking the rearview mirror the whole way.

Turning into the parking garage, I took a deep breath and exhaled, some of the tension leaving my rigid shoulders. I found a well-lit spot and quickly leaped out of the vehicle then came to a crashing halt. Maybe someone was waiting for me here. It was possible someone knew where I lived.

Feeling slightly silly at my fears, I climbed back into the driver's seat until other people pulled in. Joining a merry group headed in my direction, I made my way onto the street and into the apartment building. I wished now the building had better security for the front entrance. We had a code to punch in, but many people in the building let in anyone who hit the buzzer. Albert did his best to watch the door, but he was often called away from his desk. The night concierge usually just read the newspaper or watched a small TV. I decided to call a locksmith as soon as I got upstairs. That way, I would be safer if someone made it past the lobby.

Before I got into the elevator, I stopped. If someone was really after me, exactly who was it? And what did they want?

Mute as the bird, I had no answers.

Chapter 15

There she was! The girl in the knit hat coming out of Rita's apartment. I hadn't imagined it! Now she was back.

"Hey!" I shouted. "Hey, you! What are you doing?" I dropped my backpack in front of my door and hurried down the hall after her.

The woman carried a black plastic bag that appeared full. She took off in the opposite direction and down the back stairs. Even though the bag hindered her, she was able to sprint to the alley door before I got down the stairs, all my sore spots and aching muscles tugging on me like outraged oxen. When I opened the outside door, she was gone. All I saw were our trash and recycling bins. Had she been robbing Rita's apartment?

I turned to go back inside and ran straight into another body, dropping my keys and hitting my elbow on the door closing behind me. Instinctively, I bent to get my keys but butted heads instead.

"Damn!" I straightened, head reeling, only to find Inspector Poe holding his head as well, his Homburg hat spinning on the floor. "Inspector! What are you doing here? I was just going to call you?"

He rubbed his wavy hair and picked up his hat. "From the back alley?"

"No. I was chasing a woman who got away in the

alley."

"Chasing a woman? What are you talking about?"

"A woman was in Rita's apartment. I caught her trying to leave with stolen goods. This is the second time I saw her coming out of Rita's apartment."

"Stolen goods?" He held out his hand for me to stand where I was and then bent to gather my keys. "Can we go to your apartment? You can tell me what happened and exactly who this woman is."

Once back in the hallway to my apartment, I grabbed the backpack I had thrown on the floor. Inspector Poe stopped at Rita's door and turned the knob.

"It seems to be locked."

With shaking hands, I opened my door and ushered him in. He put his hat on the table, still rubbing his head.

"Do you mind if I sit? I think I'm a bit dizzy. You certainly have a hard head," he said.

"Please, sit. It's been a long day!" I plopped down on the couch, reeling from the encounter as well.

He took out a notebook. "So start at the beginning and tell me about the robbery."

"Well, the beginning is that I think I'm being followed!"

"Followed?" He looked up from his notebook and sat up straighter in the chair.

"I took my mother's car in to the auto shop because it looked like someone slashed my tire. When I was walking back from the library, I got the feeling that this black or dark blue car with windows that you can't see into was following me. I stepped off the curb just as it seemed to be turning, so I ran across. It sped up and away."

"Okay." He shook his head. "Didn't this happen once before, someone trying to hit you with a car?"

When I nodded, he continued, "Let's back up a minute. Someone slashed your tires?"

"I didn't know they were slashed until this morning when the mechanic told me that's what it looked like. Like someone had taken a knife and slit it."

"All four were slashed?"

"No. Just one of them. It was a puncture that made a slow leak so that when I left the Hill house, I got a flat tire."

"What were you doing at the Hill house this morning?" Poe appeared exasperated. When he saw my face, he put down his notebook and pen. "Sorry. It's just that this whole murder case is starting to be a lot more complicated than I had thought. When exactly were you there this morning?"

"Actually, it was yesterday."

"Yesterday? I'm getting confused here. Can you start at the real beginning?"

I took a deep breath. "I was feeling better, so I decided to take a drive. I happened to be going past the Hill house."

"Just happened to be going past?" Poe interrupted, his face set in a frown.

"Okay. Okay. I went there on purpose to see if I could find out anything about Rita since that might have been the last place she visited. This is all connected to Timmy's murder."

"El, most people leave that sort of thing to the police. I strongly caution you to do the same. Don't go sniffing around places that might be hazardous to your health, and don't go chasing strange women who might have a weapon!"

I felt like a naughty child getting a lecture.

"So you drove past the house and got a flat tire?"

"The car had been tugging a bit to the left on the drive there, so I guess the tire was losing air the whole time. And when I pulled over to check out the house, the tire only got worse."

He interrupted again, "Pulled over? Please tell me you didn't get out and snoop around the house?" His brows were scrunched together.

"I did not get out." I sounded a bit huffy, offended, trying to redeem my self-respect. "I only wanted to get a look at the place. Besides, the gates were closed." I remembered Jack Beane. "I did see a man go in. Jack Beane with an e at the end. He helped me later with my tire. It turns out he was the same man who helped me back to my apartment after my car run-in the other day."

Poe sat back in his chair looking stunned. "Okay. Let's get this timeline down. You almost got run over by a car, but you were rescued by a man named Jack Beane with an e at the end."

"He said it was so I could tell him from the green variety." I added lamely.

"You then go out to the Hill house to snoop around."

"I really think that snoop is hardly the right word to use."

"You then go out to look around the Hill property, see this man go through the gates, drive away, get a flat tire, and this man stops to rescue you again. Is that the heart of it?"

"And there was someone following me today." It all sounded odd, even to my ears.

"And there was the woman you were chasing."

"Oh, the woman. I forgot about her."

"I'm not sure I've ever seen one person get into so much trouble in such a short amount of time. Does this happen often? Somehow I thought you were this quiet researcher."

I went on as if I hadn't heard his last remark. "I first saw this woman the day the car almost ran me over. I was not in any state of clear thinking. That was when Jack Beane helped me up to the apartment."

"Was that Bean with an e at the end?"

"Very funny. If I may continue?"

"Please." He waved his hand in the air.

"Well, I wasn't sure where she was going or what she was doing in the hallway. I was more concerned about getting inside my apartment and sitting down." I rushed on before he could stop me or interrupt. "When I came home today, she was coming out of Rita's apartment with a black plastic bag. I think she was stealing things from the apartment."

"Can you describe her?"

"She was about my height, had shoulder length brown hair, and wore a blue knit hat."

"If you met with a sketch artist, could you give him details?"

I swallowed hard. "No." I tried to recall anything about her that stood out, but could not. "No, but I think I would recognize her if I saw her again."

He closed his notebook. "El, for your own safety, please stay away from trouble."

"Are you saying I should just lock my door and

remain inside? Become a hermit?"

"I doubt you would do that even if I demanded it. Maybe a court order?" He stood up and gave me the ghost of a smile. "But be careful."

"Has anyone heard anything about Rita?"

"It's like she just vanished. Since she was at the scene where someone was murdered and her prints were on the knife, this certainly makes her look guilty. We might have let her go too quickly."

"I thought there was a witness?" I asked.

"Yes, and that's a big reason we don't have an all-out manhunt."

"Woman hunt?" I tried some humor.

"What?" He stood up and gathered his hat. "Once again, please keep your door locked."

"Yes. I was going to call a locksmith and get a better lock. Can you suggest anyone?"

"Try Anderson Locks. They've done work for me. Quick and reasonable."

"Great. Thanks."

"How's the bird? Any speech yet?"

"No. Not yet."

He put his hat on and walked to the door. "I notice you don't play the TV or music. No background noise."

"I get too distracted by background noise. When I get involved in the research, I like to concentrate."

"Try talking aloud during the day. I think Polly would like to hear something other than silence. Hearing a human voice might get the bird going." He shrugged.

I closed the door. The apartment suddenly seemed smaller. Emptier. I realized how alone I usually was. For most of my life it hadn't bothered me. Now when someone left, the space rang hollow, the air thinner.

It wasn't until after I fixed myself some food and later changed the paper in the bird's cage that I realized I had neglected to ask Poe why he had been in the apartment building in the first place.

****

Email to El Turner

Dear Ms. Turner,

You probably won't believe this, but you changed my life! I wrote to you a while ago about finding a husband. I also asked if a name could define a person. You advised me that we define our names, not the other way around. You also suggested a shortened version: Winnie S. I did it.

I went onto several dating sites as Winnie S, complete with my picture. (Oh, by the way, I splurged to celebrate my new name by getting a new haircut, a manicure and pedicure, and a whole spa day of luxury.) I actually felt sassy! A new feeling to go with a new name.

Well, the point is I met several nice men, one in particular. We clicked immediately. When I told him my real name, he said it didn't matter. He likes me no matter what my name is. He has met my parents and friends, and last weekend he took me to a family picnic where I met his mother and other relatives. They were so nice and kind to me.

I don't know what will come of all this, but you got me to see myself in a new light, and I am forever grateful!

Thank you! Thank you!

Winnie S. (Winifred Schnickelback)

****

Email to Winnie S.

Dear Winnie:

What a beautiful email! Thank you! I am so happy for your good news. Let me also say that Winnie S. was always inside Winifred. You just gave her the chance to surface. I also experienced a perception switch and bit of relief when I shortened my name. It's funny, isn't it? We put so much stock in names when we are still the same person underneath.

Stay happy and true to the new and old you! Your email made my week, so thank you! Keep in touch, and let me know how you are doing.

Best,

El (Lana)

Chapter 16

I saw the Goth-looking guy the next day when I
went out to get a newspaper. He came out of the door at
the far end of the hallway. I quickly went back into my
apartment until I was sure he had left. His hair was
white and spiky, and he wore a studded vest, ragged
black pants, and motorcycle boots. Tangling with some
odd-appearing man was not on my agenda. I had
experienced enough of that. What was he doing in the
building? Had he been visiting a resident? I wasn't
exactly a social butterfly, but I knew the people on my
floor. The few I didn't know personally, Jenny and Rita
had filled in for me.

I didn't really need to get a paper, but I liked the
walk, and most of the time I enjoyed talking to Señor
Marquez. I liked the way a newspaper felt in my hands.
I liked the smell. Although I read so much online
information, digital news didn't appeal to me. Several
people had the paper delivered, but chained as I was to
my computer and the research, I liked to take a break
and get outside.

I had no trouble getting involved with the
intricacies of my job and forgetting everything else.
When I got into doing research, it was easier to just
open a can of soup rather than go out or take the time to
wait for someone to knock on my door holding a meal
in a sack. Getting the newspaper was one chance to

inhale the world and see what was going on outside my door. Most Saturdays I walked down to the Farmer's Market for produce. Eggs, cheese, and apples were my usual purchases. A girl can't live on soup and pumpkin seeds alone! Mingling with people, however distant we may be, also made me feel like part of the community.

I looked through the peephole but saw nothing. The bird was staring at me. "I'm just waiting for the Goth guy to get out of the building," I murmured, remembering Poe's idea of talking out loud. "It's not that I dislike Goth guys, or girls for that matter. It's just that a lot of weird things have been happening lately."

The bird tilted its head and inched to the front of the cage.

My voice got a bit louder. "Timmy was killed, people are trying to run me over, I think I'm being followed, and Rita has disappeared." I felt slightly ridiculous chatting with a bird. I know many people talked to themselves, but I wasn't one of them.

When I was sure the hallway was safe, I ventured out, ever cautious, peering at every corner on the way down. Despite Poe's warning, I wanted to get a newspaper. It was only a block or two to the newsstand and only one street to cross. What could happen in such a short time? I would be ever vigilant. Maybe I should buy some pepper spray or carry a kitchen knife with me. I imagined myself whipping out a bottle and heroically spraying an attacker. Focus! My inner mind brought me back to street attention. I admonished myself to quit thinking and just walk.

"*Buenas tardes, Sr. Marquez.*"

"*Ah, Señorita Turner, cómo está hoy?*"

"*Bueno. Bueno. Es un hermoso día.*"

"*Sí, un buen día*, a beautiful day!" He nodded his head in agreement. Most of the time he handled the store himself, a wiry, jovial man. Today, his son David was helping.

"*Qué pasa, Señorita Turner?*"

"*Nada más, David.*"

For some reason I bought not only the local paper, but five others from around the country, as well as a newsy magazine. Maybe I was anticipating locking myself in the apartment like Poe suggested. Then again, it might have been guilt at ignoring his advice.

"*Excelente!*" Señor Marquez exclaimed. "*Te veo mañana.*"

"*Mañana. Adiós.*"

After paying, I turned toward home just as a flash of something caught my eye. The sun had glinted off the studs on the jacket of Mr. Goth Guy. He was casually looking in the shop window of a nearby building. I had seen that trick in the movies. One could pretend to look in the window but be surveying the street behind.

I grabbed my purchases and almost broke a record racing home, looking behind me at every other step. There were other people around, but would anyone help if I got attacked? I didn't want to find out. I had no idea who this guy was.

When I got to the building, my hands wouldn't punch in the right code. My mind had shut down. I looked down the sidewalk and saw Mr. Goth walking my way. Hurry! Hurry! Think! My brain screamed as I continued to punch in the wrong numbers.

Suddenly a hand with a snake tattoo crawling up his arm reached in front of me, hit the right buttons, and magically opened the door. I stared into a face of heavy eyebrows and eyeliner. He winked and disappeared up the stairs. I followed slowly and took the elevator. My world was suddenly a world of what the heck was going on?

I thought about calling Poe, but I didn't want another lecture about staying inside and locking my door.

My work got all my attention for about an hour. Then I picked up the pile of Timmy notes and read them through again. When I got done, I set down a series of ideas about Timmy's murder.

He had information he was planning on giving to Rita. Something he saw at the Hill place? Something he found? Did the money he had stashed have anything to do with his murder? Was Joseph Hill printing counterfeit money in the basement?

Suspects:

Joseph Hill—I didn't even know what he looked like. There were no pictures of him online that I had found. Who would know? Note to ask Inspector Poe.

Jack Beane—What was he doing at the Hill house? He drove a dark-colored car. Why did he show up just when I almost got run over? Why did he know so much about me and where I lived? Why was he so damn attractive?

Goth Guy—not enough known but definitely suspicious.

Who was driving the car that almost hit me? Not Jack Beane. Possibly Joseph Hill. The mysterious woman? Not Goth Guy's style.

Reb Wilson—improbable, but he had anger issues and was the last to see Rita. Rita said he was the jealous type. He had been at the alley following Rita. He admitted it, and Susie Q and her husband had seen a "brick of a man" which fit his description. Maybe he confronted Timmy and they got into a fight. A crime of passion! He could have slipped the article under my door for distraction, pretending it had come from Rita.

Cassie Troy—she had clearly been angry at Timmy for trying to take the Hill picture, had even chased him down the street. Quick temper. Was it enough to kill him?

Someone from the shelter who knew he had found money? Had Danny Boy Cooper been following him to get the rest of the money? And who was the tall thin man that Susie Q had seen?

Rita—I was certain she hadn't done it, but at this point everyone was suspect. If she was so innocent, why disappear? Note: Kidnapping a possibility.

Mason Street - I hated to put him on the list, but he had acted strangely a few times and did seem overly interested in the murder and in Rita's disappearance. No motive that I can see. He was tall and thin like Susie Q's description of the man who went into the alley. He was a helpful sort, but maybe that was a disguise?

Nothing was any clearer. I resolved to go down to the police station and talk to Poe when I was thinking straight, first thing in the morning. I would take a list of questions along.

I looked at the bird. "Poe has some 'splaining to do."

****

Two phone calls started my day off on a strange note.

"El Turner?"

"Yes."

"This is Bradley Washington, editor of the *Parkville Herald Times*. I wanted to do a follow-up to Rita Starr's stories on devil worship. We got a tremendous reaction to that. People are hungry for more. Rita told me before her, ah, untimely disappearance that you had done background work for her. I'd like to send another reporter around to see what else you can contribute."

"First off, Mr. Washington, I did not do background work for Rita. She simply misrepresented me. I did not like that she used my name in her pieces. If something happened to her because of those stories, I'd feel horrible. Plus I don't want the same thing to happen to me. There have been a number of incidences."

"Incidences? Attempts on your life? Tell me more!" He jumped on my words.

I was sorry I had mentioned it. "Nothing I choose to talk about or see written in your newspaper."

"Oh, I doubt Rita's absence has anything to do with the articles. She often would take off for days at a time." His voice took on a soothing tone.

"I think this is a little more than that. How come you've run nothing about her being missing?"

"As I said, she often took little trips without letting anyone know. It hasn't been proven that she's missing. Anyway, the police have a good handle on that."

I was getting ready to say the police did not have clue one as to her disappearance but stopped. I didn't want to spill any of the information Poe had told me.

"If you won't talk to a reporter, can you at least email me a quotation or website? We'd pay, of course."

"I don't have anything." I tried to get rid of him.

"Send whatever you have, and I'll take it from there," he said persistently.

"I'm really not interested at this point."

"We'd pay for any research you have," he repeated, hoping the dangle of dollars would loosen my tongue. "Thanks for your time, and I hope to hear from you soon."

The second call came almost immediately after and was just as disturbing.

"Hello. Is this El?"

"Yes. Who's calling?"

"It's Jack."

"Who?"

"Jack and the Beanstalk Jack. Surely you remember the man who rescued you from speeding cars and flat tires."

"Of course I remember you." I was astonished at hearing his voice.

"Good. Good. I was just wondering how you were doing. Did you get your tire fixed? Are your cuts and bruises healed?" His concern radiated over the phone.

"Yes and yes. I'm much better, thank you."

"I realize we don't know each other well, but would you like to meet sometime for lunch? Or maybe just coffee?"

I felt a shiver go down my back. He was bright, charming, and funny, but I had that initial wariness. He set off a jangle of bad vibes mixed with an alluring exterior.

"I don't mean to be rude, Jack, but how did you get my number?" My number was posted in my genealogy ads, but it did not appear in the local directory.

I could hear him thinking on the other end. "I don't really remember."

"I only met you a few days ago. I would think you could remember." Things were taking a strange turn. What was he hiding?

"Okay. You caught me." I heard him chuckle. "I asked around until I found someone who had your number."

"Asked around where?"

Again the pause. "I tricked the apartment manager into giving it to me. Said I was your brother."

Anger bubbled up in me. Anger at the manager and anger at Jack for his manipulation. I considered hanging up, but he read my mind.

"Please don't hang up. I just want to get to know you better. You seem like an interesting person with the research and all." He hurried on. "Look, I'll give you all the names of my relatives and you can trace my family tree. See that I'm harmless. I just wanted to talk a bit. That can't hurt anything, can it?" He played the sympathy card. "Shouldn't a rescue or two at least merit a cup of coffee?"

"Let me think about it. I'm a bit busy at the moment." What did this good-looking man want with me? I had no illusions about myself. I had long come to the realization I was no beauty and what I did for a living would send most people crashing to sleep in under five seconds, and I was okay with that. Suddenly I had more men in my life than I knew what to do with. "I've got your number on my caller ID, so why don't I call you?"

"Great! I'll take what I can get!" He laughed once more then spoke seriously. "Take care of yourself in the meantime. Look out for speeding cars and flat tires."

I hung up, more determined than ever to talk to Inspector Poe. Then I picked the phone back up and called the locksmith with the promise of speedy next-day service.

I spent the rest of the time trying to concentrate on work, but my fingers had a mind of their own. They kept typing in Bean with an e at the end.

"What an idiot," I said to the bird.

****

Letter to El Turner

Dear Ms. Turner:

I am enclosing the information you requested concerning cities in which I lived and approximate dates.

Also enclosed is a retainer for your services. Could you contact me if you have found nothing when that money is used up and we can talk again? I want to get to the bottom of this! My contact information is on my check.

Thank you for your time and attention.

Best,

Essie Williams

Encl.

****

Letter to Essie Williams

Dear Ms. Williams:

Thank you for the information and the retainer. I will begin immediately to see what secrets I can uncover.

Best,

El Turner

Chapter 17

I got a late start the next day, delighting in the fact that the phone was not ringing and no one was knocking at my door. Bliss! I wrote my questions down in a small notebook, pondered taking a knife in my backpack, decided against it, picked up my backpack, and set off to assail Inspector Poe for more information. Determined to check out the garage and my tires before I set off, I also decided to navigate the stairs instead of the elevator. At least then I could run if I chose. I needed to ask Poe where I could get some pepper spray.

I heard the whisper of clothes too late then felt the hand pushing against my back. Reaching for the stair rail, I missed and went tumbling, keys and backpack flying. A tangle of legs and feet jumped past me with resounding clamor as I reached for something to stop my fall. I heard the thunder of footsteps. Everything seemed to be happening in slow motion, yet it was over in an instant. I saw a pair of black motorcycle boots and black pants disappear around the corner. Mr. Goth Guy! He had pushed me down the stairway!

Struggling to stand, I pulled myself up the stairs, grabbing and clutching onto the handrail. I looked back and saw blood on the floor. Some of my arm wounds had reopened, but no one seemed to be coming after me. Panic and adrenaline kicked in, so I made it to the landing without fainting. I felt something drip on my shirt. Blood. I touched my forehead and my fingers came away red and sticky. Somewhere in my plummet, I had hit my head. No time to check injuries. I needed to get back into the apartment, lock the door, and call the police. This was getting out of hand. I was seriously scared for my life.

At my door, I realized I was lacking my keys and my backpack. I inched warily toward the stairs when an apartment door opened behind me. I screamed.

"El, my word! What happened to you?" Jenny Lane pressed her hand against her mouth in surprise. "Come in. You're bleeding. Let me help."

"I fell down the stairs," I stuttered. "My pack. My keys." I pointed numbly toward the door leading down.

"I'll get them. You just go in and sit down." She went instead to her kitchen and came back with ice cubes wrapped in a towel. "Here. Put this against your forehead to stop the blood." She was gone before I could tell her to be careful.

When her door opened, I almost hollered out loud again, but it was Jenny with backpack in hand. "I didn't see your keys, but you leaked blood along the stairs and wall. I better call Mr. Hall about this."

"Who?" My brain didn't seem to be working.

"Albert. The man at the desk downstairs."

I heard her mumbling into the phone. When she returned, she took the towel and gently led me into her bathroom. I sat on a dressing stool while she removed my jacket. With soft touch and soothing manner, she proceeded to dab at the cuts on my head and arm. Old scrapes on my elbow burned their protests.

"Let me get some aloe from the kitchen," she cooed.

While she was gone, I stood, shakily hanging onto the sink and looked in the mirror. The cut across my brow wasn't deep, but I felt a lump forming on the side of my head. My fingertips patted gingerly at the growing knot.

The doorbell rang. I peeked cautiously out and saw Albert at the door. Jenny talked for a bit and then pointed toward the stairs. I closed the bathroom door, sat back down, and examined my surroundings. Her bathroom held an extraordinary display of flamingoes. The walls contained photos of the birds. Windows sang with stained glass images casting pink and flame-colored prisms over everything. Shower curtain, toilet seat cover, even floor tiles paraded the long-necked creatures. Blinding in their assembly, the birds felt almost alive. I could feel them strutting about me, craning and bobbing their heads.

"How are we doing?" I jumped a foot. I hadn't heard the door. "Sorry, dear. I didn't mean to disturb you."

"I was just taking in all the flamingo images."

"Do you like them? I was thinking of changing over to lilacs. Green and purple everywhere." She was momentarily transported. "Listen to me go on, will you? How is your head? Has the bleeding stopped?" She lifted the cloth from my forehead.

"I think it's better, but the knot on top is growing by the second."

She produced a thick stem of aloe vera and spread the sticky goo across my forehead. Then she rubbed it up and down my arm. The cool gel seemed to calm my shrieking skin. She wrapped a long bandage around the arm and placed small tight band aids on my forehead cut. She tried to put the ice on the growing lump, but it hurt too much.

"Well, that should close up the skin without a scar, but you might be wise to go to the emergency room. That bump on your head is no joke. You might have a concussion. Does it feel like you have broken anything?

I shook my head. "I'm fine. Really."

"Albert has sent maintenance to clean up the stairs. He said several people told him they saw men running out the back door of the building. Did they have something to do with you falling?"

"Men? I'm not sure, but I think I saw that Goth guy. Someone pushed me down the stairs."

"Oh. It couldn't have been Ozzie."

"Ozzie?"

"That's what I call him." Jenny shrugged. "He never told me his real name. He just moved in."

"I think he's been following me." My head began its rhythm of *pound, pound, pound.* "I wonder if Albert can let me into my apartment. I need to lie down."

"Dear, why don't you let me drive you to the hospital? I would feel so much better. Besides, I don't think you should lie down with a head injury."

She led me into her living room just as there was another tapping on the door. It was Albert.

"I'm afraid we found no keys on the stairs, Miss Turner. It might be wise to have your locks changed."

"Oh, yes. There is a man coming today." They both stared at me, questions arising in their eyes. "I called yesterday. I just thought a stronger lock might be better."

"Your lease says you can change the locks at any time. You just need to let management know," Albert said

"I'm letting you know so you can let management know."

"I'll be glad to tell the manager." He gave a strange little bow.

Jenny walked Albert to the door where they stood talking and glancing furtively in my direction. I looked around the rest of Jenny's place, something I hadn't had the chance to do before. It was the first time I had been in her apartment. Plants and flowers spilled over tables and window ledges. Pictures and posters of musicians covered the walls. Several Buddha statues were scattered around, and I saw a yoga mat rolled up in a corner. Overflowing and overpowering as the rooms were, they had a homey presence. Curtains as billowy as Jenny's dresses feathered the windows. Colorful throw rugs dotted the floor. I heard wind chimes and something like jasmine or gardenia scented the air. Then the faint music. I thought of my plain rooms. The only area showing life was the space around my computer, and that was only because of all the papers. I vowed if I lived another day to get a plant.

Albert left and Jenny came back with steaming tea in a hand-painted rose cup. "Drink this. If I had something stronger, it might help settle your nerves better, but I think this green tea will do the trick."

"What's that music? It's pleasant."

"That, dear, is a banjo genius."

"That's a banjo? It sounds like classical music."

"That's why he's a genius." She laughed.

"I thought you only liked a certain shaggy foursome."

"Well, a girl can't get into a rut now, can she? Do

you know I never listened to them until I met my husband? He said if I married him my name would be Jenny Lane which was the next best thing. So I did. We rhymed—Benny and Jenny."

Her voice along with the tea proved relaxing, and I felt my head begin to nod. The doorbell broke the mood. It was Albert and a man dressed in overhauls.

"Good timing. The locksmith is here. He has to cut off the old lock since you don't have the key. Does that work for you?" Albert inquired.

"Yes. And please ask him if I can have a deadbolt inside. Thank you, Albert."

"And I have tried to contact Mr. Johnson to see if he can add anything to the incident in the stairwell. He's nowhere to be found."

"Mr. Johnson?" Jenny and I asked together.

"Bill Johnson. The man you said you saw when you fell."

"The Goth guy? His name is Bill Johnson?" I was stunned. I had just gotten used to thinking of him as Ozzie.

"Yes."

"That sounds like an alias to me. I didn't trust that guy from the moment I first saw him." He was an instant red flag.

"He's renting the apartment by the week," Albert said.

"By the week?" Jenny seemed surprised. "You mean people can rent these places by the week? It sounds so low class."

"It must have gone through management because they approved it." Albert nodded. "It's the first time I have seen it in my time here."

To add to the confusion, Inspector Poe took that moment to make an appearance.

"El!" He stood and stared at me. "This is getting to be a habit I don't like."

"It's not any fun for me either."

"Do you think it was because of the newspaper article?" Jenny asked.

"The ones from last week?" Poe asked.

"No," she said going to her kitchen and returning with a newspaper. "The one from this morning." She unfolded it and handed it to me. "You should sue them."

I read the headline: *Researcher Digs Deeper into Past Deaths*. Poe looked over my shoulder as I scanned the story. It went into detail about the deaths of Felicity and Delilah Hill, the Hill sisters, supposed facts I had not come across. The writer claimed the two women had been fortune tellers who could summon the dead, women of such beauty they could cast enchantment spells on men and get them to do their bidding. The article implied that I had spent day after day at the library going through old records in an attempt to prove the two women had been murdered. I threw the paper on the floor. Poe picked it up and continued reading. I stood and immediately regretted it.

Poe grabbed me before I fell. "No arguments this time. You're going to the emergency room. No sense waiting for the ambulance. I'll drive you."

I nodded weakly and, once again, let him take me by the arm.

Chapter 18

Poe waited with me to see a doctor. I think his presence spurred a bit of haste among the staff because I was in and out quickly—no concussion, slight sprained ankle, stitches in forehead, cuts and scrapes treated and bandaged, pain killers dispensed. The nurses insisted I ride in a wheelchair out to the car. Service from door to door.

Poe drove me home.

I held my head and closed my eyes against the light. "I'm sorry to put you through all this bother. I know you have more important things to do."

"Watch out. You may have to put me on speed dial."

He drove sedately, and I wondered at his age. The hat, the suit, the driving created the image of an older man. Yet, the eyes.

"That was a joke," he said, interrupting my thoughts.

"It only hurts when I laugh."

"Now that's better!" He glanced over and seemed on the verge of saying more. I noticed he caught himself, shoved down the impulse to speak without thought. It probably came with the job: listen, don't speak.

"I can't wait to get home. Any more days like this, and I'll need to move to Florida and take up golf and shuffleboard."

He had a nice laugh, soft and pleasantly deep. "And all through school I thought research was dull. I guess you have certainly proved me wrong. Maybe you should think about applying to the police academy."

"Not in this lifetime!"

When we got back to my apartment, Jenny stuck her head out and handed me my new keys. She also gifted me an aloe plant with a purple ribbon. "Now you can treat your own wounds."

"Thanks, Jenny."

"I think that woman has radar," Poe whispered. "How did she know we were in the hallway?"

Once inside, Poe tested the lock and deadbolt. "Is this enough for you to stay inside for a while. At least until this batch of damage heals?"

"Yes, sir." I tried a mock salute. My elbow said not to try it again. I looked at him with tilted head. "So why do you think this Goth-looking man attacked me?"

"I don't think he did. In fact, I can almost guarantee he did not."

"How can you be so sure?"

"Just a hunch." He seemed reluctant to leave.

"Can I get you something to drink?"

He switched tactics. "When's the last time you had something to eat?" he asked, taking off his hat.

"Coffee this morning."

"That's all? How do you expect to take on the world with nothing in your stomach? I can make some passable eggs if you want."

"Really. It's not necessary. I can make something later. I'm sure you must be busy."

"Off duty and no problem." He was already

heading toward the kitchen. I hated to think what it must look like. "That is if you have eggs."

"Let me help you find things."

"You sit. Relax. I've got this. Put your head back and your feet up."

I heard him puttering around, banging pans, breaking eggs, humming quietly. I must have nodded off because suddenly he was placing a cheese omelet in front of me. He also handed me a cup of tea.

"The tea is courtesy of Jenny."

"Wow. This looks delicious." I hadn't realized how hungry I was until I dug in and finished it off in short time.

"I'm used to making food quick and easy." He sat down on a kitchen chair.

"Your wife is a lucky woman to have such a good cook in the family," I said without thinking. "I'm so sorry. I didn't mean to get personal."

He didn't look at me. "No wife."

I scraped my fork around the plate, chasing crumbs.

"Another omelet?"

"Oh. No. Thank you so much. I can't remember the last time I had something home cooked like this. When I'm doing research, I tend to eat things out of a can."

"I noticed all the soup." He sat in a chair opposite me. "That's not the best way to live."

"Well, it's the way I've been doing it for so long, I guess I can't stop now." I tried to laugh away the awkwardness.

"How long have you lived in Parkville?" He crossed his legs and settled back.

"My mother was ill, so I came last spring to take

care of her. After she died, I didn't want to return to my old life, so Mason Street told me about this apartment, and I've been here ever since."

"You know Mason Street?"

"Yes. He seems like such a nice man."

"How much do you know about him?"

"Not much. Why? Am I missing something?" My head was still dizzy.

"He lives in this building, doesn't he?"

"Yes. I think he has one of the top floor apartments."

"Not bad. For a struggling attorney, that is."

"Okay. What aren't you telling me?"

"Just making an observation."

"I think he has a lot of contacts in Europe. At least, he told me he goes to London and Paris sometimes." I wondered why I was defending him.

"Hmm."

"What? Is he mob related or something?"

He paused, then asked, "Where's the rest of your family?"

"Diversion tactic!" I pointed a finger at him. "I don't think I have any family left. I mean, the few I knew about have all passed on. The rest may take some looking into. What about you?"

"Big family. Eight brothers and sisters scattered all over the world. I'm the only one who stayed home."

"Stayed home?"

"We all grew up here, but everyone ran off to see the world as soon as they could. I'm the only one who stayed. I live in the big old house my parents owned when they were alive. It's a lot of space to rattle around in. I usually keep most of it shut off to save on heating and cooling bills."

"How long have you been working for the police?"

He got a faraway look in his eyes. "Too long." He got up from his chair and took my empty plate and fork into the kitchen. I heard him washing the dishes.

He came back with food and water for the bird, opening the cage and putting a treat inside. I watched in amazement as, once again, the bird seemed to be leaning toward his hand. Poe rubbed a finger against the bird's head.

"So, Polly, how are you doing? Are you settling into this nice woman's apartment? Is she treating you right?"

I laughed. The bird made a soft cooing sound, almost as if she understood.

"Have you discovered if Polly is a male or female?" he asked, sitting back down.

"Not yet." He was an easy man to talk to. "I've had other things going on."

"Yes, I've noticed."

"Not meaning to get back to police business, but what have you found out about Timmy or Rita?" I tried to use my own diversion on him.

"Timmy is an ongoing case, so I can't really talk about it. Not a thing on Rita. When I spoke to Joseph Hill, he claimed he hadn't seen her. We still don't know if she's missing of her own free will or someone has taken her. Since she is a person of interest, we need to be able to get a hold of her in case we have more questions."

"But I remember her saying that she was definitely going to talk to Joseph Hill." I sat up too quickly and my head started to spin.

"Easy, Tiger. Just worry about yourself for a while. I'll let you know if we find something."

He looked around the apartment. "You know, all this business about the Hill family has really brought back memories for me. I grew up here, and you would not believe how many childhood songs and taunts were traced back to them. I was just thinking about them the other day."

"Did you go to school with any Hill kids?"

"All the Hill children went to school in Europe. I don't know why they keep this house since they seldom lived there. It's so old. I guess it's the sentimental aspect."

"What do you mean?"

"Old Clark Hill. The original Hill. He just about built this town."

"His name keeps popping up over and over. My mother is buried in Clark Hill Cemetery. I had no idea it was named after a founding father when we had the service. I learned a bit about the history of the town when I was at the library."

"He bought all that land and had that huge house built for his new bride."

"I didn't realize he was married. I just heard about his sisters Felicity and Delilah, and Boris, son or brother, it's a tossup."

"The bride died a year or so after they were married. At least that's the story I've always heard. I guess he didn't have time to record her name. He rode off one day in his wagon and brought her home. No one knows where she came from or where they got married. No one claimed her body after she died. I never believed the murder part, but that's the legend. He donated the land for the cemetery."

"I'll have to take another look when I go there. Check out her tombstone."

"Oh, he didn't bury her there. She's buried somewhere on the Hill property. They have their own cemetery. Folks said he didn't want other people walking over her grave. But he saw that the town needed a cemetery."

"Rita would have a field day with that. How come I didn't find any records of that?" I finished off the tea and felt relaxed for the first time in ages. "What kind of childhood things do you remember?"

"People have always claimed the house was haunted. It was almost a rite of passage to run up to the house and touch the porch. Proved you were brave. We always thought there were vicious dogs waiting to rip intruders apart, but no one's ever seen them. That was before they put up the fence and gates. Now it's hard to get close to. My sisters and their friends made up songs while they jumped rope."

I was fascinated. This was a side of him I had never seen, but thoroughly enjoyed. He was almost like another man entirely. I wondered what it would be like to be married to such kindness, to come home to him cooking dinner, to lie in bed together.

His voice droned on, "It was something about diamonds and daisies."

"Roger 145 664 823 144," the bird squawked.

I screamed and dropped my cup, the breaking clatter echoing in the stillness.

Poe jumped to his feet and hurried to the cage. "Polly! Did you just talk?"

Polly nodded her head up and down, up and down.

"Damn bird just about caused me to have a heart attack," I said, trying to wipe the tea off my clothes.

Poe turned my way. "Let me caution you not to swear around parrots. They tend to repeat words."

"So she really can talk." I was beginning to doubt that ability, but I wasn't sure I was ready for a bird to just blurt out things. It would take a lot to get used to. My heart was still hammering away inside my chest.

Poe bent and picked up the broken cup from the floor. He took the pieces into the kitchen. "Guess you will need a new cup."

"No problem. It's not like I keep a matched set or anything."

"I noticed." I heard the faint chuckle. He wiped up the spilled tea on the floor.

I tried my own diversion tactic. "So what did she just say? It sounded like numbers."

Poe leaned into the cage. "Polly want to talk again?"

"I'm not sure I'm up for a bird to shout out words or numbers when I'm not expecting them," I said. "How will I know when she is going to talk? This could really disrupt my research time."

"Who's a good bird?" Poe put a treat in the cage. He tried cooing to the bird but could not get anything else from her.

"Well, that was more excitement than I've had in a while."

"Really?" Poe turned to face me. "You mean cars trying to run you down and strange men pushing you down stairs is not excitement?"

"Okay, okay. I misspoke. You don't have to explain the obvious, Inspector Poe."

"Poe has 'splaining to do!" Polly screeched.

"Oh no!" I cried, hand to mouth.

"What an idiot! What an idiot!" Now that she had started, she wouldn't stop. I recognized my words instantly.

"I didn't call you an idiot! Really." Poe was bent over laughing

"What a strange end to an even stranger day!" His voice choked with glee.

I suddenly felt the energy drain out of me. "Yes, what a day! And finally a bird that talks! It's almost too much."

He suddenly got up from his chair. "I should be going and let you rest. If you need anything, please give me a call." He seemed to remember he was a policeman. He wrote down his home number on a piece of paper and picked up his hat. "And keep this door locked!"

It looked like he wanted to say more as he stepped into the hall, but instead he stooped to pick up a jar with a purple ribbon outside the door.

"Seems like the woman down the hall is still tending to your scrapes and pains." He brought the jar over to where I reclined on the couch.

I read the label: *Soothing herb balm. Apply liberally to any skin irritation, aching muscles, sores, and bruises.* I opened the lid. It smelled wonderful.

Poe gave a little wave and was gone.

I got Polly's cage cover. "You certainly picked the worst time to talk, didn't you? What set you off I wonder? And what's with the numbers? I think it's time for us both to rest."

I put my new locks into action, got ready for bed,

and slathered my body in the sweet-smelling balm.

I thought about Poe for the few fragrant minutes before sleep overtook and rushed me wildly down into dreams.

Chapter 19

I woke up feeling like I wanted to sing. My body displayed only minor twinges of remembered aches. Jenny's balm had done wonders. Plus, I smelled like lavender and oranges. I began to plan my day: Item One—Do not go outside. Item Two—Finish the report I was working on. The reports were the least fun of my job. The research provided my joy. I felt like an archeologist at times—digging and carefully brushing away dirt to find the gems. One of my mentors once said, "No single document ever proved anything." The trick was to get several credible sources to confirm the fact. But reports had to be done.

The trouble with reports was how much information to give the client. I thought back to Wanda Darren, the client who wanted to spring newly-discovered information about an unknown aunt at a family reunion. I had provided her with all the information and cautioned her to read it first, but she was adamant about revealing it to everyone. I was sorry it had not worked out as she had hoped. In the future, I would have to make doubly sure to advise people in those situations. Over the years, I found that there was no such thing as a perfect family tree. Most had a few nuts mixed in. Some people never believed the facts I revealed. Often I heard, "But our family always said X, so it must be true."

When Ida Parks called, I was glad to talk to someone.

"Honey, I'm glad I caught you. I didn't want to leave a message on your machine."

"What's up, Ida?"

"I just called to let you know I had nothing to do with that last article in the paper. Honest to goodness, that reporter was asking questions all over the library. He finally got a young student worker to talk. She had been shelving books the last day you came in and knew you came to the library to do research. What kind of research you did, she had no idea. She was just excited to talk to the press."

"It's no problem, Ida. I appreciate you calling. I'm hoping the story will fizzle itself to ashes soon. It's been nothing but a headache. The editor even tried to get me to write some of that trash. Now it sounds like he has some other poor reporter trying to scare the people of the town."

"How did this whole thing get started anyway?"

"Rita Starr, the woman who wrote the first few stories, is a neighbor of mine. I'm sorry I ever opened the door to her. But now she's." I stopped, debating if I should mention Rita's disappearance.

"She's what?"

"Off my Christmas list," I added slowly.

Ida laughed. "I don't blame you. Maybe you should sue the paper."

"I don't think it's come to that yet."

"Listen, I forgot to mention it the other day, but there is a man in town who owns a small shop downtown, G. G. Marquez. He has some sketches on the wall in his store that his grandfather drew of the early town and buildings. You might want to drop by and check them out."

"Yes, I know Mr. Marquez. I go into the store all the time for the newspaper. I never noticed them, but I will certainly check it out on my next visit."

"He probably knows some of the history as well."

"I think he's a bit reluctant to talk about it. I brought it up one day and he shut me down quickly. Said he didn't mention the name of Hill in his house."

"Can't hurt to ask again. Many people do bristle at the name though. Come by the library and I'll take you to lunch. There's a new restaurant that opened nearby."

I thought about the locked door and venturing out. Another few days of healing was what I needed.

"Thanks, Ida. I'll try to come over next week."

"We're here any time for you. Take care of yourself now."

I looked over at Polly. She seemed a bit more at home today, investigating the cage.

"Polly know any numbers?" I had been too stunned to understand what she had originally spouted or what it meant. Somewhere along the line, someone had taught those numbers to her. Was it my mother? The long-gone poet? And why teach her some random numbers? Or were they random? What had my mother been up to? I vowed to be prepared in case Polly repeated them.

I turned to my desk ready to attack Essie William's childhood-imagined accident when I noticed a piece of paper near my door. When I walked over, I saw it was a section ripped from a newspaper. I picked it up ready to toss it when I saw handwriting in the margin: *Don't worry. I'm okay.*

"Now what is this?" I asked Polly. "It sure doesn't

look like my handwriting. Maybe Poe dropped it last night." But I knew it hadn't been there earlier in the day. Then it dawned on me: Could it be from Rita? Had she slipped it under my door?

I tore at the locks and opened the door, looking up and down the hallway. It was empty. I ran to her door and knocked. Nothing. Looking at the note again, I wondered if I was having hallucinations. Was I making something out of a scrap of paper that could have come from anywhere? But from where? I didn't remember what her writing looked like. If I showed it to Poe, maybe he could get the handwriting analyzed! Or check it for fingerprints! Rita must be alive! Excited and happy, I wandered back to my apartment.

"What do you think?" I asked the bird, holding the paper up to the cage. "Is Rita sending us a message?"

In an instant, she grabbed the paper in her beak, thinking I held a treat. I lifted the cage door, not concerned with safety for my fingers, and tried to wrest it back. I yelled, and she loosened her grip a bit. I pulled, and a piece tore off, but I could still read it.

"What is wrong with you?" I asked, annoyed. She retreated to a corner of the cage.

So much for plans of staying in. Surely Poe would understand. I combed my hair, grabbed my backpack, and looked for something in the kitchen to use as a weapon should I need one. All I could find was a can of cleaning spray. It would have to do. I tried it to make sure it still worked but ended up squirting it in my direction. The stuff smelled horrible. I kept it in my hand and shoved what remained of the paper in my pocket, moving quickly but ultra-cautiously through the hallway, stairs, and into the parking garage. Just because Rita might be alive didn't mean someone wasn't still trying to attack me.

****

A hand tapped on my car window. I screamed and sprayed the glass.

"El! What are you doing?" Mason Street's handsome face appeared.

I rolled down the dripping window. "Sorry. You startled me." This was embarrassing.

"Do you always walk around with a can of disinfectant in your hand?" He laughed.

"No. I just happened to, oh, never mind. It's good to see you."

"Yes. I was just leaving when I saw you get in your car and thought I'd say hello. We need to have coffee or lunch or something soon. You can catch me up on your life."

I clucked my tongue nervously. "My life has become complicated."

"Sounds interesting. How's the work coming along? Are you doing well?"

"Lately, it seems like I have more than enough work to keep me busy." I noticed the travel bag slung over his shoulder. "Going on a trip?"

"A quick one." He seemed hesitant. "For a client."

"London? Paris?"

"Nothing so exotic." He leaned against the hood of the car.

"You haven't seen Rita, have you?" I asked. He seemed startled at the question.

"No, have you?" He bent down and looked me in the eye. "Rumor has it that she's missing? Do you know where she is?"

"Not a clue," I answered. I was going to cross my heart when I remembered I still clutched the can of disinfectant.

"I sure hope she hasn't gotten into any trouble. So you don't know where she's hiding out?" he asked again.

"I didn't say she was hiding out."

"No, of course not. Bad choice of words. I just think we're all worried about her and don't want to see her come to any harm." He searched my face in earnest. "Maybe we can pool our brains and try to figure out where she would go."

"If I had any idea where she was, I would advise her to give herself up to the police." I pretended to chuckle. "We both know how Rita's mind works. No one can figure her out, much less guess where she could be."

"I'm sure you're right, but I bet the police would love to question her again."

"Me too!"

"She seemed to be involved in that murder of the homeless fellow." He tried to smile, but it fell flat. "If I know you, you're researching his background and finding out all you can about him!"

I worked to keep my face noncommittal. "Well, it's hard to research someone who only goes by the name Timmy. I'm sure there are a zillion Timmys around. How much can a person find out about a one-name murder victim?" I realized I was babbling and shut up.

"Will you call me if you hear from her?" He took a business card from his shirt pocket and wrote a number on it. "Or even if you find out anything about that murder." I wondered about his interest. "It's such a fascinating case." His words trailed off uncertainly. "Well, I have to go. Nice to see you again, El." He stared at me for a long moment and then hurried off.

"That was odd." I realized I had grown used to talking out loud. I rubbed my shirt sleeve around on the window, hoping to get rid of the dripping disinfectant but succeeded in smearing it worse.

I waited until I saw Mason duck into his car—a shiny dark blue vehicle with tinted windows. Questions immediately strangled my brain. How many dark-colored cars with tinted windows were tooling around the city streets? Not Mason Street! He was a nice man who had come to my mother's burial service. He was a lawyer. He had helped me through legal matters and into this nice place. The car was probably a coincidence. I remembered I had put him on my suspect list, but I didn't want to believe anything bad about him. Nevertheless, I looked cautiously around and started the engine. I'd deal with the messy window later, not in some suddenly-questionable parking garage.

I checked my rearview mirror all the way to the police station.

Chapter 20

I felt safe once I got to the station, but that lasted about a minute. There was the Mr. Goth Guy, or Ozzie, or Johnson, or whatever the hell his name was, sitting in one of the offices talking to a police officer. Maybe they had finally caught and arrested him. I wondered if I would have to be part of a police lineup and identify him.

I realized I had grabbed the piece of paper from my pocket and was squeezing it in my hand. The can of disinfectant was still in my other hand. Someone touched me on the arm, and I dropped the can and the paper, stepping on the crinkled wad in the process.

"Can I help you, Miss?" a uniformed man asked, eyes taking on a questioning look. He wrinkled his nose and took a step backward.

I picked up the paper only to see Goth Guy rise from his chair and head for the office door. I shoved it back in my pocket and kicked the can away.

"Poe! I must see Inspector Poe right away!" I couldn't let Goth Guy get away.

He cupped his hand around the side of his mouth and yelled, "Eddie. Someone here to see you."

I hurried in the direction the officer pointed. Inspector Poe was in his office and not happy to see me.

"Please don't tell me you've gotten into more danger! You could keep a whole unit of police officers busy." He sank down into his chair in despair and motioned me to take a seat. I paced instead, pointing toward the hall.

"No, I'm not in trouble, but I saw him! He's here!"

"Who?"

"The weird Goth creature from my apartment building. The one who pushed me down the stairs! He's here. Quick. We have to catch him before he gets away." My voice rose in a fear-induced panic.

He held up his hand for me to stop then sniffed in my direction. "No offense, but what is that smell?"

"Probably disinfectant."

"Doing a bit of cleaning?"

"Yeah. Something like that." I peered out his office window. I saw Mr. Goth stepping into the elevator. I turned toward Poe. "He's in the elevator. We need to hurry downstairs." Urgency had overtaken common sense.

Poe motioned for me to sit down and picked up the phone, mumbling something to an unknown party. "Taken care of," he said, replacing the receiver.

"Oh, good." I breathed a sigh of intense relief. Seeing him had freaked me out. My hands wouldn't stop shaking, and I couldn't stop pacing. "Do you think he's been questioned for another crime?" I was anxious to know what they were going to do with him.

"I thought I suggested you lock your door and stay inside." Poe stared me down. "I can see that didn't work for long. What hazard are you looking to tangle with today?"

"None." I tried to remember. "Oh, that's right! I got this!" I reached into my pocket. "It was slipped under my door this morning. I think it's from Rita!" I smacked the piece of paper—now a wadded ball—onto his desk as if to prove I was right in coming.

Poe picked it up gently and tried to unfold it. "What have you done to it?

"Sorry." I looked woefully at the wrinkled bit. "The bird chewed it, I dropped it and stepped on it, and then I had it in my hand when I saw Mr. Goth Guy, and I guess my hand was sweaty at seeing him or somehow it got sprayed with cleaning fluid and then I crumpled it." I trailed off, my face displaying every shade of red in the color spectrum. What had seemed a solid plan was now dive bombing before my eyes. I sounded like a lunatic.

"I'm not sure what to do with this," Poe said, squinting his eyes at the shredded mess.

"Can we get any fingerprints?" I asked hopefully.

"I can barely read it. I can decipher the word *don't* but that's all." Poe rotated the paper trying to get a better look at what was written.

"It says *Don't worry. I'm okay.*"

"What makes you think it's from Rita? Did you see or hear from her?" He leaned back in his desk chair, watching me with those penetrating eyes.

"Well, no. But who else would it be from?"

"It's not just a scrap that someone dropped?"

"No."

"How did the bird get it?"

"You said I should keep talking to her, so I showed her the note and asked what she thought."

"And she grabbed it?" Poe's sigh reverberated in the still room as he pointed toward a chair.

I sat and looked around. His office was as trim and no nonsense as he was. The Homburg hung on an old-fashioned hat rack. A new thought entered my mind. "Is your name really Eddie?"

"What?"

"When I came in, the officer called you Eddie."

He hesitated, unsure if he should answer me. "My name is Alan, but it's the old joke. Gives the boys here something to have fun with. Every once in a while someone will slip a raven picture onto my desk. One year some of the men bought me a bobblehead doll of the scare master for Christmas." He leaned forward, suddenly all business. "So you came out of hiding just to show me this crumpled note?"

"I really do think it is from Rita. That she is alive and well. I knocked on her apartment door, but no one answered."

"Leave this with me. I'll see what I can do."

"Where do you think Rita is? With that woman who was outside her apartment? Maybe you should check her family and friends."

"We can't go around checking on people who want to disappear. She hasn't committed any crime. Besides, I think someone checked with family at the beginning. No one could tell us anything."

"Maybe I should go."

"Maybe you should stay away from anything having to do with this. Certain things happened to you that are all too real. Haven't you had enough? Maybe you should leave town for a while. Disappear yourself."

"You want Polly and me to hit the road? Wouldn't that be something? I promise to stay in the building, sir!"

"Right." He rolled his eyes and played with the papers on his desk, anxious to get back to work. "Do you want an officer to see you home?"

"No, thank you. I wouldn't want to give Jenny Lane anything else to talk about."

"Yes, you might have some ''splainin' to do." He waved me off with a lopsided grin, but his eyes were deadly serious.

****

Mentioning Jenny Lane got me to thinking on the way home. She seemed to know a lot about the town and its inhabitants. Maybe I could pay her a visit and see what she knew about Timmy or the Hills and their secrets.

The parking garage was eerily silent when I got home. I sat in my car and peered in all directions. I wished I had kept the spray can. At least it was better than being empty handed. No one seemed to be stirring, so I edged from behind the wheel and tried to shut the car door as quietly as I could. My steps rang hollow and echoed throughout the concrete structure as I raced toward the street.

She was home when I knocked on her door. "Hi, Jenny."

"El! What a wonderful surprise!" Jenny wore filmy white yoga pants and a flowing lavender tunic.

I heard soft music in the background. "I hope I'm not disturbing you."

"Not at all. I just finished my shamatha meditation. Come in."

"Meditation?"

"It clears and strengthens the mind. Gets rid of the disharmony. One can focus on mindfulness."

Getting rid of disharmony sounded like something I needed desperately, but I would ask for meditation lessons some other time. "I just wanted to thank you again for the aloe plant and for helping me the other day I had my mishap."

"Any time! How is the body healing?"

"Jenny, that salve you gave me is amazing! Thank you for that as well! I don't know what I would have done without your help."

"Let me know if you need more. I have an herbalist who is a miracle worker. She puts together the most marvelous concoctions. I get all my tea from her. If you want, I can take you there one day. She's just a short walk away."

"I'd like that."

"Speaking of tea, I was just about to have a cup of jasmine tea. Would you care to join me?"

"Yes, thank you. I've never had jasmine tea."

"It's one of my favorites. It can boost the immune system and alleviate stress and pain."

"Anything that relieves stress is just my cup of tea." I smiled.

Jenny laughed. "Is that Hill newspaper business still bothering you?"

"It's been weighing on my mind and making me crazy." I remembered why I had come. "You must know a lot of the legends surrounding that family."

"Well, I think the son inherited the house, but then he left town. The house sat empty for a long time, and then a distant relative—a cousin, I believe—showed up. No one disputed her claim. You can probably check the tax rolls to get dates."

"I started a family tree of sorts, but things got too fuzzy. No one even knows if Hill is the family name or where exactly they came from. I found no immigration entries for any Hill that fit the dates of their arrivals. It would be so easy to slip into another name once you pass through customs. Records are so readily available today, but to do a back search of all men of that age who came through during that time would be exhaustive."

"Yes, it sounds thoroughly tedious. You really must come over sometime and meditate with me. It will do you worlds of good!"

"I might just take you up on that, Jenny. One thing I was really curious about is where Clark Hill got his money from." I picked up my cup. "He came here and bought a lot of land, built a big mansion, and paid people to do the work."

"That is another unanswered question. Did he come to America with it or did he arrive years before he got here, work in some other part of the country, and make a bunch of money?" She poured more tea. "I'm sure someone has told you he named the town Clark Hill?"

"No! Really? Why the name change?"

"It was just temporary, nothing official. When the tides turned against him, I think whoever was in charge thought by planting a few trees and honoring the men of the Constitution, people might not notice the new name. After all, it is fairly close in nature – Clark Hill – Parkville. Rumors! The downfall of mankind!"

"Yes, I agree. My head is spinning!"

"I guess we'll never know."

"I don't suppose you heard anything more about Timmy, the homeless man who was killed? What do you know about him?"

"Not much. Didn't he live at that caretaker's

cottage on the Hill estate? I used to see him hitchhiking into town or hanging around the park benches. I don't think I ever even heard him talk."

"Rita told me that's what he did. She even showed me the old cottage. Of course, you can't get onto the grounds anymore."

"I haven't seen her around lately," Jenny continued. "Has she gone off with that big hunk of a boyfriend of hers?"

"Your guess is as good as mine." I started to gather my things, but there was another bit of gossip I wanted to hear from Jenny. "I happened to see Mason Street as I was coming in. He was just leaving for another trip. What do you know about him?"

"It seems you came to pump me about men today." She winked. "Now, Mason Street is one beautiful man! Always on the move. I think he flies somewhere at least once or twice a month. And have you seen his cars? I love the little red sports car! I need to get one of those in purple!"

"Jenny!" The image was delightful. "I can just see you speeding around in one of those!"

She laughed as well. "You should really get to know him better. A girl could do worse. Buff. Handsome. Money." She gave me a sideways grin. "Unless you're already interested in a good-looking police inspector?"

I could feel myself blush. "Well, I don't think I'm looking at present, but Mason seems to be fairly successful."

"I think most of his business comes from outside Parkville. One doesn't get that rich in this small city. Too much competition. I think he told me once his father had also been a lawyer here. Worked for some rich family. Hmm. I wonder if it was the Hill family. That would be a bit weird, wouldn't it?" Jenny tilted her head in thought.

"That would be weird indeed." Her words gave me a jolt.

"Strange things are alive in the world, and coincidences happen all the time."

"Well, I better get home to my bird. Thanks for the tea and all the gifts, Jenny. I really enjoyed our talk."

"Come by any time, dear. I'm always ready for a chat. Namaste."

****

Email to El Turner
Hey Mrs. T.

My name is Missy, and I have a few questions.

My mother always calls my grandmother an old witch. Do you know if witches run in the family? I mean, would they show up somewhere if you dug hard enough? I'm 10 and it would be really cool to have witches in the family. I might be lucky enough to be one.

Let me know. Do you charge for emails?
Missy

****

Email to Missy
Hi Missy—

Thank you for the email.

I'm not sure if witches would show up very easily in family trees. You sound like a lively and smart young woman. I think the best thing would be to ask your mother if witches run in the family. You might ask if any of your family came from Salem. She might be able to

Allison Thorpe

straighten you out on the matter. She may not realize how her language is affecting your imagination. If I come across any articles about witch hunting in family trees, I will let you know.

Good luck and no charge!
Best,
El

Chapter 21

I patted my pockets when I got to my door only to realize I didn't have my new apartment keys. The car key was in my hand, but after searching, I did not find the ones for the door. I needed to get one ring for them all. I hoped they had just fallen out of my pack and were lying on the floor of the car. I remembered seeing all my keys when I left the police station.

As relaxed as I was after downing a cup of jasmine tea and being lulled by mind-soothing music, I did not relax my guard taking the elevator and heading back into the parking garage. It seemed to be a busy time with cars pulling in and out and people about. Still, I walked as fast as possible over to my car. Luckily, the keys rested on the floor mat. I picked them up, glad I didn't have to get another lock on my door.

I was almost back to the street entrance when I heard the whisper, "El. Over here."

Turning warily, I tried to see where the voice came from.

"El. El. Over here." I didn't recognize the speaker, but it seemed to be female. Was it the woman who had broken into Rita's apartment? Was she trying to lure me into the shadows?

"What?" I almost shouted, trying to show I wasn't afraid, all the while inching toward the street.

"Please, come over here."

My first instinct was to run. To get to my apartment and lock the door. Spend some quality time with Polly. Eat a package of pumpkin seeds. Read the newspaper.

"It's me." More insistent.

"Me who?" I whispered back this time, feeling the need for secrecy, but fear prickled the ridges of my spine.

"Rita," whispered in the hush.

"Rita!"

"Ssshhhhh. I don't want anyone to know I'm around."

I walked cautiously in the direction of the voice. "Rita?" I still thought it might be a trap.

She stepped out from behind a cement column, huge dark glasses, baggy sweat pants, oversized gray sweater, hair pulled under a wide hat. No makeup. Not the Rita I knew.

I gave her a hug. "I thought you were dead! No one knew what had happened to you! Why didn't you call or let me know you were okay?"

She seemed to have lost that confident swagger. "El, I couldn't. I was afraid for my life. I was getting death threats over the phone, and I know someone was following me."

"Where have you been?"

She looked furtively around and pulled me behind the pillar. "I was staying with my brother's ex, Zelda. It was the last place I thought people would look for me. She hates me, but she took me in. Rather, she hates my brother Scott, but that emotion transfers to all his family."

"Was she the woman in your apartment?"

"Yes. And she didn't like it one bit. I had to get some things I needed. She said you almost caught her one day outside my apartment. That was the day she told me to get out. I've been hiding here and there since—low cost hotels, a women's shelter, you name it."

"Who was sending you death threats?"

"I wish I knew, but it certainly had to do with those articles."

"I had several run-ins myself."

"Oh, El, I'm sorry you got involved in this! What happened?"

"Well, I'm still here, and so are you." I had a thought. "Did you ever make it out to talk to someone at the Hill place?"

She smiled. "I did one better. I talked to Joseph Hill. I pretended I was lost, used my sexiest voice on that intercom by the gate, and he came out to meet me. At least I know what he looks like now. When he saw me, he backed off. I think he knew who I was. I got out of there plenty quick. That's when the calls started. It has to be Hill. But why? What do those old rumors have to do with him? He can't be worried about the Hill reputation."

"Do you think he had anything to do with Timmy's death?"

"You think he killed Timmy? What reason could he have?"

"Well, what if he decided to revive the old practice of devil worship and this was part of the ritual?"

"Oh, El! Don't tell me you believe that crap I wrote?"

"Crap?"

"Oh, I knew I wasn't writing serious journalism. I have to use drama to get any kind of reaction."

"Well, it worked. Your editor said there was tremendous response. He called me to give him more information."

"Did you?"

"Of course not. But what will you do next? Maybe it's time to go to the police. We can get through to Poe. Maybe he can put you someplace out of reach. Like a safe house or witness protection or something." I glanced around, clearly nervous.

"Poe? Like that mystery guy with the black cats and the pit?"

"Like Police Inspector Poe. He's a good guy."

"Ah, so she says with a sparkle to her eye! Is he cute?"

"I think we have more serious things to worry about at present." I shifted her train of thought. "Maybe Timmy was killed because he saw or heard something he shouldn't have."

"You mean you're now in on finding the killer?" Rita was getting excited.

"Well, let's just say the police are convinced of it, and you, as a person of interest, have shot to the top of their suspect list with your disappearance," I said.

"That damn knife!"

"Tell me again what happened."

"I stepped on something when I was in the alley, almost twisted my ankle. When I reached down and picked it up, I realized it was all wet and sticky. I thought of all the disgusting things that could be lying in that alley, dropped it, and wiped my fingers on the wall. So my fingerprints were on what turned out to be the knife that killed him. I told the police I had no reason to kill him, but I don't know if they believed me."

"Let's go to the police right now. Show them you're alive. Proclaim your innocence."

"Not just yet. I don't want to end up in jail. If I come out into the open, I'm sure to be a target."

"Inspector Poe would believe you."

"You're putting a lot of faith in this guy."

"What do you plan to do then?" I wanted to get her off the subject of Poe.

"I've had a lot of time to think about this. I'm going to do more digging into Joseph Hill, and I need your help. It's dangerous, but I think that might be the only way to make this all disappear. I can't be on the run for the rest of my life. Look at my nails, for heaven's sake! I haven't worn makeup in days, and I miss Reb. He must be going crazy wondering what happened to me."

"You didn't let him know where you were?"

"I couldn't take the chance. I don't trust anyone."

"I think he followed you that night," I told her.

"What? How do you know?"

"He told me. I think he did a lot of trailing after you."

"Surely you don't think that Reb killed Timmy, do you?" Rita grabbed my arm.

"He came to my apartment and told me about a fight you had. He had some pretty odd moments, but then again, everyone around me seems to be acting oddly."

"You know, I often had the feeling of being watched. That man does get insanely jealous, but I don't think he could have killed anyone. Timmy and I certainly were not involved."

"Maybe he confronted Timmy after you left, and there was a fight. Maybe it was accidental."

"But wasn't Timmy dead when I went into the alley? If Reb followed me, he couldn't have attacked Timmy after I left." Rita shook her head.

"At this point, everyone is on my list of suspects," I said. "Susie Q and Hubie saw two men in that alley: one they described as tall and thin who stayed in the alley the longest, and then one they called a brick. I thought they might be talking about Reb."

"Susie who? All these unknown names are swirling around my brain like geese gone dizzy in a storm!"

"They are people who live near the alley and saw you go in and come out. Hubie had a pair of binoculars where he watched from their porch."

"Well, the only thing to do is to solve this mystery." She stamped her foot. "Are you with me? Are you up for it?"

"Exactly what are you going to do and exactly what do you want me to do?"

"I'm going into the Hill house and look for clues."

"What?" My voice rose to such a pitch, I was afraid I might shatter a few car windows. "Excuse me, but what?"

"I'm still working on a plan for that, but I think I found a way into the caretaker's cottage where Timmy lived. I'm sure there are clues there. I just didn't want to venture in on my own. With the two of us, it might work. One can be lookout, and the other can search the cottage."

"Rita, get real! We aren't police or even detectives.

What makes you think we are up to doing a house search?"

"Like I said, I'm sick of running. We have to do something! Now are you with me?"

"What do you want to do?" I wasn't sure I wanted in on her craziness, but she was right. I was tired of looking over my shoulder as well.

"Let's go there right now. I think I found a way through the bushes so we can avoid the fence. No one's living in the cottage, so that shouldn't be a problem."

"But it's late in the day. Shouldn't we wait until tomorrow?" My body was starting to ache, and I longed for another soothing bath and Jenny's balm.

"Now. We can be in and out quickly. I have a flashlight in my pack. Let's do it now!"

"I'll drive there, but I want to look it over first before rushing in."

"It's up to us, El! Let's do it for Timmy!"

I nodded and got in the car, wondering if I had hit my head harder than I thought. At the moment her plan actually made sense.

Chapter 22

I remembered the last time I had come this way. It was not a pleasant reminder. But this time I had Rita with me and new tires on my car. I hoped Jack Beane was nowhere around.

We pulled up on a side street some distance from the Hill house. Rita pointed out the bushes with a miniscule path between.

"We might have to duck a bit or even crawl to avoid the thorns. It's not too bad. I went through the other day, but chickened out at the cottage door, afraid someone might come along and find me. That's why it will work with one of us as lookout." Rita hit her fist into her open palm.

"Isn't the cottage locked?" I was getting nervous. What did we know about breaking into a house? If Joseph Hill was around and had killed once, what was to say he wouldn't do it again?

"No. So, let's go. Now or never." She slipped out of the car. "And don't appear suspicious. There's an old woman who loves watching things out of her window."

"Didn't you talk to her?" I asked.

"Yes, and she had gossip about the whole neighborhood, but I have a feeling she was dramatizing much of what she said." She looked at me and shrugged. "Who does that?"

I held back a comment about Rita's own

melodramatic moments and tagged along behind her.

"This way." She appeared to be walking along the road when suddenly she bent over and disappeared through the bushes.

I tried to follow, but couldn't see where she had gone. The bushes menaced thick branches and thorns. "Rita?" I didn't relish the idea of scrambling through them.

A hand poked through the dense greenery and yanked at my sleeve. "Here! And duck low or you will get scratched!"

I did as she said and came up on the backside of the caretaker cottage that had once been Timmy's home. I survived with only a few minor scratches. I crept around to the front. Rita already had the door open.

"I'll go in and scout; you stand watch. Then we can switch places."

I tried to make myself as small as possible and stand in the shadows, out of sight from any of the main house windows. I hoped Joseph Hill did not like to take late afternoon walks around the grounds. A dog barked in the distance, sending my nerves to the edge of sanity. Were there dogs on the premises? I remembered Poe's childhood fears. I didn't want any surprises like giant wolves rushing at me. Or fierce Dobermans or Rottweilers with their teeth gnashing ready to take a giant bite out of my behind.

"El." Rita touched my elbow.

I screamed.

"El, it's me! Shut up! Please!" She came around and stood in front of me. "What's up with you?"

"I was just imagining guard dogs rushing at me.

Sorry." I surveyed the property. "Do you think someone heard me?"

"Probably not, but don't do it again."

"What did you find?" I tried to bring my mind back to the task at hand.

"Nothing that looked like a clue. Just a big mess in there. It looks like someone might have already had the idea to search the place. Go in and tell me what you think. Here's the flashlight." Rita was all business.

My nerves still raw, I took the light and eased inside the cottage. I let my eyes adjust to the limited light. Rita was right; someone had already been here and made no effort to hide it: papers scattered around, drawers left open, mattress askew. I wish I had worn gloves. Dust coated surfaces and danced its molecules about in the dimming light that filtered through the small windows. I was sure if any clues had been there, they were long gone. Who had searched? Joseph Hill? The police? I wondered if they would be back looking for fingerprints. I tried to remember what I had touched, wiped off some areas with my shirt sleeve, then went back outside.

I shook my head, and Rita nodded toward the bushes and escape.

"Who do you think got there first?" I asked once we were back in the car and safely driving away.

"Would the police make that much of a mess? I think Hill got there first, and he made no effort to hide his hunt."

"I wonder what he found. Someone thought Timmy had evidence worth killing for."

I felt Rita shiver beside me, but a moment later she said, "Time for Plan B!"

****

"I've been watching the house," Rita explained on the drive back. "Joseph Hill has a crew of three women who come in every Friday. I think they clean and cook for him or something. He goes out when they are there. I tailed him. He visits a bar down by the river—The Staggering Pelican. He stays there for two or three hours. That's going to be our chance." She looked more determined than ever. I parked the car back in the garage, glad to be home and safe. Rita's ideas made me rub my temples.

"Our chance? Our chance to do what?" I burst out. Rita had clearly lost her mind. "I don't know if I can do this again. And how are you going to get us in with some cleaning crew? Besides, that house is huge. Where do we even begin to look? Are we looking for a murder weapon? Some written confession? Shouldn't we leave this for the police?" We got out of the car. I stopped and checked the garage. "Wait!" I thought I saw something and pulled Rita farther into shadows. "Was that Goth Guy?" The tea and meditative music Jenny offered seemed like centuries ago. I was back to nervous wreck.

"Goth Guy? What in this weird world are you talking about?"

"It's this guy who moved into an apartment on our floor. I think he pushed me down the stairs?"

"Oh my goodness! Are you sure? You mean like one of those dark and broody men with tattoos and snakes and stuff? He pushed you down the stairs?"

"I'll fill you in later. Now why shouldn't we call the police?"

"You know they need a search warrant to go in and

for that they need proof of some kind."

"Aren't these threats on our lives proof?" I asked.

"We have no proof who is doing it. I suppose they could trace my phone calls, but people use burn phones these days. Besides, it would just show someone from the Hill house called, not that they threatened me." Rita lowered her voice as a group of people walked into the garage.

"I don't know, Rita. I think it all sounds like an iffy plan, and what if something goes wrong? This man could be treacherous, even lethal. We would be going in blind. This isn't like the caretaker cottage. This is the main house where a killer might live!"

"El, you don't have to do this, but I am definitely going in! If you don't want to, that's fine. It would be good to have someone on the outside in case something did happen to me. Then you can call your precious policeman Poe to come in and rescue me." Rita had that do-not-try-to-change-my-mind face, a look I knew too well, like when I would try to talk her out of buying another pair of shoes or one more designer handbag.

"Listen, I thought I lost you once. I don't want to go through that again! I worried about you day and night!" This was a crazy plan, but Rita was right. I didn't want to have to peer into shadows forever.

She reached out and gave me a hug. "You don't know how much that means to me. I've been living on the edge for weeks."

"Me too."

"What else happened to you?"

"I'll tell you some other time. Friday is a few days away. Tell me your plan."

Rita clapped her hands and squealed softly. "Does

this mean you'll help?"

"Let's hear your ideas first."

"We go in with the cleaning crew. It's usually three women. Hill leaves soon before they get there, so the gates are open for that time. I don't think there is anyone else in the house—no butler or maid. We dress like the cleaners and walk in like we belong. Once inside, we act like caterers or interior decorators or someone who should be there. Let me do all the talking. What do you think?"

"Okay. How do we get out?"

"We walk out before or with the cleaners. He usually comes home about half an hour after they leave. It's the only time the gates are open."

"So in and out very quickly?"

"Yes. I suggest we wear dark clothes and shoes for running, just in case. Today was a warmup." This was a new Rita.

"But if we're there as caterers or interior designers, shouldn't we be dressed better?"

"Yes, you're right. Hmmm." She stared off into the distance for a few minutes. "Okay. I got it. Do you still have that awful painting hanging in your apartment? The one I hate?"

"The one that was in the apartment when I moved in?" I had no idea where she was going with this crazy plan.

"Yes. The one you were too lazy to take down."

"I prefer the word busy, but yes. It's still there. Right next to Polly."

"Polly?"

"My bird."

"You have a bird? How long have I been gone? I

feel like that Rip Van guy who slept for years and woke up and nothing was the same."

"She's been in a cage next to that painting since I've known you."

"That's a live bird? I thought that was some stuffed art thing with creepy eyes that someone had left behind but you hadn't gotten around to throwing out."

"After all this we can sit down for a heart-to-heart, but for now what do I do with the painting?"

"Bring it covered with a sheet. We'll pretend we're there to arrange the art work. That way we have to dress for work and climbing ladders."

"Plan B sounds very sketchy to me."

"Believe me. This cleaning crew won't care. They come to work. They don't worry about what else is going on."

"Why do we wait for them? Can't we get in earlier?"

"I'm not sure if the front door is locked. They may have a key."

"All right. I'm in. Maybe we can find some more of the money Timmy found."

"Money?"

"A man at the homeless shelter told me Timmy had a stack of bundled money that he implied might have been the cause of his firing."

"And you waited until now to tell me about this?" Rita put her hands on her hips.

"The man I talked to thought it might have been stolen."

"Timmy stole it?"

"Well, Timmy had it as proof of something. I think he was going to tell you the story when he got killed."

"Damn. Who has the money now?"

"It was stolen."

"So Timmy stole some money that may have been stolen only it got stolen?"

"I guess that sums it up." I wondered if anything in life would ever make sense again.

"Why would anybody in the Hill family steal money? Aren't they all rich?"

"Maybe they're not all rich. Or maybe the money wasn't stolen at all."

"Then why would Timmy take it? And how does that figure into the hot story he had?" She gathered her things. "You know I keep coming back to Joseph Hill. He seems too simple to be behind this whole thing. I think there is someone else behind the curtain pulling the strings."

"You mean like a mastermind?" I asked.

"Yes! A mastermind! That's it. You just wait. When we solve this, we will find a mastermind at work!"

"It seems the more we know, the more questions we have."

"It's up to us, El. I know once we get inside the house, we'll find answers. See you here on Friday at seven. We'll go early and be ready." She gave me one final hug and disappeared into the night.

I shook my head. What was I getting myself into? I checked the garage for Goth Guy, but it appeared empty. I moved carefully, sticking to the wall until I was inside my building. The evening concierge was on duty. I nodded to him and went uneasily up in the elevator with a couple who had obviously been out celebrating something and now couldn't wait to get each other into bed.

I couldn't remember the last time I had that feeling.

****

Letter to El Turner

Dear Ms. Turner,

I am returning the refund you sent me. I have had time to review everything and look back at your letters, and you did warn me. I guess I was just too excited to pay attention to it. There were so many wonderful endings that could have been revealed; I never thought for one moment it would be something as bizarre as what you discovered.

Despite fainting, Grandmother Tootie declared this reunion to be the best one she could remember. She said that since the gatherings had become so dull and boring, I was a genius to come up with something that was startling and memorable. After her blessing, I have received flowers and good wishes from the rest of the family.

I must apologize for my previous letter. You have made me the family hero of the moment, so I thank you. Sometimes I just can't figure life out!

Sincerely,

Wanda Darren

Encl.

****

Letter to Wanda Darren

Dear Ms. Darren:

Thank you for your letter and returning the check. I am so happy things worked out in the end. It's often difficult to know what our ancestors have been up to, and family trees do produce some interesting branches!

I agree with you about life. We never know where it will lead us. I am glad for your happy ending.
Best,
El Turner

Chapter 23

The day was eaten up researching the hit-and-run incident of Essie Williams, which helped the time pass. I looked through a ton of old newspapers online, trying to find a lead. If she had indeed seen something, I hadn't found it yet. I was amazed by how many hit-and-run reports there were.

I didn't answer most of the calls, letting the machine pick up.

"Hey, Miss Turner, this is Bradley Washington again calling to see if you were interested in sending over an article on the Hill family. Give me a jingle. Remember, we pay for stories!"

"Still waiting for you to call me back." Jack Beane's voice was all honey. "I found a really great place for lunch and would love to take you. See how you are feeling. Catch up on our lives." He repeated his phone number again in smooth and inviting tones.

"Well, he certainly seems interested in getting together," I told Polly. "He's cute in a ragged blonde sort of way. Great shoulders. Handy with the rescues, and he knows how to change a tire. I get a strange feeling around him, though. And he was out at the Hill house. I'm not sure I believed that stuff about asking for directions. But why would he lie?" The bird bobbed its head as if it understood.

I took a break from Essie's search to try to find out

who owned the Old World Inc. company. They were listed as paying taxes on the Hill property. I didn't get very far. It seemed someone was playing a shell game.

The phone rang again. "I know you're thinking about me. I can feel it." Jack Beane laughed into the machine. "Still waiting."

"He does try hard at being charming," I said aloud.

I took the next call. Poe. Then was sorry I did. "How are you doing?"

"What do you mean by that?" I said, edgy and certain he was onto my plans with Rita.

"El, I just asked how you were doing. There's nothing wrong, is there?"

"No." I let out a deep breath. "You just caught me in mid-research. I sometimes have a hard time getting back to the present." I hoped I didn't sound too nervous.

"I just wanted to tell you we got nothing off that note Rita may or may not have left for you. Not enough there to do any testing."

"Oh, that's all right. I realize it was just a long shot at best. Sorry to have bothered you with it." I hurried on, knowing now that Rita was alive and well.

"Okay what have you done with El Turner?"

"What do you mean by that?"

"You keep asking me that. I mean the El Turner who came into my office and was adamant about finding her friend. She insisted I examine a tiny shred of paper that had been chewed by a bird, sprayed with cleaning fluid, stepped on, and heaven knows what else. That El Turner."

I overplayed my hand, brushing off a problem I had brought to him. "I've had time to think about that whole thing and how unreasonable I was. You were right. It's best for me to stay home and keep out of trouble."

"Now I know something is going on." He paused, examining my words. "Did Rita contact you?"

The man was reading my mind. I didn't want to lie to him. If I told him our plan, he would definitely lock me up. "At the moment I am sitting here talking to Polly, buried in research questions, and thinking about making a bowl of soup."

"You didn't answer my question."

"I told you what was going on." I tried to think of some way to get him off track. "By the way, has anything come of the Timmy Russert investigation?"

"I see you found out his last name."

"I guess I happened to hear it somewhere."

"The case is still under investigation. You know I can't talk about it," he answered.

"Did anyone from the police inspect the caretaker's cottage where he had lived before he was fired?"

"Back to telling me my job, are we?"

"Sorry. I just wondered if anything came of it."

"So back to my question about Rita? Any word from her?" He was like a bulldog with a chew toy.

"I showed you the note." I answered hoping to sound innocent.

"You know what I was asking."

"El. It's Jenny Lane." I heard her gentle knocking at my door.

"Coming, Jenny."

"Who's that in the background?" Poe asked.

"Oh, Jenny's at the door. I have to go." I told Poe.

"Nice out, El. Be safe. I'm serious. If something

comes up, call me. Don't try to handle it by yourself."

"You bet. Thanks for calling." I did enjoy talking to the man; now just wasn't the right time. If we had spoken longer, I probably would have blurted something out I didn't want blurted.

I put down the phone and went to the door. Another little box tied with a purple ribbon. "I brought you some jasmine tea. You seemed to like it, and it will be good for your nerves."

"Jenny, how thoughtful! My nerves are in desperate need of this calming tea. Do you want to come in? You can meet Polly."

"Just for a minute. I'm running late for my drumming circle." She looked around for a person named Polly. Finding no one about, she turned to me with raised eyebrows.

"Polly, meet Jenny." I walked over to the bird cage.

"What a marvelous parrot! Aren't you the pretty bird?" she cooed his way.

"Pretty bird," Polly echoed.

"Amazing. She has only just begun to talk. I think she likes you!"

"I'm glad you have such good company," she said to me. "Now I must really leave. I don't want to lose my drum spot. Very nice to meet you, Polly."

"Thanks for the tea. Happy drumming."

I envied Jenny and her carefree life. When this was all over, I swore to take up yoga or meditation. Drink more tea. When this was all over, however, seemed to be a long way off.

****

Before I could catch my breath, the phone rang

again. I considered yanking the cord from the wall, but the call was from Ida.

"Hey El, how you holding up? I've been worried about you."

"I'm not sure how I'm doing at this point, Ida. I've been meaning to get back into the library. I seem to still be hung up on Parkville history and how it connects to Timmy's murder. I'm at a loss at the moment."

"Have you talked to the lady who lives across the street? Beatrix McGregor keeps the closest eye on the Hill house. I think she owns a telescope or something. She's been around forever and might know something about the Hill history."

"I haven't talked to her yet." I made a note to ask Rita exactly what the woman had told her, gossip or not.

Ida's next words brought me quickly back to reality. "By the way, word is going around there's been another murder."

"No!" I almost shouted the word. "Who got murdered?" *Please don't let it be Rita,* my brain screamed.

"It was another homeless man. People are starting to think a serial killer is out to murder homeless people."

"Did anyone know a name?"

"Just someone who had been staying at one of the shelters. Danny someone."

My heart crashed ten stories. "Danny Boy Cooper?"

"That could have been it. Do you know him?" Ida sounded concerned.

"I just heard his name mentioned. Where did it

happen?"

"That's all I know. The news hasn't made the papers yet; it's just the word on the streets, which I'm sure will swirl with all kinds of insane rumors. So whatever you do, stay home, lock your doors, and be careful!" were Ida's parting words.

"That's probably good advice. Thanks, Ida. I'll talk to you later."

I wished I had taken it.

****

I remembered what Ida had told me concerning Señor Marquez and the prints in his store and decided one quick trip to his newsstand couldn't hurt. At least I hoped I wouldn't get hurt. Living with a banged up body had become the norm. How did action stars do it? At least the day was bright and sunny and seemed as far away from murder as the moon. Maybe Señor Marquez or someone in the store had more news about Danny Boy Cooper. I hoped his demise wasn't connected to Timmy in any way.

No one bothered me on the race over to the store. No one tried to run me over or push me down the stairs or into the street. No one tried to save me.

The small bell jangled as I pushed the glass door open, and a figure turned from the register, leaned on the counter, and gave a flirtatious smile.

"*Hola, Chica!*" He winked.

"Is Señor Marquez here today?"

"*Emergencia. Familia. Soy manuel, su sobrino.*"

"Family emergency? And you are Manuel?"

"*Si*. But I can help you, *Chica.*"

"*Que es sobrino?*"

"I am his nephew, *Chica.*"

"*Hola, Manuel.* What's the word on the streets? Any gossip today?"

"Gossip, *Chica?* I spend the day watching television."

He obviously hadn't heard about Danny Boy, so I changed subjects. "I wonder if I could see those pictures."

I looked beyond him to the wall where a series of drawings hung. Why had I never noticed them before? I moved around the end of the counter to get a better look.

"*Quiero tomar una copa, Chica?*"

"Drink?" I asked, not exactly sure what he was asking. "No thank you."

The drawings were small but detailed. Someone had a deft hand at capturing a scene. One certainly outlined what could very well be a worker camp. Another showed what I took to be the Hill mansion. Several held men with shovels and pickaxes. Before I could get a glimpse of them all, the boy behind the counter moved closer, cutting off my access.

"Do you know anything about these drawings?"

"Those old dusty things. They've always been hanging there."

"When will Señor Marquez be back?"

"Don't know." He tried the wink again. "*Vamos de fiesta?*"

I reluctantly moved back, my eyes returning to his face. He grinned wildly and wiggled his eyebrows.

"Party?"

"*Si. Soy el fuego. Eres el Diablo*"

"Fire? Devil?" I began backing up.

"*Da miedo! Da mucho miedo, Chica.*"

"Be afraid? Be very afraid?" I gripped the edge of the counter. Could he be part of the group trying to hurt me? Was he involved with the murders? Was I being too paranoid? "Why would you say that to me?" I wondered if I should scream. Just then a family walked in off the street, and I made my way hastily to the door.

"*The Fly.* That's a quote from the movie. That film was just on the television. Great movie, huh, *Chica?"*

The family moved to the back of the store.

"Hey, *Chica*, I mean nothing by it. Don't tell my uncle I was watching such things. He imagines they are bad for the brain. I'm really a nice guy. I didn't mean to scare you."

His last words faded because I was running down the block for home, and I was very afraid.

****

Letter to El Turner
Dear Ms. Turner,

My daughter reminded me that I had mentioned living in a small area called Millertown, IA, for a few months between Madison and Atlanta. I don't know if that will help you or confuse you more.

Sincerely,
Essie Williams

****

Letter to Essie Williams
Dear Ms. Williams:

Bingo! I think I found the event you were asking about. Since Millertown is so small, it was easy to access their newspaper. I am enclosing an article which I believe to be the one. As you can see, it mentions a young girl witnessed the accident but remembered nothing when questioned. I was glad to see that no one was badly hurt, and the driver of the hit and run was caught.

Please let me know if you agree. If so, I hope you will now be able to put the issue to rest.

Best,
El Turner

Chapter 24

Friday came way too quickly. I spent hours babbling to Polly. I'm sure she thought I was crazy. I took the painting down from the wall, covered it with a sheet, uncovered it, and put it back on the wall a dozen times. Thought about all the things that could go wrong. Got together the dark clothes I had used when I originally staked out the house. I knew I should call Poe and tell him what we planned to do, but I also knew he would hit the roof. If I had some way of contacting Rita, I would have called the whole thing off.

I tried to keep my mind off Danny Boy Cooper being the new victim. Maybe it was some other Danny. Maybe there was a serial killer after homeless people and not Joseph Hill trying to cover his tracks. I had a gut feeling it was Danny Boy Cooper. Why kill him, I kept asking, but I knew the answer. He had some of the stolen money.

"I'm going to the Hill house, Polly. Can you believe that?" I asked her. "Why did I let Rita talk me into this? This is really a stupid move!"

The bird came to the edge of her cage and stared.

"We have to solve this murder!" I repeated like a mantra.

I jumped every time the phone rang and usually let the answering machine take messages. Jack Beane called several times.

"Lunch invitation is still on," the message said.

"Still waiting," said the second and third call. "I'd really like to talk to you again."

At least he wasn't outside stalking me. Sometimes I would hide behind the curtains and peer out at the street to see if he or someone suspicious was lurking around. I saw nothing out of the ordinary. I stayed inside, glad I had enough supplies to hold. Two new clients called, but now was not the time to be searching for Lincoln links and Indian princess connections.

At twilight, I dressed in black and left the apartment before I could change my mind again. Forgot the painting and had to go back. The worn frame contained a generic seascape, but if one had no eye for art, it might pass as something valuable. I stowed it in the trunk and sat in the driver's seat waiting for Rita. I began to get edgy when she didn't show. At one point I held my watch up to the light of the parking garage when a tapping at the car window almost made me die right there from heart failure. Being frightened in my car was getting to be as bad as all the early morning door knocking. I unlocked the passenger side, and she threw a bag in the back seat before hopping in.

Rita gave me a nervous smile. "Ready or not!"

"You want me to drive?"

"My car is a bit too obvious." I remembered she had a bright yellow sporty Mustang. "It's been here the whole time I was gone. Too many people know it."

We drove the rest of the way in silence. I didn't think now was the time to tell her about Danny Boy Cooper. We were already nervous as two pumpkins on Halloween. The days were getting shorter, and the sun had long gone home when we pulled up near the house.

"Why do we have to wait for the cleaning crew to walk in?" I asked.

"I told you originally I was on my way to interview a woman on this street who said she saw some weird comings and goings. I think she watches out the window all the time. If we go in with the cleaners, it won't look unusual. Besides, the door might be locked even though the gates are open."

"Wouldn't someone going in with art look less suspicious than someone coming out with artwork?"

"Good point. We can go in now if you want. Take our chances that the door is open."

Just then the cleaners pulled up in the driveway. Rita and I jumped out, grabbing the sheet-covered art from the back and heading across the street. She waved to the women; I nodded and just kept going. When we got to the door, we struggled as if to get a key out of our pockets while holding a large painting. One of the women stepped up and used her key to gain entry, then held the door for us. She lifted a corner of the sheet, saw the painting, and smiled. Once inside, they moved off toward the kitchen; we slowly made our way down a long hallway, unsure of where to go next.

"Should we split up?" Rita whispered, not waiting for my nod. "You take this floor and I'll take the stairs to the next floor. See if there are any hints of who the true mastermind is or any clues to Timmy's murder. Split up."

"Might be better. More ground to cover. If you find anything unusual, give me a call. I'll put my phone on vibrate." I inched away.

"Let's stick this painting in one of these side rooms. One that looks unused."

"Meet back here in an hour? Have you got a watch?" I was ready to leave before we even started.

"I've got my phone, Silly."

"Right. Your phone." While my landline and answering machine were my main connection to the outside world, I did have an outdated flip phone. I was glad I had brought it along and made sure Rita had the number.

"Okay. Good luck." She held out her hand. "We do this for Timmy!"

I took her hand in mine. "For Timmy!" Then I saw her move off into the dimness.

The house was extremely large. I had no idea how we expected to find anything. I tried a few of the doors, but they were locked. We had spent so much time planning our entry I wasn't even sure what we hoped to discover. More of the money? A bloody knife? A handwritten admission of guilt?

"Look for a den or office," Rita murmured from the shady stairwell.

I checked several open rooms and then crept further down the hallway until I came to a closed door into what looked like a library. Slipping inside, I kicked myself for not bringing a flashlight. Or gloves. When was I going to learn to be a competent snoop? I used my shirt sleeve to wipe off the door handle in case my fingerprints should linger there. I moved aside one of the curtains, and the moon lit up the room. There was a desk, but nothing was on it. Again using my shirt sleeve, I tried some of the drawers, but they were empty. A globe stood in one corner of the room. I wondered if anyone used the space for anything. Shelves of old, dusty books were everywhere.

What now? Should I do a good job of searching the area or move on to another space? I glanced at my watch, careful to keep track of time. Ten minutes had passed. I heard footsteps in the hallway as the cleaners went by, talking and laughing. I wished I had a map to this place. Maybe there was one in the court records building downtown. I'd have to check the next time. Surely there would be blueprints on file. Probably not for when the original house was built, but there might be for any additions.

Uncertain which way to go, I tripped over a throw rug on the floor and grabbed at a shelf on the bookcase to stop my fall. A panel opened behind me, and I fell backward. My grip loosened from the shelf. I clutched at whatever was around me, but I ended up on my butt with a solid whomp.

The panel door shut with a resounding clunk, leaving me in total dark.

****

I picked myself up, rubbing my backside. I had felt something crack in my pocket and remembered my phone. When I flipped it open, I saw the glass was splintered. The electronic light still lit and let me examine the door that had just closed. I felt around the outside, but I could find no way to open it back up. If I beat on the door, maybe one of the cleaning ladies would hear me. But how would I explain what I was doing snooping around instead of hanging artwork? Maybe I should phone Rita. I tried her number, but I could get no service. The light seemed to be fading on the phone. I wished I could scream.

Turning around, I pointed my phone in the other direction. A twisting dirt path led back into darkness. I followed it guardedly, hoping to find another way out. What I came to was a workroom of sorts. There were tables and a desk and jars on the shelf. I felt my phone vibrate. Rita!

"Rita? Thank goodness! I tried to call you, but my phone didn't work."

"El. I think we should get out of here. I don't want Joseph Hill to find us. If we slip out before the crew, we won't have to worry about locking the door. Did you find anything?"

"You wouldn't believe what I found!"

"El, you're cutting out. El?"

"I'm in some sort of secret room. Off the library."

My phone flickered then went dark. So did the room. I had not charged the phone in ages. Great! That was really smart. Now what was I going to do? Had Rita heard where I was? Hopefully she would get me out of here. I tried to feel my way back to the library panel door, but a blast of cold air in the face told me I was going in the wrong direction. Working to calm myself, I leaned my hand against one wall and closed my eyes. The room was already dark, but closing my eyes brought everything more into focus. Think! Which way did you come? Slowly, I inched back. It seemed like hours until I felt the edge of the wooden desk.

Just as I oriented myself to the right path, lights went on around me. The shock blinded me for an instant. Rita had found me! The thud of footsteps, however, indicated a heavier step, and that heavier step was marching toward the room where I stood frozen as a popsicle. Maybe Joseph Hill or someone else was home!

Quickly, I ducked back into the tunnel I had just

left, feeling only marginally safe in the dim passageway. What had I gotten myself into? I had only a partial view of the room. I didn't dare step out too far, but I had to see who was approaching.

The man who strode into the room was not what I expected. He was tall and attractive, but very thin, almost gaunt in the muted light. His clipped hair was dark, and there was something vaguely familiar about his profile. He wore a neat sport coat and blue jeans. He didn't look like a monster. Or like someone who would run me over or push me down the stairs. Or like someone who would kill Timmy.

The lights were muted decrepit-looking lamps hung on the wall. The man had his back to me, so I took a chance and peeked out. Now that I could make out the room, the contents became clearer. The desk I had happened upon was an old wooden affair covered in grimy magazines, papers, and used coffee cups. Metal tables and shelves covered half of the room. I couldn't make out what was in the jars on the shelf. The floor was hard-packed dirt. A damp sandy basement atmosphere. I wouldn't have been surprised to see Dr. Frankenstein come walking out in a white lab coat.

When he turned, I quietly shuffled back into the gloomy recess. I couldn't see anything, but he couldn't see me either. For an eternity I stood there, crouched in blackness, afraid to breathe, afraid to move further into the tunnel. My back and legs became rigid sticks. This man could be a killer, and I was in his house illegally. I heard a clicking then the rustle of paper, almost as if he were rapidly turning the pages of a book. My legs groaned in agony, and I felt faint. My body began to shiver, whether from fear or the damp cold, I couldn't tell. At last I heard him rise from the chair behind the lab table and move off. Once more I heard the clicking sound. I became one with the wall behind me, molding to every clammy curve and jutting stone. Soon the lights went out, and I heard the scrape of the panel door. Still, I remained where I was, teeth chattering in the dark and musty passageway.

Finally I moved my body, snail-like, stretching taut, unyielding muscles a millimeter at a time. My legs refused to listen to my brain. Afraid I would stumble, fall, and break aching bones, I steadied myself in the blackness until confidence in movement returned. I had never known such fear. What was I doing breaking into a man's house? Was I insane? I was an unassuming, ordinary, take-no-chances researcher. I wasn't a superhero in the slightest. I began to think about snakes. Did snakes live in damp basements? Rats? It was all Rita's fault!

Then I remembered why we had started this folly: someone was threatening us, maybe even trying to kill us. Still, witness protection seemed like a Hawaiian vacation at the moment. I wish I had confided in Poe. I pressed the button on my watch that lit up the time—half the night gone—but the glow was not bright enough to navigate by.

Once more I moved on toward where I remembered the desk, felt its splintered edges, and continued along the tunnel toward the library. I knew there had to be a light switch there somewhere. I came to the panel and backtracked, expanding my search against all the walls. Then I found it. A single switch, higher than I expected. Should I turn it on? Would someone in the library see the light?

Again I hesitated for what seemed like years. I lost all sense of time. Had Rita made it out? Had she gone to the police? We had driven in my car. Was she waiting there for me? If not, how did she get home? I asked all the questions that had built up in my brain but were too terrifying to consider before.

When I could stand it no longer, I tentatively flipped the switch. The lights were lower than I remembered, possibly because the dark had been so absolute. I was used to it now. I checked the panel again but there was no lever or knob I could find that would open the door. I pushed and pulled against the entrance, but nothing worked. If I didn't think someone would hear, I'd kick my way out. I resolved then and there never to leave my apartment again. I would chain myself to my computer! Eat soup and pumpkin seeds and be totally happy. To get to that point, however, I had to find another way out. What were my options? Possibly one of the passageways led to a door to freedom. I decided to check out the lab/desk area.

The desk drawers squeaked and groaned, sounds I had not noticed when I was cowering in the tunnel. In the bottommost one, I found a journal. It was old and filthy, and the paper was yellowed. The handwriting, when I gingerly opened it, was in looping letters. The longhand smeared and hard to read. I carefully turned to the beginning. The pages looked ready to self-destruct at any moment.

Today I started a town. Read a journal entry on the first page. I gently turned to the back, trying to decipher the nearly illegible scribbles.

A terrible fire. Dreams destroyed. The words jumped out of the uneven lines. Was this Clark Hill's handwriting?

I heard a noise above my head and halted, doing my best to imitate a statue. Should I hide? Move to turn out the lights? Run down one of the passageways? In the end, I stayed put for another hundred years before deciding I was imagining things.

I put the journal down and turned to the shelves behind me. The jars held odd random things like stickpins, screws, and buttons. Then I noticed several suitcases just visible in the opening of one of the tunnels. I lifted one. It was so heavy, I wondered at its contents. Abandoning any caution I had left, I laid it on the ground and opened the latch. I recognized the clicking sound. Opening it, I was stunned to find it full of money. Was that the shuffling noise I had heard? Why was he counting money in the basement?

This must be the money Timmy had found. What had made him be suspicious? Maybe the Hills just traveled with a lot of cash. Maybe they were printing their own counterfeit money. I didn't see any printing machines around. Had Joseph Hill robbed a bank? Was he hiding out until it was safe?

I had to get out of the house! I grabbed the journal and surveyed the labyrinth before me. There were five entrance points. The faint light did nothing to help with the decision. I looked around. There was a flashlight on one of the shelves. I clicked the on/off switch, and it worked. Shaking out a grungy piece of cloth nearby, I wrapped the journal in it and placed it inside my shirt, I went with the middle passage. Being careful on the damp, slick, dirt floor, I made my way as quickly as I could.

At the end was a heavy metal door that was locked.

I thought of every cuss word I had ever heard and forcefully whispered them a dozen times each before starting back toward the lab area. The passageway I had hidden in looked to be the larger, so I started a new journey. The farther I moved along, the stronger the drafts of wind on my face. Several twists and turns took me eventually to an old kitchen. I wondered if this had been servant's quarters when the house had originally been built. The underground puzzle of trails could have been their entry into the main house. Surely there was a door that led to the outside here!

It was a sooty old coal chute that saved me. The bin was full of the dust and filth of ages, but the chute was bent and worn. When I lifted it, it came away in my hands. I found a rusty dented bucket I turned over and stood on, balancing precariously while trying to worm my way into the chute. A snake shedding its skin would have been faster and more graceful. After a tiresome struggle to wiggle my way out, I rolled over and settled miraculously in the damp welcome grass of outside. Nothing had ever smelled so sweet! I wept and would have shouted to the heavens but for the fear that came roaring back. I wasn't home yet.

Light was just beginning to crest the horizon. I had been here all night! I hobbled up and leaned against the house. I had to get away, but my body refused to move. My arms and legs shuddered, and spasms shot through my muscles. I clutched the flashlight. Remembered too late that I had left the lights on. Joseph Hill would know I had been there! I calmed down a bit. He would have no idea who had been in his house. He hadn't seen me. Maybe he would think he had left them on. Or maybe he would blame the cleaning women.

Ever vigilant, I inched my way around the side of the house. Why did this house have to be so big? Every time I went around a corner, there would be another attached addition. I had no idea where my car was. After it seemed like I had circled the house several times, crouching all the way, sometimes crawling through the grass, I spotted my car. Nearly ran right toward it. Then I remembered the gates. Would they be open or closed? I tried to stay under cover of bushes and tree limbs as I worked my way toward the metal entry. When I tried them, they were locked. Would nothing work in my favor?

I retreated and looked around for Rita. Nothing moved. Surely this massive wall of metal with the spiky tops could not encircle the entire property. Several hundred feet along, I found an ending. A massive fencerow of thorny bushes rose skyward and blocked view and access to the property. I took out the journal and held it in front of me. Risking what little skin I left uncovered, I struggled on my stomach, wiggling and worming my way through the thorns. They showed no mercy, tearing at hair and clothes, now shredded facsimiles of their former selves. I kept my face as low as I could get it, protecting my eyes. Old wounds ripped open, stinging like fire. Wishing I had worn armor and a helmet, I managed to make it through, putting the journal back inside my shirt. I used the fencerow as a shield working my way back toward the car. The sky was lightening at an alarming rate, and I didn't want to attract any unwanted attention. I patted my hips. For a second I panicked. Did I still have the car key in my pocket? I checked the side of my jeans. The pockets had ripped away from the pants. No car key!

Tracing my steps, I worked my way back to the thicket I had crawled through, hoping with all my heart I did not have to tackle it again, hoping I had not lost it somewhere in the dark tunnels. There were tears in all my clothes, and I could feel blood running down my arms and legs. The gods were on my side for once. As I looked down, I saw a shiny object on the ground. My key! It had fallen out as I stood up. Fighting down the desire to race to the car, I again imitated a snail, creeping inch by painful inch.

Ducking across the street, I could only pray Beatrix McGregor wasn't an early riser with her telescope or Joseph Hill hadn't decided at that moment to look out a front window. Once at my car door, I could not get my fingers to work. My hands shook like I was in the middle of an earthquake. I had to use both hands to get the key in the lock. Why couldn't my mother have had a keyless remote to open the door? I stepped up into the seat, not caring how dirty and broken I was. Desperately hoping I hadn't used up my lot of prayers, I folded my hands and pleaded with the car to start. The engine sounded like a jet plane taking off when it ignited, but no one came out to give chase or stare at me. With heartfelt thanks to whatever forces were now on my side, I drove quickly back into town. The traffic had begun to swell as people set about their day going to work or taking the kids to school. It all looked so normal.

I saw no sign of Rita.

Chapter 25

When I pulled into the parking garage and turned off the motor, I laid my head on my arms on the steering wheel and bawled loudly. I sobbed like I had lost my best friend, my body heaving and convulsing in relief. Hysterical and nauseous down to my toes, I thought I might die then and there. The tears seemed to be washing away some of the blood on my face, stinging as they settled the fluids into the cuts and scrapes.

My car door abruptly flew open, and Rita grabbed my arm.

"Oh my God! El! El!" She kept repeating my name in a frantic wail while trying to hug me.

"Stop! Ouch! Rita, get away!" I tried to push her off.

She jumped back in shock and amazement. "What's the matter?"

"Rita. I'm sore in every inch of my being. There is no place you can hug me that I don't hurt!"

"You look horrible. Did they beat you? Tie you up? El, what happened to you?"

"Thanks for the positive reinforcement. Help me out of this vehicle. Let's go up to my apartment, and I'll tell you all about it." I put my arm around her shoulder, feeling every cramping muscle scream. In the last month I had put my body through every known bit of torture. I was thoroughly drained and sick of all this mystery solving.

"I thought you were dead! I didn't know what to do." Rita started to sob in relief.

"Well, I'm alive. At least for the moment." I limped through the garage, both of us sniveling and blubbering. "Did you go to the police? Call Inspector Poe?" I managed to get out.

"Who? No. I didn't call anyone. I thought about calling Reb, but I was terrified we would land in jail." She got a good look at me, her eyes widening in alarm. "Oh, Lord, you're even worse in the light."

"Please, Rita, no more compliments. I just want to get out of these clothes and see what my wounds look like."

"Was it Joseph Hill? Did he do this to you?"

"No. It was a fencerow of evil thorns."

"Huh?"

"The gates were locked, and I had to crawl."

Rita screamed and grabbed my arm, propelling me forward. "Run!"

I stumbled, almost falling as she tried to jerk me into a faster pace. "What are you doing?" I managed to shout at her.

"It's Hill." She yanked her head to point behind us.

I caught a glimpse of a man running in our direction. A flash of silver in his hand got my attention. "He's got a gun!" I yelled.

"He must have been waiting for us. I've been in the garage most of the night, but I didn't see him come in."

"Did he follow you?"

"No, but he knows where we live." She struggled for breath, her small body almost carrying me along.

I saw the entrance to the street ahead just as another shadowy figure moved into sight, blocking out the light. "There's someone!"

"Let's see if he'll help! Yell!"

We both hollered, waving our arms, and shouting in his direction. "Help! Help us!"

I saw the man's face as we got closer. "It's Jack! Jack! Help!"

Jack Beane stepped into the light and motioned us forward. Gratefully, we hurried over to him. I could have kissed him. My rescuer once again! What a beautiful sight!

"What's the matter? Are you both okay?" He gathered us in his strong arms.

"Someone's after us! A man with a gun!" We pointed behind us. Joseph Hill slowed to a walk.

"Get us out of here! Please!" Rita cried, tugging at his arm.

"I'll be glad to do just that," Jack replied, turning toward our pursuer. We huddled against him, feeling safe in his certainty.

It lasted all of one second.

"Well, Joe, you've made a right mess of this, haven't you?" He tightened his arms around our shoulders in a sort of locking grip.

Joseph Hill approached. "How was I to know these birds would fly?" Up close, his face had a pinched look, a cruel mouth.

"Bring the car around and let's get them out of here." Jack's voice had taken on a low, threatening quality.

"Jack, what's going on?" I shook my head, my brain numb, trying to make sense of what was occurring. Too little sleep and too much fear combined to create chaos in my thought process. We had stepped into an alternate reality!

"That, Miss Turner, is what you are going to tell us." He clamped onto my arm and gestured for Joseph to seize Rita.

She broke and ran, but Joseph was ready, hitting her on the head with his gun. She went down like a burst piñata. He picked her up and roughly slung her over his shoulder.

"Do you have to make everything as difficult as possible, Little Brother?" Jack snarled.

"Brother?" I felt like I had been dropped into a dense corn maze with no way out. "This guy is your brother? Your brother?" I kept repeating the words in confusion.

"Unfortunately, yes. My no-good, kicked-out-of-the-house, always-in-trouble brother."

"But I thought you were nice," I stuttered. "I mean, you saved me and everything."

"Just a doorway in, that's all. I thought I could get the information out of you simple and easy, but you never called me. I even offered lunch, but nothing. How was I to know you were a real life, stick-in-the-mud, boring researcher?" His face twisted into an ugly scowl. I couldn't imagine how I had found him handsome. "Now get moving." He shoved me toward the car.

"Where are you taking us?"

"Somewhere we won't be interrupted," Jack replied.

"Oh, I think Miss Turner has already been there," Little Brother said as we stopped in front of his vehicle, a dark blue car I had seen before.

Déjà vu danced before me like an ugly circus clown.

****

Rita came to on the road back. "Waz with my head? It hurts."

"One of these dismal excuses for a man knocked you out."

"For a researcher, she's got a right smart mouth," Joseph said over his shoulder. He slumped into the front passenger seat.

"She's smart all right." Jack sneered.

"I can hear you," I said. "So is Jack your real name?"

"Yeah. But it's not Beane." He looked at me in the rearview mirror. "And, Miss Researcher, it's not Hill."

"I told the police about you," I tried, hoping to scare them a bit or at least get them thinking.

"So? They don't know much about me. I've never been to this backwater berg before. And besides, there's tons of Hills running around the world."

"What do you want with us? We don't know anything."

"You two bloody birds have stirred up trouble for us! We can't have you two digging into our business. We wanted to lay low, but you had to go put the spotlight on us with those articles. Bring the police right to our door. Now we're going to make some trouble for you." Joseph seemed obliged to get in his two cents while doubling down on his brother's anger.

"Joe, if you hadn't been out getting sloshed, these two would never have gotten in the house."

"I can't stay in that bloody old mansion all the time. A bloke can go bonkers." He slumped even further down into his seat. It was clear who was boss in this relationship.

"Bonkers like killing a homeless man or two?" I taunted them. If they were going to harm us, I figured I'd go down swinging.

"Can't prove a thing!" Jack roared, clearly upset and swerving all over the road. "We will bury these two in the back woods. No one will ever discover them."

"We could just leave the bodies down in the low basement. No one would find them there for a hundred years," Joe suggested.

"She found her way there, and so did that snooping Timmy guy, so I guess it's not as foolproof as you think, Little Brother. How you have stayed off police radar this long is beyond me." Jack pointed threateningly at his brother.

"I move around a lot. They can't catch me. I'm really invisible." Joseph sat up straighter and puffed his chest. "I can take care of myself, Big Brother!" He seemed to be mocking Jack with the tone of his voice.

"You're a stupid, stupid man, and I'm sick of following you all over the world cleaning up your messes. That bank job was the last straw!" Jack yelled, waving his fist. The car sped up.

"It's plain neither of these men is the mastermind you thought was behind all the crimes, huh, Rita?" I hoped a little goading would get them to reveal their secrets.

"What makes you think we didn't plan this ourselves, Miss Smarty pants?" Joe shouted.

"All the things you did wrong, for starters." I laughed.

"Let me tell you something, Missy."

"All right, Joe. That's enough. She's just insulting you hoping you will spill your guts to them." Jack punched Joe in the shoulder. "Let her talk. It means nothing to us."

I hoped some friendly policeman was out with his radar and would stop us. My scrapes and scratches were beginning to stiffen anew. Dried blood rubbed raw against my clothes. I moved around to find a comfortable spot, massaging my sore areas when I felt the outline of the journal under my shirt. My clothes carried a few tons of dirt and grunge. I would have done anything to transport myself into a nice hot bath. I had a few layers on and so much had happened, I had forgotten about shoving the journal in my shirt. It was old and flimsy, but I hoped I wasn't bleeding all over the cloth I had wrapped around it. The writing was hard enough to read as it was.

Rita elbowed me in the ribs. The two men continued their argument in the front seat.

"Ouch! Watch it!" I cried.

"Let's make a run for it," she whispered out of the side of her mouth, looking furtively out the window.

"How can we run when we're in a car?"

"The next time they stop, let's open the doors and run."

"Rita, I couldn't run if this car was on fire. I've been up all night, I'm sore in every bone of my body, and all I want to do is lay down. Besides, you have a lump on your head the size of Texas."

Rita put her hand to her head. "Mother in heaven, what did those goons do to my head? This really hurts."

Joe turned around. "Hey, you birds, what are you cooking up back there?"

"Nothing," I said. "I'm bleeding."

"And my head hurts from where you hit me. Wait until the police get you!" Rita seemed to think we were getting out of this mess. I wasn't so sure.

"Won't matter much in a little while." Jack began snapping his fingers, laughing, his anger suddenly forgotten.

"Why did you keep calling me? I thought you were nice." I tried again to get information, some understanding.

"Thoughts don't exactly add up to much now, do they?" Jack threw off.

"So we wrote some hogwash about the Hill family. So what? Why should that bother you?" Rita seemed to have gained some bravado.

"You don't get it. Little Brother here got into some trouble, and now that you two busybodies are bringing up old wounds, the police are looking our way."

"Why not just leave town? Slip away in the night?" I asked.

"Because the second time the police came out here about your red-haired friend being missing, they told him not to leave. That they may have more questions. It would look mighty suspicious if we left now." He turned to his brother. "And we need to get rid of all the evidence they could find if they came with a search warrant." He slammed his hand against the steering wheel. "I still don't understand why you had to kill that man. You just can't help but call trouble down, can you?"

"Timmy!" Rita shrieked from the back. "You killed my friend Timmy!"

Joe turned around in his seat. "If you want another

jolt to the head, Missy, just keep yelling. Can't stop snooping, just like that old man." He grinned wickedly.

"He found the money," I said, hoping to get them to talk more.

"That sneak poked in places he shouldn't have been. I found him in the basement. He must have known another way in 'cause he sure didn't walk through the front door. I fired him on the spot, but he must have seen the money before I got there. I followed him and overheard him arrange a meeting with that busybody reporter."

"Hey!" Rita shouted. "I am not a busybody!"

"Pipe down or I'll give you another lump on the head."

"Brother, I think you talk too much. Don't admit to anything." Jack admonished Joe.

"Awww. Where these ladies are going, they won't have no one to tell." Joe made a slashing motion across his throat. "Yah. I killed your little snoopy buddy. It was so easy, especially after you picked up the knife and put your fingerprints all over it. A perfect patsy. Now shut up."

"I bet you killed Danny Boy Cooper too, didn't you? Did he try to sneak away with some of that stolen money?"

"Danny Boy Cooper? What are you talking about?" Rita looked at me as if I were trying to conjure unicorns.

"Is that what that other little sneak's name was?" Joe laughed. "I told him I would pay him to tell me where he had gotten that money. It was too easy. Greed will get you in trouble every time."

Jack sounded weary at this point. "Joe, will you

please shut it? These women don't need to hear all our secrets."

"Oh, another rap on the bean, and the rest will be history." Joe gave us a menacing look and shook his gun in the air.

Rita slunk down in her seat, rubbing the side of her head. When this was over, if we were still alive, we could compare head bumps. She squeezed my hand.

"El?" she murmured, tears running down her face. "Are they really, really going to kill us?"

"What I really, really wish was that you had called the police. At least then someone would know where we were."

"Next time I will! Promise!" She huddled against me, rubbing all my painful aches the wrong way. I tried to push her gently away, but she clung even harder.

The car pulled into the long driveway. The gates were wide. When the car door opened, I was surprised to see it was fully light outside. The tinted windows obscured the time of day. I was exhausted. It was all I could do to pull myself out of the vehicle. Adrenaline was my friend. I was battered and bruised, and my stomach rumbled either out of fear or hunger. Jack seized my arm. I saw Joe haul Rita through the front door.

"Please, please, let Beatrix McGregor be staring out her window," I murmured under my breath.

"No time for prayers now." Jack pushed me ahead of him so hard, I almost fell.

Seeing the house in daylight hours made it appear less spooky inside. Still, motes of dust floated through the air as we passed, but the well-polished furniture suggested a regal appearance, and the draperies hung dark and velvety. Obviously, the cleaning women excelled at their job.

The library, when we entered, jogged my mind. Even though I knew where the secret door panel was, I would have had a hard time finding the opening. Joe put his hand under one of the shelves, and the door slid open. The all-too-familiar scene hit me hard. I had struggled so badly to get out of that place; now I was back. Joe dragged Rita roughly along the passageway until we came to the desk area. He threw Rita to the ground.

"Leave her alone," I managed to get out. Jack still had a death grip on my arm. At least it felt numb at this point.

Joe took out his gun and aimed it at Rita. Hand to mouth, she screamed.

Then the world exploded.

Chapter 26

We heard the door panel crack and splinter. The air filled with shouts and the thud of running footsteps. Both Joe and Jack spun in alarm toward the noise. In turning, Jack let go of my arm. Not sure of what was happening, I kicked out at the back of his knee, sending him sprawling on top of Rita. Men in blue uniforms with guns drawn invaded the room, spreading out to encircle us.

"Hold your fire!" Inspector Poe shouted.

I had never been so glad to see someone in my life. "Poe! Poe! Poe!" I couldn't stop repeating his name.

One of the officers pulled Jack off Rita and backed him against the wall with Joe. "I think you have a fan there, Eddie."

"What's happened to Rita?" I cried, struggling to reach her.

Officer Reb Wilson got to her first, kneeling and checking for a pulse. "I think she just fainted." He gently shook her. "Rita? Rita, can you hear me?"

"Well, Gentlemen, would you care to explain what you're doing with these two women?" Poe stepped in front of the brothers.

"We ain't saying nothing." Joe stuck his chin out belligerently, gun no longer in sight.

Jack, quicker on the uptake, shook his head. "Officer, we found these two women snooping around our house. They broke in and were trying to steal items from the house. As you know, this house holds many antiques and irreplaceable items. We have no idea who they are or how they got in. I'm glad you're here so you can arrest them for trespassing." He tried to step away from the wall, but several policemen trained their weapons on him.

"Are you okay, El?" Poe asked, coming over to stand next to me.

"I'm all bruised up again, but I'm more worried about Rita."

A low moan worked its way into the scene, and Rita's arm went to her head.

"Rita!" I ran over and knelt down. Reb helped her to sit up.

"Am I dreaming or is the room full of wonderful, beautiful policemen?"

"You're not dreaming!" I smiled and watched Reb help Rita to her feet.

"I could kiss you all!" she cried, patting her hair and pulling at her clothes. "I'm sure I must look a sight." I was hoping she wouldn't giggle.

"Just glad you're all right, ma'am," a nearby officer said.

Reb Wilson wore a dopey grin on his face.

Poe stepped toward Rita. "Can one of you ladies tell me what happened?"

"They kidnapped us!" Rita and I shouted together.

"They're liars! They broke into our house! I insist you arrest them!" Jack demanded. He bristled and huffed and seemed so sure of himself, I almost believed him.

"And who would you be, sir?" Poe asked.

"That's Jack Beane, the man I was telling you about," I spoke to Poe.

"Is that Beane with an 'e'?" Poe questioned. I could almost see him smile.

"My name isn't Beane, no matter how it's spelled," Jack said firmly. "I have no idea what this woman is talking about. I live here with my brother. We are part of the Hill family who practically built this town. Our taxes go toward your salary, so, again, I must insist you arrest these women for trespassing."

I marveled at his defiance in the face of conflicting evidence. "If we broke in, how come Rita has a knot on her head where you hit her with your gun?"

"Gun?" The police weapons became serious as several officers came forward and frisked the two men. The gun was in Joe's pocket.

"My brother got his gun when we heard these two scrabbling about in the house." Jack kept up the façade of virtuous homeowner. "We heard glass breaking, so I think they must have come through a window. If we can just go upstairs and check, I'm sure you will see the evidence."

"Yes, that's why I went to get my gun. Never know who's after what." Joe tried to summon some of Jack's bluster but succeeded only in getting a dirty look from his brother.

"What exactly do you think these two women were looking to steal down here in this damp basement?" Poe asked, looking around him.

Jack wouldn't be dissuaded. "We have valuable antiques, priceless art, everywhere in this house. I have no idea what they were after. As I said, we came in and found them rifling through our things."

"Men, let's take everyone down to the station and sort this out. Sir, we'll hold your gun for you until we determine what occurred. Take the two men in separate squad cars. Call for an ambulance for the ladies."

"Nice way to treat intruders!" Jack valiantly continued his righteous indignation. "And I hope the Police Department will be paying for all the damage you have done in this house!"

"They'll be under our supervision the whole time, sir. If they are as guilty as you say, we will make sure they are properly dealt with." Poe shepherded the group down the tunnel toward the library, ignoring Jack's request for damages.

While attention focused elsewhere, I slipped the journal from my shirt, unwrapped it, and slid it on top of the papers on the desk. I picked it up like I had just discovered it, "And this might be of interest as well." I held it out to Poe.

"Put that down," he ordered. "Now it's got your fingerprints all over it."

"Oh, I'm sorry." I rubbed it against my clothes like I was innocently trying to get rid of fingerprints. "I guess I'm so shook up, I forgot I shouldn't touch anything."

Poe looked me up and down. "Yes, I'm sure you forgot. Now your fingerprints and your blood are on it." He started to say something else, but changed his mind and shook his head. "I can see, once again, you are in need of medical treatment. Both of you need to go to the hospital to be checked out. Then you can come to the station to give your statements."

"Inspector, I also noticed those suitcases in that tunnel. Why would someone hide suitcases down here?

Maybe they should be checked out."

"Hmm. Another intuition of yours?"

Poe gestured to one of the policemen to bring a suitcase forward.

"Hey," Jack yelled when he looked back. "You can't touch those. That is private property."

"I just want to check them out," Poe said. "Make sure that these women didn't take anything valuable from inside. It's for your own good, sir."

Jack could do little but nod his head.

The policeman lifted up one suitcase. "It's really heavy, Inspector. Should I open it?"

"Yes. Let's make sure the property of these two gentlemen is still intact."

The policeman snapped the latches and opened the case. His mouth dropped. "It's full of money!"

"Well, I see someone doesn't like banks," Poe exclaimed. "Check the other cases."

"I've never seen those cases before," Jack shouted. "I have no idea where that money came from."

"I thought you said it was your private property?" Poe asked.

"I just meant it belonged to the owner of the house, not that it was mine." Jack said, not quite as adamant as he had been before.

"Well, we better take them down to the station while we sort out this mess. We don't want anyone to steal these cases that belong to the owner of the house now, do we?"

Jack turned away, suddenly at a loss for words.

"I'd really love to go home first and clean up," I said to Poe. "I'm exhausted."

"Hospital. Station. Then we will see you home."

I started to ask him how he had found us, but the ambulance arrived, and someone escorted me gently inside.

****

The nurses remembered me; I was getting to be a regular. Once more, they dealt swiftly with my injuries. This time, they were mainly related to scratches from the thorns. My arms, legs, and face got a thorough cleaning and bandaging. Poe had directed an officer to take photos of the bruises on our arms, clearly finger and hand prints. One of the nurses, full of pity for my sorry state, retrieved a shirt and pair of pants from her locker and gave them to me. The clothes were several sizes too big, but my cuts and scrapes would welcome the room.

"Changing into something different will have you feeling a bit better. Those clothes are ready for the trash barrel," the nurse said.

"Please put them in a bag as evidence." I heard Poe instruct the nurse who took them out of the room.

"Thank you," was all I was able to get out when she came back in. I asked her to help me change. My arms and legs felt like dead logs.

"Keep the cuts clean," was the parting advice.

"Will do. Can I put aloe on them?"

"Absolutely."

Rita was not as lucky. The doctor recommended she stay a few nights in the hospital. An armed guard stood outside the room. Poe let me speak to Rita before he took me to the station. The guard stepped into the room with us.

"Don't worry," she said. "I feel safe here. Finally. I think I'll just sleep and sleep some more." She gestured toward the guard. "Lieutenant, I wonder if you would mind getting a nurse for me."

The young man blushed. "It's just officer, ma'am, not lieutenant."

"My mistake," Rita simpered. "You look so experienced and so much in charge."

The officer nodded and moved away into the hall.

"What did you tell Poe about us?" I whispered. "Hurry, we don't have much time."

"I didn't say we had been in the house. All I said was the two men grabbed us in the parking garage this morning. I said I knew one was Joseph Hill because I had tried to interview him for an article. I had never seen the other one. I told him I couldn't imagine why they had taken us."

"How am I going to explain all these cuts and scratches?" I moaned.

"You can tell them you were worried about me, so last night you decided to go to the Hill house and look around. Say you tried to get in but the gates were locked, so you wiggled under the thorns only to find the rest of the house was locked as well, so you wiggled back and then went home. You saw me in the parking garage just as the two men grabbed us." She kept her voice low and conspiratorial.

"What about the cleaning women? What if they say they saw us come in with that painting?"

"Well, if anyone gets around to asking them, then we will deal with it. At this point we evade any mention of going into the house." Rita moved around in the bed trying to find a comfortable spot. "I made sure I didn't leave any fingerprints."

"My painting! It's still in the house."

"We put it into a room that looked like Columbus was the last person to visit. There's so much stuff in that house, I doubt they will dwell on that painting. Just say as little as possible."

"Oh, Rita! I don't think I can lie to Poe."

"Remember, say as little as possible. Stick to the story that they kidnapped us. Which they did. That they took us into the basement. Which they did. Maybe they won't ask the hard questions."

"What are you going to say about where you were this whole time?"

"I'll tell the truth, the places I stayed, all because of the threats, which were very real." Rita placed her head back on the pillow just as a policeman came into the room with a nurse.

"Thank you, Officer." She gave him a mega-watt smile. "Nurse, my head hurts so much. Can you give me something for it?"

"After we finish our tests, I can give you a pain reliever."

"Is she getting x-rays for the goose egg on her head?" I asked.

"Next up," the nurse said and left us alone with the officer.

"Is it that bad? How horrible do I look? Is there a mirror around?" She painted on the pouty face I knew so well. "I hate that the lovely policeman here has to look at ugly old me for hours on end! Officer, you should ask for hazardous duty pay."

We heard the gulp echo around the room. "Nothing ugly about you, ma'am," he stammered and turned to look out the window.

"Well, you can't do anything about it now. I

certainly have no makeup on me. Or a brush for that matter." At this point I could have cared less what we looked like. We were safe and away from the Hill brothers.

"What if Reb wants to see me? I look just too awful." Rita couldn't let it go.

"I think Reb's already seen you. Remember he was in the basement trying to revive you from your faint and fall." I smiled at her. "He didn't run away in horror at the sight of you."

"Oh, that brave boy!" She stared dreamily off into space. "All those officers in blue were wonderful! They're all heroes!" The officer in the room scuffled his foot along the floor in an aw-shucks manner.

"I'll let you get some rest, Rita. Take care."

"You too! Good luck, El!"

I gave her a gingerly hug and walked into the hall, not quite ready to meet Poe and whatever fate he held.

Chapter 27

"So how did you know where to find us?" I asked Poe a bit later. I was sprawled on a chair inside his office. Exhaustion swept over me like a tsunami.

"This is going to sound really strange."

"Okay. Nothing at this point will seem anywhere near fantastic." I took a drink of coffee someone had placed in front of me. The Greek gods couldn't have provided anything sweeter.

"Polly told us."

"Polly?" I thought I had misunderstood. I was totally loopy at that point.

"Well, not us exactly, but Jenny Lane."

"Now it's my turn to say start at the beginning."

"It seems like your bird started talking sometime during the night. The only problem was that Jenny had some ocean sounds playing in her headphones, so she didn't hear it. Rita wasn't around, and another lady on your floor was on vacation. When Jenny got up in the morning, Polly really turned up the volume by screeching and interrupted her morning meditation."

"How did Polly screaming help you find us?"

"She was screaming 'Murder' over and over. Jenny called the station. The switchboard relayed the message to me, and I came to her apartment. We listened to the bird and figured out you must have seen Rita. A reporter and a researcher. Where else would you go but to the Hill house? I gathered the troops. We had some unmarked cars already in the area when you drove in. It was lucky timing seeing as how Joe Hill had a gun pointed at Rita."

"Polly!" I exclaimed again. "I am going to get that bird the biggest treat I can find!"

"Oh, and I owe you a new lock and door. We had to break in to quiet the bird and to see if you left any note behind. I do believe Polly would have awakened people two counties over. That is quite some bird. Jenny took the bird and cage home with her until we could find out where you were." He smiled. "I guess it was our day for breaking down doors."

"Have those two guys started talking yet?"

"Jack and Joe lawyered up immediately. And you aren't going to like this."

"What?" I wasn't sure how much more I could stand. I already felt like I had used up a lifetime of adventures.

"Mason Street is their lawyer."

"No! Not Mason." Another shock.

"We traced the serial numbers on the money, and it's stolen all right."

"Joseph admitted firing Timmy for snooping around. Then he killed him. He told us that after he kidnapped us," I said. My head and whole body were so tired I felt like lying down on the floor in Poe's office and sleeping for a century or two. "Do you think Timmy discovered the money and that they weren't really any relation to the original Hills?"

"And just how did you know Timmy found some of that money? Who told you?"

Drat my big mouth! "I was worried about Rita and

just happened to be passing by this shelter place where Timmy had stayed."

"There seem to have been quite a few places you just happened to be passing by. I guess the money part was some information that didn't make it into Officer Wilson's report."

"I would suggest speaking with Will Pepper at the shelter. He not only saw the money but knows who stole it from Timmy. You might be able to find that man and see if he still has any left. OH!" I put my hand to the side of my head.

"What?"

"I forgot that he is dead."

"Who?" Now Poe seemed confused.

"Danny Boy Cooper! The man who stole the money from Timmy. Joe also admitted he killed him as well." I took a big gulp of my coffee. "I'm getting muddleheaded."

"And you know his name how? Did you just happen to be passing by his house?"

"No. He lived at the shelter where Timmy was staying. Will Pepper told me about it."

"It looks like Will Pepper knows quite a bit about what is going on." Poe got up from his desk and stared out the window. "It seems you love to do our jobs for us. Are you sure you don't need an application for the police academy?"

"What about the diary?" I tried to switch it up, but Poe wasn't misled.

"Ah, yes, the diary. Nice misdirection. There is some dynamite reading there. The lab thinks it might have been Clark's. They will analyze the handwriting. His signature might be on a document at the historical society to use as comparison."

"Wow! You're going to ask Cassie for that information?"

"Not me, but I'll send one of the officers." Questions clouded his eyes, but he didn't ask how I knew about Cassie.

I bit my tongue. "Will we ever know what was inside? Is enough legible?"

"Let's see what the lab comes up with."

"Can I go now? I am sick of these odd clothes, and I feel like my hair is a mat of mud. I think I might need to soak for a week to get all this slop off me."

"I'll have someone drive you home. I see you gave your statement to the officer. It seems to match Rita's account pretty closely." He looked directly at me. "The officer in charge should not have left you two women alone. He's learned an important lesson."

"Don't be too hard on him. Rita said she needed a nurse, so he went to find one. You know how she can smile and flirt. "

"And gave you both enough time to get your stories straight?"

I remained silent.

He moved over to help me out of my chair. "I'll let you know how things work out. Jenny and Albert promised they would get someone on your door and lock, so hopefully it might be done by now. If not, Jenny offered her place until it's fixed."

"I might just sleep for a week, but you can leave a message." I gave a half wave and started down the hall.

There was Goth Guy! Sitting in one of the offices. They had caught him! I felt lightheaded and happy. Safe for the first time in ages. He looked up and saw me then rose and came out into the hallway. I turned and ran back to Poe's office, slamming the door behind me.

"What's the matter? You look like you've seen a ghost."

"It's Goth Guy! He's here! He started to follow me down the hall. You have to arrest him." I leaned against the door.

Poe came around his desk and pealed me gently away. I heard the door open behind me and turned around. Goth Guy was standing behind me. I screamed and jumped toward Poe, ready to run.

"Whoa there!" Poe stood and held up his hand to steady me.

"It's him!" Adrenaline again had me going over the edge.

"El, meet Sergeant Little, undercover Goth Guy."

"What? What? He works here?" I stuttered. "What?" Nothing made sense. This clearly was beyond imagination!

"I put Stew in your building temporarily to watch Rita's apartment and to keep tabs on you."

"But he pushed me down the stairs. I saw him. If he didn't push me, who did?"

"*He* is right here and can answer for himself." Sergeant Little grinned. "I'm sorry I didn't stop to help you, but I thought catching this guy was more important. He disappeared in the alley before I got outside."

"So you have no idea who it was? And he could still be out there?"

"It was Joe Hill, or whoever he turns out to be. I got a good look at him. It's one more charge we can add to his list. Great work, by the way, El. We might have to make you an honorary sheriff or something."

"Don't give her ideas. Thank you, Sergeant." Poe nodded for the officer to leave.

I plopped down in one of the armchairs. "This is all been too much for me!" I put my head in my hands and started to cry. Uncontrollably. I didn't think I had tears left.

I faintly listened to the door close behind me, and then Poe came around his desk and handed me a box of tissues. He sat down next to me and took my hand in his. The warmth of him radiated through my fingers, up my arm, and straight to my heart.

I had never been so happy and so drained all at the same time.

****

Letter to El Turner

Dear El,

I don't know if you remember me or not, but several years ago you did a search of my father's family after he and my mother met their end in a plane crash. He had run away from home at a young age (remember the car episode?) becoming estranged and burned all pictures, letters, and documents relating to his family.

You tracked down the family, and I am glad to say we just had a big family reunion! Well, my father was an unusual man, and his brothers and sisters fit with that theme!

Uncle Autry spent most of his adult life as a bronco bull rider. (He amused us for hours with his stories!) Since his fall and broken leg, he has taken up poetry, specifically cowboy poetry (Yes, there really is such a thing!). We were treated to some of his poems later in the evening around the campfire. Once a year he goes

237

to a poetry roundup where people from all walks of life read their cowboy poems.

Aunt Onnie writes greeting cards for a living. She peppers her speech with things like "Even though we live miles apart, you will always be in my joyous heart" and "May your days be sparkly and sprinkled with cupcake cheer." You can't help but smile at her positive outlook. She promised to send us all one-of-a-kind-Onnie-original Christmas cards this year.

But Uncle Zarsha (everyone calls him Dagger) holds the record for being the most unique. He makes fancy knives and has mastered throwing them. He put on quite a show for us throwing knives at trees. He even got Onnie to stand next to a tree with a top hat on as he hurled the sharp blades at the hat. She confided later that he had been doing that sort of thing to her since they were little, and she had five scalp scars to show for it!

Sorry for the long newsy letter, but I am so happy you found this part of my family for me. I can't thank you enough. I talked it over with everyone, and we want to invite you to our next gathering. (Bring your own top hat! Only kidding!)

Thankfully yours,
Annie Oliver

****

Letter to Annie Oliver
Dear Annie:

Of course I remember you! Thank you for sharing your good news with me! I'm so happy you were able to connect with family, and it turned into a positive experience. They sound like a fun-loving bunch of folks. I'm sure their stories and adventures will make for many interesting gatherings in your future.

Thanks again for the newsy letter. Those kinds of responses make my day joyous and sparkly (as Aunt Onnie might say). I will check my mail for that invitation!

Best,

El

Chapter 28

They kept Rita in the hospital for two days, during which time I took long baths, ate chicken soup that Jenny insisted on feeding me, fussed over Polly, answered my emails, and slept. Poe took a morning off and drove me to pick up Rita and take her back to her apartment. I was dying to know what had transpired with Jack and Joe Hill and if Poe had read the journal, but he refused to say anything until we pulled up in the hospital parking lot.

"I'm trusting you to keep this to yourself."

I nodded.

"I think I might need a Girl Scout pledge or something." Poe was clearly enjoying himself.

I held up two fingers. "I promise to serve my country, help people, and keep my mouth shut."

"I guess that will have to do." Poe looked over the dashboard and out the front window.

"Ahem! The journal?" I turned all the way around in my seat to look at him.

"Ah, yes. The one you just happened to find on the table in the basement and managed to get your fingerprints on and then smear blood from all over your clothes? You mean that journal?" he teased.

"So?"

"We believe the book was Clark's originally. We have his signature on one letter Cassie had, and it matches the writing in the diary, at least a handwriting expert seems to think so."

"Clark Hill? Really? What a find for this town!" I looked over at Poe. "At least I hope it was a good find for this town."

"Miss Turner, it might just change minds about the man."

"Why? What was in it?"

"It seems Clark Hill has been viewed in a poor light. Unless he was hiding some evil genius, he seems to have been someone who cared about his family and the workers who came to help him build the town. He worried about his sisters, and he paid the labors a decent wage. He often gave them credit at the trading post and made sure they were fed and sheltered. Those with families of their own were given rooms in one of the boarding houses." He smiled. "Some of that has also come from Cassie who happened to have some ledgers from her grandfather. He kept meticulous track. I'm astounded that these documents survived over all the years."

"That's amazing! So what else are you holding back?"

"Clark was clearly upset when his wife and sisters died. He just wrote they caught the illness. It might have been influenza or pneumonia. Who knows? It certainly wasn't murder."

"I'd say that's earth shattering." I realized I was tense, almost ready to spring. "So Cassie Troy was right all along!" I stared wide-eyed at Poe.

"It's all fairly bland. No murder or bad blood I could find. About half of it is unreadable, at least for us mortals. Clark paid a fair wage to the men; he seems to have been a penny pincher on everything else. We found a few detailed accounts of expenditures from Cassie's ledger. Just a man with a dream of starting a town. The journal ends with the fire, but Clark seems to have been losing hope after his sisters died."

"Señor Marquez said his grandfather was part of the labor crew that had worked to help build the town. I wonder why Señor Marquez hates the Hills. Does the diary make any mention of his grandfather?"

"Not that I could find. I don't think Boris was the man his brother or uncle was. It's still up in the air which he was. He might have taken over for Clark before he died. Seems Clark had to discipline him a time or two. Maybe Boris caused some hurt feelings? Was rough with the workers? We probably will never know."

"Cassie said he was a brother, so maybe she has inside information."

"She has seemed to be open to providing what knowledge she has in that house."

"When are you letting this information out for the public?" I couldn't wait to read it. "People need to know about Clark!" I persisted. "At least his name can be cleared."

"We'll see."

"Any chance I could look through the journal?" I asked hopefully.

He shook his head. "Not much. We'll have it in evidence for quite a while. I don't know what will happen to it after the trials."

"But it's town history!" I declared. "It should be put where everyone in the town could read it."

"Well, it is pretty harmless and does show his

passion for getting the town built."

"You have to do something!"

"I'm sure something will eventually be worked out." He grinned. "Even to your satisfaction."

"Wait! Did I hear you say trials? You mean Joe and Jack?"

"You'll like this. With the hint of a deal, Joe spilled everything against his brother." Poe seemed pleased with himself.

"What? Why?"

"It seems Jack strongly insisted Joe stay inside until the story of Timothy's death died away. Jack had gotten Joe out of trouble before, but nothing he cared to expound upon."

"You mean Joe could have murdered other people?" I could see another story stirring around in Rita's head.

"I think Timmy's death may have been an accident, but he definitely killed Danny Boy Cooper."

"But he confessed to the murder of Timmy."

"I don't think it was premeditated. Joe tried to bribe Timmy into not going through with the story he was about to tell to Rita. Timmy refused. They fought, and the rest is history."

"Wow. What did Jack do? He really acted like the dominant one. I bet he went nuts. Why didn't their lawyer keep Joe from talking?" Tons more questions popped into my head.

"First of all, we kept the two brothers separated. We couldn't talk to either without their lawyer present. Mason Street sat on them for a morning, not letting them answer. Jack stayed with the story of your trespassing in their house. Joe didn't say much. When we began to suggest a deal, Joe started talking."

"But why did Mason let Joe babble on instead of stopping him?"

"Well, with Mason Street we come to the strange part," Poe continued.

"Now it's getting strange for you? I thought it was strange from the beginning!" The whole adventure seemed like a fantastic story Rita might have envisioned.

"Do you want to hear about him or not?"

I nodded.

"After we supplied evidence the money was stolen in a bank robbery and their descriptions were in law enforcement hands, Mason asked to speak to Joe alone. He came out of the interrogation room and said he had to get a document from his office and would return shortly. We took a break, but time went on and he never returned."

"He never returned?" I felt like Polly, echoing the last words said.

"No, El, he never returned."

"Did you look for him? Send for the police?" I got excited again.

"I am the police, and he was in a police station."

I stared at the floor, chastised for the moment.

"We sent a car out to his office and one to his apartment. By the time we got the supers to let us in each place, he was gone."

"Gone? Where would he go? And why?"

"We should have seen it coming, although we've never had a lawyer skip out on us. If he is attached to them in any way, I can see him not wanting to get involved. He must have been spooked by what Joe admitted to him and didn't want any part of it. Clothes, papers, you name it, were scattered about his apartment. Looks like he left with what he could carry."

"But you can set up road blocks, put out an APB, check the airports."

"Yes, El, I do know my job."

"What would you charge him with? He didn't kill anyone or steal the money?"

"He does manage the Hill accounts, so he knew when the house was going to be empty and offered it to Jack when Joe got into trouble. Since he knew about the robbery, he could be charged with being an accomplice. I think if we do more digging, we might find he used the Hill place as a safe house for many criminals. A place to lay low. I think he also arranged false documents for people. All for a price, I'm sure."

"I did find records that a company called Old World, Inc. paid the bills and taxes on that place. I tried to trace ownership, but it evolved into a sequence of shell companies. What do you want to bet he's behind it?"

"I'd say the man was smart enough to get away with a lot over the years. He certainly had an exit strategy!"

"What a shame! He was so nice to me. It's hard to believe he had anything to do with hurting me or Rita."

"I don't think he did. I think that was the two brothers on their own," Poe said.

"So are Jack and Joe named Hill?"

"I think we'll find a string of names. Mason had a good thing going and tried to live a straight life, but he did like the extra money. Now, any other suggestions on how I should do my job?"

"Sorry, it won't happen again."

"Yes, it will, but I'll try to be ready in the future." He reached out and patted my knee.

When I looked up in surprise, he cleared his throat and put his hand on the door handle. "I guess we better get Rita home. I'm sure she's more than ready to leave the hospital."

I got out on my side of the car, but he wasn't through yet.

"Remember your promise, El! I would hate to throw you in jail!"

"It's not the first time I've had to keep a secret," I countered. "I'm pretty good at it."

"Well, just don't tell any of it to Polly. We found out what a blabbermouth she can be!"

Chapter 29

We gathered in Rita's room. She smiled and simpered like her old self. The space was bursting with flowers. Roses and carnations of all colors dominated the scene.

"Reb," Rita replied when I raised my eyebrows. "Seems he missed me." She let out a shy giggle. "We had a bit of a tiff the last time we saw each other. Then I disappeared. He thought it might have been his fault."

"He came by my apartment looking for you. He was really worried."

"Oh, what a sweetie he is!" She cooed. "I still remember waking up in that awful dark basement at the hands of those two killers and seeing his angelic face, feeling his muscled arms around me."

I could see she was still the drama queen, but I let her have her moment of enjoyment.

"I'd say he's just a little bit enchanted," Poe agreed.

"So tell us," she cried eagerly, not wanting to wait another minute. "What's the word?"

"What word would that be?" Poe asked, looking around as if he didn't know where she was heading.

"Those horrible men who kidnapped us!"

His eyebrows took a serious downward turn when he looked at us, especially Rita.

"Don't take this lightly. This is totally off the

record. This is a town where word gets around quickly, and I'm sure Reb will let you in on bits and pieces, but you keep it out of the paper, you hear? I don't care if you write about being kidnapped or what came after, but this next part is just between us."

"I get it." She stared at the floor, but we both could see her brain churning out headlines.

"If word gets out, you have my solemn oath that I will lock you up. Somehow I don't think you would like that."

"She wouldn't like that. I'll keep her quiet," I said. Too much had happened, and I'm sure it finally dawned on Rita the trouble we could be in if Poe chose to reveal what we had actually done.

"She won't say anything about the journal."

"What is this about a journal?" Rita asked. I had not had a chance to explain, and she had been carried out before I presented it to Poe.

"Amazingly, El discovered an old diary in the basement where you two ladies were taken. And since you hadn't been in that basement very long, it was equally amazing that she spotted it among all the stuff scattered on the desk."

"Well I thought it looked important." I tried to sound insulted. "After all, I am a researcher. I'm used to spotting old papers and such."

"Yes." He nodded his head. "Good answer."

"And was it old and important?" Rita asked.

"Very old and very important."

"Oooo. That certainly sounds noteworthy." Rita's nose actually started to twitch.

"For a one hundred-plus-year-old journal, it is very noteworthy. It seems Clark Hill jotted down how he started the town. His entries read like the work of a kind and impressive man." Poe looked at me, and I knew he wouldn't reveal any specifics.

"But what about all the rumors about killing people and being rotten to the workers?" Rita asked, sounding disappointed at this turn of events. I could see her journalistic career melting before her eyes.

"Probably just that, rumors."

"Hopefully they will prove Cassie Troy was right all along." I felt glad that Cassie would be vindicated.

"Who's Cassie Troy?" Rita interrupted. "I swear I wasn't gone that long. How come I'm so out of the loop?"

"All will be revealed," I assured her.

"Remember, this is all off the record, Rita," Poe said sternly. "I'll let you know when we do release some of the facts, but don't hold your breath."

"Once the information is made public, can I get first shot at the story?" she asked Poe.

"I'll keep you in mind, if, and that's a big IF, that becomes public."

"You can even get a quote from Cassie," I mused.

"If you let me know who she is, I'll interview her." Rita wrote her name down in a notebook by her bed.

"She would make a good interview even without the journal information," I told Rita. Poe shot me a sideways glance, but I ignored him.

"Maybe the town will even do something to honor him. Have a parade or some sort of celebration," Rita gleefully contributed.

"That's a possibility." Poe nodded thoughtfully. "And Clark might get a street or building named after him in the future."

"Can I write about my attack in the basement of horrors?" Rita's creative flair was in overdrive.

"Sit on it for a few days," Poe said. "We don't want to spill any beans and compromise our case. Right, Rita? You don't want those boys walking now, do you? They might end up walking in your direction."

"I will sit on that information like a chicken brooding over an egg." Rita flapped her arms like wings. "I certainly do not want to be the cause of those mean men getting out on some technicality." She looked straight at Poe. "You have my word."

"Girl Scout promise?" Poe laughed.

"I was never a Girl Scout," Rita said, "but what the hell!" She held up her hand.

Poe turned to both of us. "Seriously, I'm glad nothing happened to either of you. What you did was beyond stupid, and don't even think of doing anything like that again. Understand? The next time I will arrest you!"

"Yes, sir," we both chorused quietly. We were a step away from a meeting with the judge ourselves and we both knew it.

Suddenly Rita sat up. "Wait! You know they admitted killing my Timmy!" Rita exclaimed.

"Yes, we heard it from Joe's mouth. Several people came forward with Timmy's name after your article in the paper." Poe told her. "We have tried tracking down any family."

"You mean other townspeople? They came forward because of *my* article?" She was almost purring.

"I'm not sure of their status, but they did seem to want to do right by him."

"I'm glad my Timmy had people who cared." She leaned back on the bed again and crossed her arms in front of her like a hug.

"I guess that's the most we can hope for in this world," Poe said.

Rita was thoughtful for a few moments then spread her arms wide. "I still wish some of those old rumors had been true! What fantastic copy they would have made!" I could already see Rita's headlines about madness and murder. "I don't suppose Boris was crazy either, huh?" Rita said, ever eager for theatrics.

"Probably not," Poe answered. "El did point us toward some suitcases filled with stolen money though."

"Stolen money?" Rita came alive again. "Murder and money. I can see the headlines now."

"Seems Joe would spend a lot of his time down in the basement counting the money and dreaming of what he could buy with it."

"Yes. I remember now that when I was in the basement I heard something," I started to say, but Rita jumped in.

"You mean what a relief it was when we were in the basement with our kidnappers, and you heard the police break in to save us? Isn't that what you were going to say? I know it was the greatest feeling in the world for me. Wasn't it for you, El?" She made a *Watch what you say* face as she turned away from Poe.

'Yes! Absolutely the greatest feeling in the world!" I agreed, not sure I could look at Poe with a straight face. He would know I was lying. What I had been remembering was the sound of money being counted while I was plastered to the dank wall, afraid to make a move.

"It's so nice of you two to be in sync on everything," Poe murmured.

"Can we tell her anything about Mason Street?" I tried to change the subject.

"Mason Street? What does he have to do with this? Isn't he the lawyer who lives in our building, El? I tried to get him to work on my case, but he was too busy. Don't tell me he's mixed up in this. Nobody tells me anything!" She grumbled.

"Well, he turned out to be Jack's and Joe's lawyer," Poe said.

"What? How could he be mixed up in all this?"

""I don't know if we will ever find out," Poe said. "He disappeared."

"Wow. A person hides out for a few weeks and comes back to chaos."

"Rita. One day we will sit down with several bottles of wine, and I will tell you every gory detail."

"Yes, you girls can work some more on your story," Poe continued.

"What story?" Rita asked, a questioning pout to her lips.

"Okay. Play it your way. I know when I'm beat." Poe raised his hands.

"Okay, now what's going on? What's with you two? What aren't you telling me? How come I missed all the good stuff?" Rita's sigh of exasperation filled the room.

Poe immediately stood, turning his back on us. This time he changed the topic at hand. "You know, I don't think this is the first time Mr. Mason Street has been on the run. He seemed smart enough to have a plan for everything." He turned around, the formal police chief once again.

"I still can't believe it," I wailed. "He was such a nice guy. He helped me with my mother and the apartment, and we had coffee." My voice trailed off.

"Charm was a large part of his persona," Poe said.

"What is it with the men that come my way? They're slimy lawyers or kidnappers."

"Or kind police inspectors?" Rita batted her eyes at Poe.

I felt myself flush down to my toes.

"Anyway," Poe coughed and cleared his throat. "We offered the two brothers in custody another lawyer. Jack agreed, but Joe waved his rights. You could see how pleased he was to tell someone how he almost got away with robbery and murder. Jack was livid when he heard that Joe had confessed."

"Gross!" Rita exclaimed. "To think that grubby little man could have killed us." She shivered, but I saw her reaching for her pen and paper.

"That's enough for today. Let's get Rita home. I'm sure she can't wait to get back to her apartment. Remember, Rita, this was for your ears, not the world's. We will get the information out when we see fit."

"I swear by my designer bag! Which, by the way, cost me a fortune. El, you are my witness. On penalty of jail, I promise not to reveal everything we said today." She held up her hand and laughed. "I feel like someone in those spy movies. Will I self-destruct?"

"Well, I don't know what I would do with a big designer bag, so I'll hold you to your word," Poe said.

"Changing the subject, I do want to take some of these flowers home," Rita declared. "I'm sure my apartment is stuffy as a sick dog's nose. These beautiful roses will help make it seem more like home."

Just as we gathered up as much as we could carry, Reb Wilson sauntered through the door.

"Oh, hello, El. Inspector. I didn't expect anyone to be here. I just thought I would see if Rita needed a lift back to her place." He glanced over at Poe. "I'm on my lunch break, sir."

"Oh, Reb, you came to give me a ride. What a gallant thing to do!" Rita simpered.

An aw-shucks expression lit up his face, and then he reached for the flowers Rita had in her hand. "Leave these for the other patients," he said, a grin spreading from ear to ear. "We'll pick up some fresh ones on the way home." He held out his arm for her.

"You two don't mind, do you?" she asked Poe and me, but her eyes never left Reb's face.

"No at all," I answered. "We'll talk later."

They swept out the door, leaving Poe and I in a room full of flowers.

"Well, Miss Turner, it seems like you're stuck riding home with me. Do we need to stop and get you some fresh flowers as well?"

"Not flowers, but I do have one stop if you don't mind."

"I don't mind at all."

Chapter 30

He laughed when I told him where to stop.

"I need to stock up on bird food. Besides that, I think Polly deserves a bigger cage, toys, and a cartload of treats! I think I should get one of those rolling carts."

"Amen!" Poe agreed. "That bird is your lifesaver and deserves all the goodies you can carry!" We walked into the Ravin' Pet Store.

"Absolutely a lifesaver!"

I introduced Josh to Poe.

"Are you in the market for a bird as well? Maybe a puppy?" He gestured toward Poe.

"I work too many hours to keep a pet," Poe answered.

"We have fish. You can outfit a really beautiful fish tank. Very low maintenance. Or maybe a turtle?"

"The only fish I bring home are the ones I can eat." Poe laughed. "And the last time I checked, I was not a turtle person. Sorry."

"No problem. Just thought I would ask." He cheerfully bagged up all our goodies. "Did you ever get the bird to talk?" Josh asked. "I seem to remember some interesting tidbits."

"Oh, yes. Polly's a very smart bird. And you're right. She came out with some very surprising language."

"She?" Josh appeared baffled. "I thought I

remembered it was a he. Let me check our records a moment." He clicked a few buttons on his computer. "Yup. Albie. That's the name written down. Albie. His original owner, Mr. Taylor, was interested in poetry and named him Albatross." He looked at our startled faces. "I guess your mother never mentioned it to you, did she?"

A light bulb went off in my head. "Albie! Of course!" I recalled all the times my mother had shouted out in her waning time to "Take care of Albie" and "Watch over Albie." I had always assumed she meant the long-gone poet. Now one mystery was solved. "My mother spoke of someone named Albie, but I didn't connect it with the parrot."

Josh made a forgive-me face. "I was positive I mentioned that to you when I delivered the bird, but it must have slipped my mind. Anyway, she is a he." He finished wrapping all our goodies. "For future reference, males are usually bigger with a smaller neck and head than females. The tail feathers in males are all red; females have a bit of silver mixed in. And the underside feathers are a darker gray than the females. Check it out when you get home just to make sure Polly is really an Albie." He chuckled at his own joke.

"We will do that, Josh, and thank you for all your help!"

"Come on," Poe said picking up the bags. "Let's get all these treasures hauled home for you. I'm sure Rita isn't the only one anxious to be back in her apartment."

"It's true. These last few days have been blissful. Jenny packed me full of soup and tea, I slept, and only occasionally went near the computer; it was wonderful."

"Your new door and lock are in place."

"Excellent. I even think most of my wounds are healed. Jenny got me some more of her miraculous salve from her herbalist. I really have to visit that place one day."

"So it sounds like you'll be staying around for a while." Poe smiled.

"Guess I'll have to." I smiled too but remembered what else lay ahead. "We still have the trial to go through."

"You have a lot of people supporting you on this. It shouldn't be too bad."

"I just wish it was all over." I was so weary with the whole thing. It would be great to have a delete button like my computer.

"Even though we have the two brothers locked up, Mason Street is still out there." Poe turned serious. "It will pay to be cautious for a while." He opened the trunk of his car, and we filled that and the back seat with Albie treasures.

"I don't think Mason is the killer type. I think he ran to save his own skin."

"And maybe to save those expensive suits he wears. We found several pieces of luggage missing as well as clothes, items from his dresser, desk cleaned out, and laptop gone."

"That car of his will be hard to miss."

"It's still here." Poe pulled into the garage. "See, there it is. That was one of the first things we checked. I think he probably had another one stashed somewhere. Probably a plain old beater. He probably also had another set of ID's handy."

For the first time in what seemed like a decade, I wasn't afraid to get out of the car and walk to the apartment building. The sun radiated a shy warmth into the fall crisp air.

"Glad to see you smiling again," Albert shouted as we made our way to the elevator. With the new cage and all the bags of treasure, we almost didn't fit. "Do you need a hand?"

"I believe we can manage, but thanks, Albert." Poe nodded.

I used my new key on my new door and dragged our purchases inside.

"Who's a good boy, Albie?" I sang out. "Guess I'll have to get used to having a male in the house."

"Albie!" the bird cried.

We both laughed. "It seems like he knew his name all along," Poe said. "Did he ever mention those numbers again?"

"No. I still don't know what they were or what set him off."

"Someone must have taught them to him. If he spouts them again, be sure to write them down. They may be a clue to something. We should have asked Josh if Albie ever spoke while in the shop."

"I don't care what they were for. I'm done with clues and solving anything but a plain old family tree," I said. I looked over to the shut door where my mother's boxes waited. What was ahead for me there?

"What's the matter?" Poe saw my hesitation, but I just shook my head.

While we set up the new cage and filled it with the toys, I told him about the note my mother had written, about her papers and how they might change my future, about never really knowing my mother or father.

"The past is just that," Poe offered. "You are still El and always will be. Although your family tree might have some broken boughs or crooked limbs, you remain the woman I know who can survive anything. Look at what you just went through. You think a little joggle to the family tree will cause all the apples to fall off?" Poe attached the mirror, new water and food dishes, and placed paper on the bottom.

"I guess I'm afraid of what nuts might fall out?"

Poe looked at me, trying to decide if I was making a joke. "On the other side, there might be nothing there. From what you said, your mother didn't leave much information lying around." He rubbed my shoulder. "How are you going to proceed?"

"After all this is over and I can breathe, I'll be in the right frame of mind to tackle what she left behind. First, I'm going to see if my birth certificate is real. Then check if my mother's name is real. There are adoption agencies I can check, chat boards, registries, orphanage records, missing children sites. I'll do a DNA test and see if it matches anyone out there." I shrugged. "This is what I do for other people. I always put off doing it for myself. Maybe I had inklings something was off. If my mother wasn't my mother, who was she and why did she drag me around with her all those years? There are a million questions I'll have to consider, but not today." I looked at Albie. "Today it's Albie's day!"

"You know I'll always be around if you need help or want someone to make you an omelet when the work is too much." He picked up his hat and coat. "I'll come by one day and build a wooden ladder for Albie that connects the two cages. He can have himself quite the mansion."

"Please!" I stopped him there. "I think I've had enough of mansions for one lifetime!"

"Well, maybe we won't call it a mansion. How about a castle? Albie's castle."

"Now that sounds exactly right for a prince of a bird."

I saw my message machine was blinking and pressed the button.

"Hello, Miss Turner. I got your name from Ida Parks at the library. I think I'm a few clicks away from a certain celebrity. Can you help me prove it?"

"I'll have to talk to Ida about this."

"Sounds safe enough." Poe shrugged.

"I could do with safe! I love safe! No more danger for me."

"Danger!" Albie squawked then went back to his new toys.

"But maybe next year. Right now I think I need a little vacation. A lot of me time."

"How about Christmas in Hawaii?"

"Now that would be a vacation!" The room suddenly got quiet. Even Albie sat on the edge of his perch, seemingly waiting. I glanced over at Poe. "Are you offering?"

"I have some built-up vacation time. It can get mighty cold here in winter. Snow. Sleet. Slushy roads. Boots. Scarves."

"So knowing my track record with local men, you want me to fly halfway around the world with you?"

"You have to break that losing record sometime."

"But I don't know anything about you."

"Well, your bird likes me; I can't be all bad."

"I can never tell when you are joking."

"Can't hurt to think about it." His face was set to serious.

I thought about what had led me to Parkville, the roads that converged to bring me people I could call friends, the unknown bridge that awaited me with Poe. "Seems I have quite a bit to think about."

****

Letter to El Turner

Dear Ms. Turner,

Yes! You found it! I can't tell you how happy I am to have this information. All these years, people I mentioned it to thought I was crazy. My parents hid it from me my whole life, and even my children thought I was batty. I imagined that man dead or dying and it being all my fault. This has brought a peace to my soul. I have carried that weight with me for so long. Now that it is gone, I feel like I could dance all night and sing from the rooftops. If you ever get to my neck of the woods, please come and see me. I would like to give you a huge hug.

I am forever in your debt. Thank you! Thank you!

Your truly,

Essie

PS: Encl. a check for your wonderful services

****

Letter to Essie Williams

Dear Ms. Williams:

Thank you for your letter and check. I'm so happy this has resolved a lifelong problem! Once we had that last town and address, it was easy to find. Glad your daughter remembered you talking about it.

Allison Thorpe

It has been a pleasure working with you, and I wish you happy dancing and singing!
Best,
El

Chapter 31

"I want to buy Timmy a marker," Rita announced one morning. She had fallen into her old habit of dropping by unannounced, but this was a different Rita, more subdued, thoughtful. Her voice now hit the air in waves, not tsunamis.

"A grave marker?"

"It's the least I can do. He did start this whole thing rolling; I owe my journalistic career to him." I thought journalistic career rang a bit heavy handed, but she did make a good point.

"Do you know where his body is now?"

"Reb told me the body is still in the morgue while the city diddles its thumbs trying to figure out what to do, waiting to see if anyone claims him."

"I researched him once the police had a name. You wouldn't believe how many Timothy Russerts there are in the world! I think I traced yours to Sheboygan, Wisconsin, but if there was any distant family left, they wanted nothing to do with him, especially when it came to shelling out money for burial. Poe said they weren't even sure if that was the man they were related to. I didn't find any military service record, which was odd, but for most of his life, he was off the grid. He might have been one of the protesters who went to Canada during the Viet Nam War. Or he may have just been a drifter, working here and there for cash. The pathologist could only guess at age. They are checking teeth records for a match. Poe said Timmy had no identification on him."

"How in the world did you find information?"

"I went by process of elimination. Some of the others had already died. Some were still alive and had families. You just keep sifting until not much is left in the sifter. We are only assuming that was his real name. His prints were not on file anywhere."

"What kind of things do people put on tombstones anyway?"

"We have a death date. Anything else you want to put on is up to you." I watched her walk over to Albie's cage. Since finding out he was a live creature and one who saved our lives, she had taken a greater interest in him, cooing gently to his tilted head. "Sometimes people put phrases, quotations, sayings."

"Like what?"

"I don't know. Faithful wife and mother or Beloved child or Salt of the Earth. Do you want me to look up tombstones on the internet?"

"Let me think about it."

"How about Someone cared?" I asked.

"I like that. Or at least words along that line of thought."

"I'm sure you'll think of something that will suit both you and Timmy."

"Let's call him Timothy from now on, okay?" Rita moved toward the window.

"Fine with me." Personally, I was glad to see the shift in her thinking.

"How did you go about arranging a service for your mother when she was buried?"

"Mason Street handled all that for me."

Rita whipped around. "Did Poe say if he had turned up on their radar? Did they find him?"

"Vanished like a dandelion spore in the wind."

"That man sure had everyone in town fooled." She was still good at pacing, but her energy was now more controlled, less flighty.

"Me included. We used to have coffee. I even considered dating him."

"Okay, we won't get into your track record with men." She waved her finger in front of my face. "Besides, you have a good one now."

"I don't *have* anyone; we just talk now and then."

"Whatever you say, sweetie. Just don't let that one go."

"To get back to Timothy and his service, I think I still have the numbers of people you can call to arrange burial."

"Thanks." She snapped her fingers. "I just realized something."

"What now?"

"You're Al and El. Hilarious!" She clapped her hands. "Al and El Poe. No. El Poe sounds too much like elbow. In fact, Alan is Al Poe. Yikes! But you might have to go back to Lana. Lana Poe. Do you realize that Lana starts with Al, but backward."

"Okay. You have seriously too much time on your hands!"

She shrugged and then giggled. "Al Poe! That is funny."

"What about you? Would you change your last name?"

"Nope. No matter what, I'm staying a Starr." She

affected a dramatic stance. "I'll always be a Starr!"

"So are you and Reb serious now?"

"He's been serious from the start. That boy would have married me on the first date."

"Are you talking marriage?"

"No way! I have an important mission in life."

"Really?"

"Don't laugh, but ever since we survived our little adventure," she whispered the last word, "I've thought I was destined for bigger and better things. In fact, I have a plan."

"Spill. A plan for what?"

"Still in development." She giggled again. "And now I better get on with my day. I have an article to write."

"Another one? How many does that make?"

"Well, I couldn't give all the details at one time now, could I?"

"Just be sure."

"I know," she interrupted. "Be careful. You know I will run this one by you just like the others. Although with all the hours we have spent going over and over our story, I have no intention of incriminating you or me! Which reminds me!" She started for the door. "I have something for you. A thank you of sorts. Wait here."

"What do you think, Albie?" I asked after she had left. "Will it be a new toaster? An electronic pen? A CD of Reb's country western band?"

Back she came, struggling through the door, a painting in her hand.

"For you!" she announced. "To replace the one you left. Ah, the one you lost, that is. The landlord will never notice, and this one definitely will help with your social life."

I looked at the abstract monstrosity she was proudly holding out to me. It appeared to be a robot in clown makeup riding a space ship. The thing could have put Rorschach out of business. At least it was on the smaller side.

"I'm slowly getting rid of my things, and I just knew this was right for you! Doesn't it scream cutting edge?"

She went over and hung it on the wall where the other had been. The nail was still there. I glanced over at Albie; he hurried out of his cage, onto his ladder, and crossed into the cage farthest from the canvas. I didn't blame him. I wondered how long I would have to keep it.

"Thanks, Rita! You really didn't have to do this. I hate to break up your art collection." I thought back to what she had said. "Wait a minute. Getting rid of things in your apartment? Are you going somewhere? Are you moving?"

"Well, I've said too much already. That's part of my plan. And now I really have to go." She grabbed her briefcase—gone were the designer bags—and put on her coat. "Toodles." She waved. "I really should get a new farewell, shouldn't I? Maybe I could try Adios or Auf Wiedersehen. No, that last one is already sewed up. I know—'Ciao'! Yes, that's it. Ciao!"

And she was gone.

"Why do I still feel exhausted after she leaves?" I asked Albie.

I walked over and turned the new painting to face the wall.

"Ciao!" he answered.

****

"Will Pepper here," came the voice over the phone. "Don't know if you remember me or not."

"Mr. Pepper! Of course, I remember you." His phone call was a nice diversion from the steady stream of reporters.

"Seems like you've been a busy lady, at least according to the newspaper stories." He paused. "Hope I wasn't one to lead you into trouble."

"I'm afraid I did all the leading myself. And I'm sorry I had to give your name to the police. How have you been?"

"Been fine. Been fine." He paused. "And no problem with the police. Figured they'd get here sooner or later. At least this time, I talked to someone who seemed to have his wits about him. Just wanted to let you know that we did some cleaning here and came upon a small satchel that belonged to Timmy."

My heart rate went up a couple million points. "Wow. How do you know it was his?"

"Had some pictures inside."

This time my heart stopped.

"You still there?" he asked.

"Wow and double wow."

I heard his chuckle. "Thought that might get you going."

"I guess the man who stole the money under Timmy's mattress didn't find that."

"Yup. Old Danny Boy missed it. Timmy tossed it in a back closet full of junk."

"By the way," I told him, "I'm sure you heard he was killed because of that money."

"Not much for brains, that one."

I was almost afraid to ask. "What can you tell me about the pictures you found?"

"Only two there. Rest was a change of clothes and an old coat."

"And?? Don't leave me hanging."

"Still got them here if you're interested."

"You didn't turn them over to the police?"

"Guess I will in due time."

"I'll be there before you can put down the phone, Mr. Pepper."

I heard "Call me Sarge" as I was running out the door.

****

I stared at the photos, my smile like a lighthouse on a dark night. Dog-eared and finger-smudged, the black and white pictures showed a high school graduation close up of Timmy and his mother, both grinning with pride. The other was taken on the front steps of the Hill house where a young girl—obviously Timmy's mother—stared uncertainly at the camera. She wore a stark maid's uniform with frilled apron and dust cap.

"So Timmy's mother worked as a maid for one of the Hills. She looks so young. I wonder if she was born here or came here with the family?"

Will Pepper sat with me on the front porch as I marveled over his find. "Hard to say, but that other picture is definitely Timmy. Hair darker, face softer, but he's got the same crooked bend to his mouth, the full lips. Some things don't change. He didn't look you square in the face often, but when he did, he'd set them green eyes to almost look through you." He took the graduation picture from me. "Yup, that's him."

"It's a pity there are no dates on the photos, nothing to show where the school picture was taken. It's not here in Parkville. His mother was very pretty. I wonder how long she worked for the Hills. Maybe I can show them around and see if anyone recognizes her. This might explain Timmy's knowledge of the old house. Maybe even why he came back here to work."

"See no reason why not. Police got their case in hand. Don't know what a few pictures could do to change that."

I knew I should turn them over immediately to Poe, and I would, just not this soon. I wanted to show them to Rita first.

"Thanks again for calling me."

"You seemed to have a wish to do right by Timmy. It's all a man can ask for in this life." Will handed the picture back. "Almost didn't find the pictures. They were squirreled away in a small inside compartment. Just about got thrown away."

"I'm so glad you found them. Hopefully it will help us learn more about Timmy. The leads I had to a family in Wisconsin didn't pan out. Either they weren't sure if they wanted to claim him, or they truly didn't know who he was."

"So you found the rest of the money?"

"Yes! It was stolen during a bank robbery in Wyoming. These two men tried to hide out until the heat was off. One even disguised his looks." I glanced at Will. "Didn't you tell me that you thought Timmy was doing the same thing? Pretending to be older than he actually was?"

"Appeared that way. All gray and hunched over so you couldn't get a good look at his face. Walked with a bit of a limp like an old man. His voice seemed to give him away. It sounded sure and steady. Deep."

"You said he mentioned his mother at one time. Do you remember what he said?"

"Sorry, ma'am. Can't rightly think on it. I got a mind that don't always work."

Suddenly I sat up in my chair. "Oh heavens! I must have a mind that doesn't work either. Look at this picture of Timmy's mother and tell me what you see." I handed it to him.

"A woman in a maid's outfit in front of the Hill house. What am I missing?"

"Look at her apron." I pointed with my finger.

"I don't see." He raised his head and met my eyes. "She's pregnant."

"With Timmy?"

"He never mentioned brothers or sisters."

"I wonder who the father was? Do you think it was someone who lived in Parkville?"

"We didn't find a picture of any father." Will snapped his fingers. "It must have been someone local."

"You did say he hated the people who had lived in the house." An idea swam slowly into my head. "Did you say he had green eyes?"

"Yup. They were green. So what?"

"I remember Cassie Troy telling me that all the Hills had dark hair and green eyes."

"He was a Hill?" Will seemed stunned. "Why didn't he ever say anything? Why live in the caretaker's cottage and work on the grounds?"

"Maybe he couldn't prove it, especially if his mother had him out of wedlock."

"That would explain how he knew back ways into

the house."

"Yes! And why he knew Jack and Joe didn't belong to the family. They both have brown eyes. He must have gotten suspicious."

"And that's another reason they had to kill him."

"I'm going to keep on trying to find out his story. There must be a birth certificate somewhere. I'll check out the records here." I was getting excited.

"Lots of people had kids at home without a birth certificate." Will shook his head. "Maybe Timmy's mother even got sent away to have the child. Maybe the family didn't want her around, especially if one of the Hills was responsible. They might have paid her off."

"Too many ifs," I said. "I deal in certainties. This riles me up to find solutions to the puzzle."

"Strange work you do there." Will laughed. "Digging around in roots and trees without any soil."

"Well, that's a way to look at it that I've never come across." I laughed with him, feeling so at ease in his company. "Do you know all about your family?"

"Know as much as I want to." He glanced up at the sky. "Not many left, but my mama was one to keep a Bible in order. She recorded everyone in there."

I nodded. "One of a researcher's best tools."

He looked me over. "What about you? I bet you got every leaf on your family tree organized and filed away."

I looked down at my shoes. "Not yet, so far it's just a twig, but one of these days I'm going to have to fill it out."

"Sounds like a story in that one."

"Might be."

"Well, if you get there and feel like sharing, you

know where to find me."

"Thanks, Sarge. I might just take you up on that!"

****

Email to El Turner

Dear Mrs. Turner,

My name is Jacques Cousteau Miller. I have a rather astounding story that I hope you can help provide with an ending.

My mother recently died. She always told me my father was a sailor and was lost at sea. She even named me after one (at least it wasn't Popeye lol). All my life she fed me his tale, taught me sea shanties, and took me on vacations to lighthouses. She gave me gifts of books like The Old Man and the Sea, Moby Dick, and The Voyage of the Beagle. I embraced that life to honor my father.

Now comes the hard part. On her deathbed, my mother told me my father hadn't been lost at sea. That he had never even been out to sea at all. That he was a deadbeat louse who went out for cigarettes and never returned. My mother suffered her last few years with dementia and often said strange things.

So here's my dilemma: my father was either a heroic sea figure or a jerk. I struggle with the pros and cons of finding out the truth, but I think I need to know. My mother and I have lived in one house, one town, one state all our lives, so it might not be too difficult to trace him. Either way, I have to know.

If you will let me know if this search is even feasible and what your rates are, I would be glad to send any information you may need.

Thank you for listening,

Awaiting your response,

Jacques Cousteau Miller
****

Email to Jacques Cousteau Miller
Dear Mr. Miller:

What a story! I can honestly say this is by far the most intriguing request I have ever gotten. I can see why this is troubling, especially since your mother's mental state may not have been accurate. It's also interesting because my mother died earlier in the year and said some puzzling things as well.

I would be happy to do what I can to solve this mystery should you choose to go ahead with it. Enclosed you will find a list of questions and a list of documents it would be handy to have, as well as my rates. If you choose to proceed, would it be possible to scan the documents and email them to me? If not, we can work out some other option.

I look forward to hearing from you. Please ask if you have any questions or concerns regarding this endeavor.

Best,
El Turner

Chapter 32

"Ida! It's so good to hear your voice!"

"Honey, if half of what I read in the newspaper is true, you are lucky to still be walking among us!"

"It was unreal, that's for sure. When I think back on it, it feels like a dream."

"More like a nightmare."

"Well, that too. What's happening with my favorite librarian?"

"I called for several reasons. Knowing you like I do, I figured you would be laying low for quite a while. This hasn't been a great time for you, but I just wanted to let you know we were still here for you."

"You've always been there for me, Ida, and I thank you for that!"

"Second, the library is working with the police department to get some copies of Clark's journal so we can display them."

"Really? That is so cool."

"Third—and you will like this one—I am working with Cassie Troy and Mr. Marquez to find a spot in the library where we can combine what we have and display our treasures: the diary prints, Cassie's pictures, and Mr. Marquez's pencil prints. There may be other people holding onto things they were afraid to talk about because of the stigma attached to Clark."

"That is amazing! I tried to get a look at the prints

Mr. Marquez has, but he wasn't in the day I went, and his nephew kept trying to hit on me. But from what I did get to see, the prints look spectacular. I would love a chance to view them up close. He must be so proud."

I had given up my daily walk to his shop for the newspaper. Too many curiosity seekers. Jenny Lane had been leaving her copy outside my door after she read it.

"He kept and displayed those drawings for years, but his distaste for Clark Hill was well known. Fortunately, Cassie changed all that."

"Cassie? How?"

"She produced two documents, short notes from Clark to her grandfather. Remember he ran the company store. After Clark's sisters died, Clark turned some of his duties over to Boris. The first letter says as much. One of the duties was to see the workers got their pay. The fire seemed to take all the life out of Clark, and it sounds like he let Boris do more and more in regards to rebuilding. The second note was more serious. Clark had heard Boris wasn't paying the workers and had even let a lot of them go. He wanted confirmation from Cassie's relative. Soon after, Clark died and Boris left town. Mr. Marquez wondered if his grandfather was one of those who did not get his pay or had been let go. It would explain the bitterness. At least from the journal entries, Clark wanted to do right by the workers. Mr. Marquez saw that."

"It's a miracle she still had those letters."

"Deep down, she's a good historian. She kept them in the right kind of sleeves and folders inside a document case."

"Those poor Hills. At least some good has come

from all this. I sometimes think this town was built more on rumors about them than the actual foundations."

"Honey, this town would fall apart if it didn't have something to talk about!" Ida said.

"I thought that was a very insightful piece in the paper the other morning about the diary and Clark Hill and his efforts for the town." I was amazed at how much Rita's writing had grown.

"Yes, that's your friend, isn't it? Or should I say your partner in crime solving? She did a good job on the article. Hopefully it, along with the exhibit, will change some people's minds."

"Yes. Her name is Rita Starr, and I think she is on her way to becoming a serious journalist."

"For living in this town such a short time, you do seem to have made friends in all the right places. I don't think the police would have been so anxious to release those original journal entries if it hadn't been for Alan Poe and his insistence on their historical relevance."

"So tell me about Poe."

"It's about time! Well, I went to school with some of his sisters. He's the only one who stayed around."

"So I heard."

"He lives in a big house down on River Road that belonged to his parents."

"Isn't he a bit young to be Inspector?"

"I think after his wife died, he put his head down and just worked. Lived, ate, and breathed that job."

"Whoa. Whoa. Whoa. Wife? He was married?"

"Sorry, El. I thought you knew."

"What happened?"

"She was killed in a car crash. Drunk driver. Just

one day going out for groceries."

"When was this?"

"It must be almost ten years now. Not long after, his parents both got sick and he moved in to take care of them. It was a really hard time for him."

"Oh, my goodness. I had no idea. Wow. Now I understand a bit more about him."

"Ah. So getting serious, are we?" She chuckled.

"I was just asking a simple question. Can't a person ask a question without having a motive behind it?"

"Here we go again! So you just go around quietly slipping questions about men into the conversation?"

"No. I don't do it about all men."

"So it's just this one?" I could hear her cracking up over the phone.

"Ida, you are blowing this all out of proportion. I was simply—"

"Yes, I know," she interrupted. "You were simply asking a question about a man. A man, from what I hear, who saved your life. Nothing wrong with that." She couldn't stop snickering.

"Let me know about the exhibit." I tried to get her off the subject of Poe, but she continued to giggle. I still was not ready to confirm there was a relationship.

"Yes, ma'am! And you invite me to the wedding, you hear?"

With that, she hung up the phone.

I went to the kitchen, poured a cup of leftover coffee, and thought long and hard about the man who had saved my life.

"Who's a good boy?" was Albie's only contribution.

****

The exhibit opened to a great turnout at the library. I saw Rita giving an interview across the room. We had been through a lot together.

The trial behind us, I was glad our part did not require much testimony. I didn't like seeing Jack and Joe again. Rita had thrilled at the courtroom drama. Somewhere along the line, she acquired a severe black suit jacket, a white blouse secured at the neck. She still wore the short skirt, but seated ramrod straight in the witness box, she looked credible and convincing. Her audience listened wide-eyed to her breathy, vivid tale of kidnapping and terror. My testimony, on the other hand, came through as short and dry.

In the news accounts, I ended up being the friend dragged along on Rita's shocking adventure.

Our statements provided the whipped cream on a mixed bag of crime. Jack and Joe were brothers, but they weren't named Hill. When their prints were run, the police had discovered a lengthy list of transgressions. Since Mason Street's sudden disappearance, the boys had thrown him into the alligator pit: that wasn't his real name, and he had set the whole thing up. There was an old house, hardly used, where they could lay low after their last misdeed, the bank robbery. All they had to do was say their names were Hill. He arranged for housekeeping once a week and would contact them only in case of emergency. They even claimed he had planned and engineered the robbery.

They hadn't counted on Timmy poking around and overhearing them. After Joe fired him, Jack had managed to follow him to the homeless shelter. They feared he might talk, so when he left to meet Rita, they trailed him. While Jack waited in the car a few streets away, Joe met Timmy in the alley, they fought, and Joe stabbed him. He dropped the knife when Rita showed up. With her fingerprints on the knife, Joe figured he was safe. He hid in the alley until he knew it was all clear.

Rita was winding down her question and answer session. With her around, no one bothered to ask me my opinion on anything. In fact, no one noticed me at all anymore, which was just fine. I wandered around the mounted pages from Clark Hill's journal, marveling at the history.

Today I started a town. I recognized the first page, read in the dim, dank basement of what seemed like a million years ago. The other entries appeared to have been written in few words and at infrequent times.

First run of logs floated down river to sawmill.
Guido's wife had a boy.
Building finished for trading post.
Sisters and brother arrive soon.

The majority of the pages proved much harder to decipher. The writing had faded, the ink had smeared, and the moisture had done its work on the old paper. Some of the weathered entries dealt with expenditures for supplies or a listing of accounts for the workers. The partial sentences were teasers that would keep historians and townspeople busy for some time, me included.

"So, where's lover boy?" Rita whispered into my ear.

"And to whom would you be referring?" I asked, looking around to make sure we weren't being filmed or quoted.

"Our illustrious police inspector." She adjusted her glasses, dark-framed clear lenses she had taken to wearing, believing they gave her a more studious look. Often she would let them slip down her nose a bit and glance over the top, a gesture she had seen a university professor do in a movie.

"Working." My eyes scanned the displays. "What do you think of all this?"

"I'm glad something good and honorable came out of my suffering." She repeated a line I had heard her say to numerous reporters.

"Okay, Rita. It's me. You can drop the act."

"Sorry." She giggled like the girl I used to know. "I don't know how they brought this together, but it certainly has given this town a shot in the butt."

"Your writing has certainly captured the attention of the world!"

"Well, the diary turned out to be a DAD story, so I had to punch it up."

"DAD story?" I asked.

"Dull as dishwater!" she proclaimed. "A good man built a town. Where's the drama in that? No murder. No intrigue. But at least old Clark is back on top, just where he belongs."

"All thanks to you two women!" Ida exclaimed, joining us.

"It was all El," Rita said, turning credit my way. "If she hadn't discovered that old book in the desk when she was trapped in the basement, we wouldn't be here now."

I gave her a sideways look. "You mean the old book I found *on* the desk when the police broke in and rescued us in the basement."

"Yup. I got my propositions mixed up."

"Prepositions."

"Yup. Those too." She skimmed the crowd. "And now I have to run. I see another reporter coming my way." With a whiff of perfume, she was off.

"Whew! That girl is a whirlwind!" Ida uttered.

"Always has been!"

"Well, I don't care where or when you found that journal, it's priceless!"

"Ida, you've done a fantastic job arranging these tributes to the town's history. It's a hit!"

"I have Cassie and Mr. Marquez to thank. They organized and arranged everything. I just provided the library space."

"Will you walk through everything with me?"

"You bet, hon. We should have included a plaque to you."

"A tour will be fine."

We stopped in front of the journal entry about the log run down the Roma River. One of Señor Marquez's prints showed the scene. Men stood on the banks watching the logs. Several held long gaffes to prod the wood on its journey. One broad-shouldered man stood atop a log raft pointing down river.

"Do you think that's Clark on the logs?" I asked.

"It's a good possibility," Ida replied as we moved on, photos and prints interspersed with journal pages.

"I didn't see Cassie or Señor Marquez. Are they here today?"

"I think they're busy talking to the press. So many folks have questions for them that they are trying to answer."

Then I saw them: Cassie in her brown bustled dress. Señor Marquez gently holding her elbow. Both wearing wide smiles.

"By the way," Ida said softly so as not to be overheard, "quite a few people have told me they think the man named Guido mentioned in Clark's journal is their ancestor. I expect some will be calling you about researching their family trees for the connection."

"I'm not sure that is good news or not." I wasn't sure I needed an overload of work. "It looks like Cassie is holding her own among so many people."

"She's been really good helping set this up. I think she feels vindicated after all these years defending Clark when no one would listen. Now her great man finally got the recognition she felt he deserved all along. She even agreed to search through her things to see if she has any more pictures or documents."

"Wow! That's amazing!"

"I knew that would get you excited." Ida gave my shoulders a hug. "Maybe one day she will even let you through the door to help! I heard a new historical society has been formed, and Cassie will be on the board. I also heard this group has asked you to do more research about the town."

"As much as I would love going through all her stuff, I think I'm going to take a break from town historian for a while. I've got a disappearing sailor to deal with and then a big project of my own to tackle. I'm about to uncover the real El Turner, whoever she may turn out to be!"

"Hmmm. I'm not sure what you mean by that, but I kind of like the El Turner right in front of me! However, I don't blame you in the least, hon. You deserve a break." Ida rubbed my arm then continued, "I've been hearing some very interesting wedding rumors about you and a certain police inspector." She smiled mischievously.

"Not you too!" I wrinkled my brow. "Honestly, Ida. I'm not sure what I'm ready for at this point."

"I said it once, and I will repeat: Don't let that one get away. He's a keeper!"

"*Señorita Turner, gracias por venir.*" Señor Marquez had worked his way over to our corner.

"*No me lo hubiera perdido,*" I replied, repeating, "I wouldn't have missed it."

I extended my hand, but he gave me a hug instead. "We have you to thank for all this."

"*Si, gracias,*" Cassie Troy said, smiling shyly. "Mr. Marquez is teaching me Spanish."

"He's a good teacher," I agreed.

"*En español por favor, Seniorita Turner,*" Señor Marquez prompted.

"*Él es un buen maestro.*"

"*Excelente!*" He bowed in my direction.

"I just had a thought!" Ida cried. "Señor Marquez, I know you are busy, but would you be willing to teach a beginning Spanish class here at the library?"

I could see he was clearly honored by the suggestion. "Thank you. I will think on it." He turned toward the exhibit. "And now, if she agrees, Señorita Troy and I will once more visit the displays."

Cassie Troy's cheeks turned bright pink, but she took his arm and went off.

"Maybe we should call you the miracle worker?" Ida mused.

"Just researcher would be fine."

Chapter 33

The delicious smell of chicken roasting had my stomach doing flip-flops. I couldn't remember anything ever smelling so good. Even Albie was giving off little cooing noises. I wasn't sure if it was because I was humming or because an alluring food aroma was actually coming from my kitchen. I scored the potatoes and put them in the oven to bake. Everything seemed under control.

For good or bad, I had invited Poe to dinner to thank him for all he had done to help Rita and me, which included saving our lives. I had seen the questioning eyebrow lift when I asked. He knew my shelves contained canned soup and not much else; this meal would surprise him.

Earlier in the day, I ventured out to the Farmers Market. I didn't journey into the world much these days. Even Mr. Marquez was kind enough to have his nephew deliver several newspapers to my door each morning. This particular day rose bright and sunny and seemed to call me forth. My favorite stop at the market had always been Billy Tell's Farm booth. His cheery manner was infectious. Some Saturdays he even sang along to the bluegrass music that burst from his old boom box.

"Why, it's El, our very own town hero," he shouted when I approached. He must have seen the scared look on my face because he lowered his voice and tried again. "Sorry! Didn't mean to startle you, but you are a celebrity now."

"Don't remind me," I murmured, embarrassed.

He got the message. "Don't crowd the lady now, folks. Give her space to do her shopping. She doesn't need you all gawking at her." He laughed to take the sting out of his words. "Everything is on me today, El. You choose whatever tickles your fancy."

"Oh, no, Mr. Tell. I insist on paying." His kindness astounded me.

"Nope. I won't hear of any such thing." He leaned over the vegetables and held out his hand to shake. "And the name is Billy."

I shook his hand and smiled. "Thank you, Billy. I don't really know what I want. Everything looks so good."

"These fall crops do really well. Are you cooking any kind of meal in particular?"

"I thought I might try roasting a chicken."

"Well, then, you need a few herbs. Parsley, rosemary, and, of course, thyme." He picked out several bunches and placed them in my bag. "What else are you having?"

"Maybe a salad?"

"Ah! Then you will need lettuce. Do you like arugula? Endive?"

I could only nod my head. I had no idea what was what, but the lettuce he was adding to my swelling bag certainly looked tasty.

"If you want some color, just take some of these carrots and grate them over the lettuce. I still have a few red peppers back here, and you can slice them thin to make it really special."

"Oh my goodness, Mr. Tell. No! That is way too much. You can't give me all that! I really must pay for these things."

"Now, El, I told you the name is Billy, and I won't be taking no for an answer." He got a reckless expression on his face like he had just received a grand idea. "I do have one tiny little request, though. Maybe we can call this a trade. A barter. Would that make you feel better?"

"What's the request?" I was suddenly wary he might want my autograph or something.

"I'd like to display a sign on my booth. Would you be okay with *El Turner shops here*?"

I had to laugh. "Yes, I would be honored, Billy."

He reached out to shake my hand again and continued, "Now, what are you having for dessert? These apples from my orchard would make a great pie."

"I don't know about a pie. I'm not much of a cook." I knew my limitations, and I was already exceeding them with a roast chicken and salad.

He snapped his fingers. "Baked apples! Easiest thing in the world to make! Slice them in half, take out the seeds, and sprinkle with brown sugar and cinnamon."

"Well, I can't argue with that."

He loaded five or six apples in the bag. He saw my look. "Once you've had one, you can't stop."

"Billy. This is so generous of you." I tried again. "Won't you please let me pay?"

He pushed the bag toward me. "Remember our trade. I get a great sign out of this. It will be a one-of-a-kind treasure!"

"Thank you, Billy. You just made my dinner much easier."

"A dinner for two, is it?" He had the look of a proud father.

I blushed, grabbed my bag full of goodies, and managed a wave. Did the whole town know I was cooking dinner for Poe?

****

"El, I could smell that chicken as soon as I got out of the elevator." Poe took off his hat and coat and hung them on the pegs. "No offense, but I was expecting soup." He laughed at his joke.

"We are having soup," I said, deciding to play along. "Those smells must have been coming from another apartment."

"You can't fool this nose when it comes to roast chicken. It's one of my favorites. And do I smell rosemary and thyme?"

"Fresh from the Farmers Market!" I said. Actually, I was impressed that he could differentiate the herbs. To me, it all just smelled good. "Wine?" I asked.

"I would love some, but unfortunately, I'm on call if needed. Do you have coffee made?"

"Always." I smiled and poured him a cup. The salad was all made and in the refrigerator right next to the ready-to-go-in-the-oven apples, coated with brown sugar and cinnamon. I turned the soup to a slow simmer. "And actually we are having soup," I said, handing him the coffee. "Canned soup."

"Really? I was kidding before."

"I'm not. Canned soup is our appetizer."

"Well, the chicken smells so good, I can handle canned soup," he said taking his place at the kitchen table. "And I can't believe there is really a table here. I've only seen four legs covered in a computer and tons of books and papers. Now there's a tablecloth and real dishes. Did you raid a kitchen and housewares store?"

"Aren't we in a jolly mood tonight," I exclaimed. "And now let me get you a nice big bowl of canned soup." The place settings were Jenny's. I marveled at how everything matched. After the market and grocery store, I had spent the morning hitting up the internet for recipes. When I came across one for enhancing canned soup, I knew I had a winner, especially with Billy's extras. I added some of the cream I had gotten for coffee and some of the fresh herbs.

"I see you were joking about the canned soup. This is delicious. You'll have to share the recipe. It's homemade, isn't it?" Poe had half his bowl gone before I could answer.

"Should I show you the can?" I volunteered.

"Okay, tell me how you doctored it."

"My secret." I smiled mysteriously. "Let me check on the rest of tonight's meal." I took out the chicken and potatoes and put the primed apples in the lower part of the oven.

When I came back in, he had pushed his bowl away and was licking his lips. "Cream of mushroom with parsley and thyme with a hint of dried paprika?"

Damn his tastebuds.

We didn't talk much during the meal. Poe seemed ravenous.

"The life of a police detective," he explained. "It's been a busy few weeks, and I've had to catch food here and there. I wasn't sure what to expect tonight." When he saw my look, he went on. "You didn't exactly prepare me for this, especially after I got a good look at your cupboard and refrigerator. This is all just fantastic!"

"I didn't do it alone. Billy at the Farmers Market suggested the herbs and salad. When I went online, I found out how to jazz up canned soup and that one chef always recommended rubbing butter all over a chicken before roasting," I said. "That woman does love butter!" I continued, but I was secretly pleased. I never expected to be any kind of whiz in the kitchen, but even I finished off my plate.

"Do I smell something burning? " Poe asked.

It took a minute before I remembered. "The apples!" I jumped up and ran to the kitchen, Poe not far behind.

The tops were a bit charred, but I caught them in time.

"They're just well caramelized," Poe explained away the error.

I vowed to remember that word for any future almost-accidents as I took them off the tray and put them onto plates. I stopped short. Was I anticipating more dinners like this? At one time, I imagined he could be doing the cooking. At this rate, I would have to get a desk so the kitchen table was free. I could move a desk and all my work into the spare room. A shiver went down my spine as I recalled what was in the room now.

"Problem?" Poe asked as he grabbed the plates and took them into the next room.

"No." I sighed. "And I don't want to spoil this nice evening."

"Spoil away," Poe said as he attacked the apples.

"These are the perfect dessert, El! The least I can do to pay you back is listen."

"But this dinner is to pay you back for saving Rita and me!" I protested.

"Well, I'm going to steal this dessert idea, so now I owe you. I might even try putting a few sliced almonds on the top."

I shook my head. "I can't believe I lived on canned soup, coffee, and pumpkin seeds for so long when just a bit of effort and experimentation can produce this!"

"A whole new El is born?" Poe carried his empty coffee cup to the kitchen. "Can I bring you some more coffee or a glass of wine?"

"Coffee, please. With cream. And a new El is what I am dreading." Now that things had calmed down with Rita and the town, I knew I would have to explore my mother's boxes. I just hadn't pictured the topic surfacing tonight. I had hoped things might take a more romantic turn.

"Are you thinking of getting into those boxes in the spare room?" Poe was reading my mind.

"Thinking of it. Not sure I can actually do it." I sipped the coffee he placed in front of me.

"You told me about your mother's note. Do you really think she might not be your mother?"

"It's hard to say. She never was a good mother. Oh, she took care of all my needs, but she wasn't a snuggle-under-the-covers-and-read-to-me sort of mom. I always had the feeling she was using me for something, but I never knew what." Poe moved his chair closer as I continued. "Even when I came to Parkville and saw she was dying, she treated me more like an employee than a daughter. I was there to wash and style her hair, make sure her lipstick was next to the bed, and give her the medicine."

"When people are dying, they often just think of themselves," Poe offered.

"It's more than that. Bits and pieces of my life have been appearing at random in my brain since her death. It's as if some floodgate has opened into my past. I don't remember her ever working, and there was usually a man around. Lots of whispering at night when they thought I was sleeping. As if they were planning things." I looked into Poe's eyes. "I think she was a criminal of some kind. Oh, not a killer or anything, but more like a thief, maybe. Or involved somehow in a scam or robbery."

"What are you going to do?" Poe took hold of my hand. It calmed my thinking and felt really nice.

"I have one more project to research, and then I will probably put my ads and web page on hold. Say I'm not taking new clients. Then devote a month or two to seeing what I can come up with. Work on it full time. I remembered a friend of my mother's—Hillie. She might know something if I can find her. I guess I won't know until I get into her things."

"Prepare yourself either way." Poe rubbed his thumb against the back of my hand. "There might be nothing there. After all, you said your mother was very secretive. She may have destroyed all evidence."

"I definitely will start with my birth certificate with a hospital listing. If there is such a hospital, there should be records. I'll try the courthouse records. If it's fake, I'll have to start elsewhere." I sighed again.

"Isn't your father listed on the birth certificate?" Poe asked.

"Just the name F. Turner. Many years ago, I tried to find out about him, but it was a dead end, and Turner may not even be his real name."

"DNA testing? I heard that can bring about some matches." Poe drained his coffee.

"More?" I asked.

"Sure." He gave me a smile. "Looks like I might be here a while, but let me get it."

"I think you'll need to make another pot."

I heard him in the kitchen, stacking the dishes and then running water.

"You are not doing those dishes," I shouted.

He walked back into the room. "How about I wash and you dry? We have to make sure Jenny gets her dishes back clean."

"How did you know?" I asked.

"I saw her initials on the big platter the chicken was on." He looked affronted. "I am a detective, you know." He leaned toward me, and I thought he was going to kiss me, but at that moment his phone rang. He turned and walked into the other room.

"Poe." He listened for a bit and then I heard him say, "Yes. I'll be right there."

My singing heart sank to my toes.

His face was troubled when he returned. "I am so sorry, El, but I have to go. The life of a policeman." He shrugged as if that said it all. "It will be something you might have to get used to." He left the sentence hanging.

"I understand," I answered, but he was already heading for the door, the job.

He put his hat and coat on. "Leave the dishes and I'll come back tomorrow and help you with them."

"Don't be silly," I said. "Go. I'm glad you could come to dinner."

"It was great, El! Thank you. I'll call when I can."

And then he was gone. I locked the door and went back to the table. I ate the other two apples without even blinking. Billy was right; they were addicting.

****

On a cold and windy day in early December, we stood at the airport and said goodbye to Rita. She was New York bound.

She had surprised me with her decision a few weeks earlier.

"Well, I'm getting out," she had declared.

"Getting out of what?"

Our past traumatic adventure was over, and things had settled back to normal.

"Out of this town." She paced around my living room, stopping every once in a while to look into Albie's cage.

"Taking a trip?" I was back to half listening.

"I'm moving to New York."

"New York?" I choked on the pumpkin seed I was chewing and jumped up from my computer.

"I'm moving to New York. I gave notice at work today and talked to the manager. My lease is almost up, so now is the time."

"What will you do in New York?" This wasn't at all like the Rita I knew, but since the Hill fiasco, she had slowly changed. Well-cut suits were now her fashion uniform, she had gotten a more flattering cut to her hair, and the makeup looked natural. The skirts were still short and the heels high, but her look was now polished, the colors definitely more somber in nature. The dark-rimmed, non-prescription glasses always on her nose or on the top of her head.

"Don't laugh, but I'm going to be a serious journalist." She stopped walking and put her hands on her hips in an effort to look stern.

"Well, I think that's a wonderful goal." I wondered if this was another fly-by-night scheme or if she had given it much thought.

She didn't leave me in suspense long. "I've considered this long and hard. I've talked to my editor, and he suggested taking a few courses at one of the colleges. He also called a friend of his who edits a city paper, and he's made a job offer. My name is a bit golden right now with all the publicity I got over the Hill affair. Those first-hand accounts really upped our circulation, and several outside papers ran my stories as well. I also had a request from a woman's magazine to write a how-to guide of things to do if a woman gets kidnapped. I appreciate you helping me with the spelling and grammar and all. It was hard not to blab the whole story."

"Well, I was never one to blab, but, yes, that whole story thing needs to stay buried in the back woods of the Hill estate." We hadn't brought up the subject once.

Poe had gone light on us since we helped solve the local Timmy murder case, and our trespassing charge didn't stick. We had both been inundated with requests for interviews and quotes, but I never had the urge to tell all. Rita's boss let her have free reign with the articles, and she even got several front-page bylines. I chose to stay out of the limelight and forget the whole thing.

"Where we almost ended up—that back wood of

the Hill estate." She went over to Albie's cage once more. "I can't believe this dang bird saved our lives. I will send him a Christmas treat every year for the rest of my life! Who's a good boy?" She cooed to the cage.

"Good boy!" Albie cried. "Good boy!" He had quickly learned that usually garnered him a treat. I walked into the kitchen and got the good boy a reward.

"For the minute, I'm hot," Rita said. "I've had offers from several other papers, but I wouldn't leave my editor unless it was for something much bigger.

"How does Bradley feel about you leaving?"

"Mr. Washington," Rita said looking gravely my way, "thinks I have great potential. He suggested the courses I should take and offered his help with any problems I have at the new job. His recommendation is the best."

"And what about Reb?"

"He's okay with it. Better than I expected him to be. He says he loves New York and can't wait to visit again. You wouldn't believe how nice he's been to me since all this happened."

"I seem to remember he was always nice. You were the one who treated him so cavalierly."

"Guilty." She shrugged. "I take a better picture of the world today than I did several months ago."

Now, the wind whipping the bare trees outside, our group of four was saying goodbye to one. Poe and I had brought her a gift: a sweatshirt that said *Serious*. Reb came with an armload of magazines and newspapers for her flight.

"He seems happy to let her go," I remarked.

"For the moment. I expect once the realization sets in, I'll find his transfer papers on my desk and the New

York police force on his radar."

We watched her board the plane, give a dramatic wave, and disappear.

"Let's go someplace warm." I shivered, looking outside. "I don't much like winter."

"Like Hawaii?"

"I was thinking more like inside for a coffee or a hot chocolate. This cold weather came on too suddenly for me."

"I know for a fact that there is coffee in Hawaii. And I can shut off my phone."

"Very funny. Ask me again when the first snow comes."

As we stepped outside the airport, a snowflake fell on my arm, then my nose. The kiss came to catch the one that landed on my mouth.

A word about the author…

Allison Thorpe published six collections of poetry before turning her love of writing to cozy mysteries. She and her husband spent several decades enjoying a homesteader lifestyle in rural Kentucky where they built their own home and tended an organic garden. She taught college courses in English Literature, Creative Writing, and Women's Studies before moving to Lexington, Kentucky, where she works as a writing mentor at The Carnegie Center for Literacy and Learning. https://www.allisonthorpe.com

Thank you for purchasing
this publication of The Wild Rose Press, Inc.

For questions or more information
contact us at
info@thewildrosepress.com.

The Wild Rose Press, Inc.
www.thewildrosepress.com

www.ingramcontent.com/pod-product-compliance
Lightning Source LLC
Chambersburg PA
CBHW051142030726
47504CB00004B/991